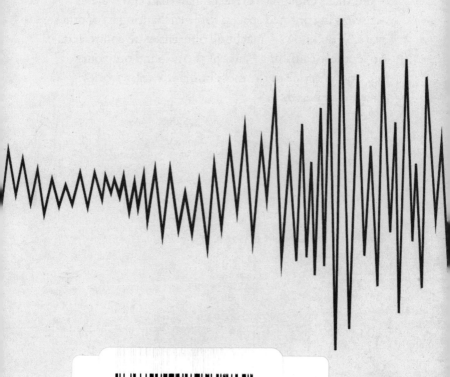

A MESSAGE FROM CHICKEN HOUSE

Sound is the last terrifying frontier. It's beguiling, dominating, and has effects we can only have bad dreams about. We can't even hear half the spectrum – but that's enough to drive animals mad and scare us senseless in confined spaces, while enchanting us in other ways. Who knows – maybe all our senses are connected? So let the astonishing Paul Southern sound out your sensations in one of the most brilliantly scary stories I have ever heard.

BARRY CUNNINGHAM
Publisher
Chicken House

KILLING SOUND

PAUL SOUTHERN

Chicken House

2 PALMER STREET, FROME, SOMERSET BA11 1DS

Text © Paul Southern 2014

First published in Great Britain in 2014
Chicken House
2 Palmer Street
Frome, Somerset, BA11 1DS
United Kingdom
www.doublecluck.com

Paul Southern has asserted his right under the Copyright, Designs and Patents Act 1988 to be identified as the author of this work.

Cover and interior design by Steve Wells
Typeset by Dorchester Typesetting Group Ltd
Printed and bound in Great Britain by CPI Group (UK) Ltd, Croydon, CR0 4YY

The paper used in this Chicken House book is made from wood grown in sustainable forests.

1 3 5 7 9 10 8 6 4 2

British Library Cataloguing in Publication data available.

PB ISBN 978-1-909489-08-0
eISBN 978-1-909489-90-5

For Maddy and Zain

'The forthcoming end of the world would be hastened by the construction of underground railways burrowing into infernal regions and thereby disturbing the devil.'

Reverend Dr John Cumming, 1860

PART ONE: GHOSTS IN THE MACHINE

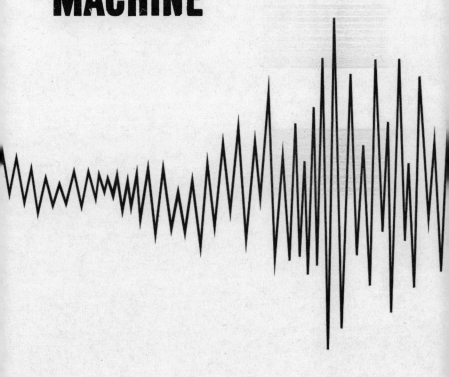

1

The black cab tore through London's rain-washed streets, slicing through the late-night traffic. It was 1.33 a.m. and Malcolm Lawrence was feverish with anticipation. The clamp of fear that had gripped him all day was gone, the blackened tunnels all lit up. He stared at the readings in his red notebook and a triumphant smile appeared across his face. William would be furious about this. He held up the spectrum analyser and turned it on. This little device had proved his theories and would change the world.

The digital display above the driver blinked back at him. He looked out at Camden High Street. He knew Kate would be up and that she'd be cross. She'd told him a million times he'd been overdoing it, and he had, but there were some things you had to do – for science.

The streetlights along Haverstock Hill flickered intermittently, then sank behind the dark waterline of trees as they

3

approached Hampstead. Grand Victorian houses clung to the shadows on either side. If what he'd discovered was accepted, he'd be able to afford one outright and give his family a better life.

He closed the notebook and paid the cabbie, then walked up the drive of a large three-storey house where they rented the ground-floor flat. He turned the key in the door and let himself in.

Kate was asleep on the sofa.

He touched her hair. 'Darling?'

She looked up, bleary-eyed. 'You're late.'

'I'm sorry. I had to finish up. It was important.'

'Are you ever going to stop this, Malcolm? Your ridiculous fight with William Habborlain has to end.'

'I think things *are* coming to an end.'

She sat up. 'Well, so am I. I'm going to bed. You coming?'

'Give me a minute.'

She looked at him sadly. 'Can't you give it a rest for just one night?'

'I will, I promise.'

He headed for the basement.

'Don't forget to say goodnight to Jodie.'

He turned to look at her. There were priorities other than work. He set his briefcase down, pushed open the door beside their bedroom, and tiptoed in.

A faint breeze stirred the Mary Poppins curtains. Jodie was asleep. He stared at the mobiles on the ceiling and the pictures on the wall. For a five-year-old, they were quite brilliant. Kate and he thought she had a fantastic imagination and would grow up to be a famous artist or writer. And they weren't alone. Everyone agreed that Jodie was special and destined for great things.

He sat on her bed. Every night he came in to tell her stories. It was part of the ritual. He'd talk about the pictures she'd drawn and try to bring the characters to life. She'd watch him, wide-eyed, and drift off to sleep to the sound of his voice. But not tonight. He regretted that. He felt her cheeks and kissed her forehead.

'I love you, darling. Sweet dreams,' he whispered.

She stirred and he tiptoed out.

Kate was waiting outside. 'I kept her up as long as I could.'

'I'm sorry,' he said. 'Really.'

He picked up his briefcase and went to the end of the corridor. There were some steps down to the basement. It had been a pantry when the building was one house – it had that cold, storeroom feel – but he used it as his laboratory. Every spare moment he had, he spent there. Some men had their train sets or cars. Others spent their lives in pubs or on the golf course.

Malcolm had his gadgets.

Kate pulled her dressing gown around her and followed him.

There was a bench on one side of the room. On it was a large electronic device connected to a battered conical speaker. Opposite, and sticking up from the edge like an antenna, was a fencing foil held in a vice.

She looked at him, bewildered.

He smiled, wheeled out a chair from under the bench, and sat her on it.

'You're going to tell me what this is all about?' she said.

He could hardly contain himself. 'It's going to wow the world.'

She pointed to the electronic device. 'That?'

'Yes, I know it looks a bit primitive. I borrowed it from

the lab.'

'What is it?'

'A sine wave generator.'

'And that?'

He patted the speaker affectionately. 'A self-amplified subwoofer.' He put a finger to his lips. 'Just watch.'

He set a dial on the generator, turned another, then pointed to the foil.

Nothing happened.

Kate looked at him sceptically. 'What am I looking for?'

He turned the dial some more. At first, nothing happened; then, very gradually, the blade began to quiver. After a few minutes, it started rattling. Malcolm placed a glass of water next to it. Soon, that too was shaking.

'That's amazing,' she said. 'What's doing it?'

He smiled. 'Sound waves.'

'But I can't hear anything.'

'Precisely. It's a sound you *can't* hear.'

'I thought your experiments were to do with the paranormal? What's this got to do with it?'

He stared at the glass of water. 'I might just have found the link between the two.'

*

Jodie opened her eyes suddenly and looked around the room. She thought there was something in there with her and had a strange feeling like she was going to be sick. The Mary Poppins curtains and mobiles swayed in the breeze and the shadows lengthened across the floor. She felt scared.

She went to her mum and dad's bedroom but they weren't there. She looked in the kitchen and the living room, then opened the French windows on to the patio and stared into the shadows. They weren't there, either. She ran back inside.

It was then she heard the voices coming from the basement. She ran to the end of the hall and felt her way down the steps in the dark. There was a sliver of light coming from round the door. It was partially open. The voices were clearer now. She could hear something else, too. It was in her head. She wanted to tell Mum and Dad to make it go away.

As she peered through the gap in the door, she began to shake. There was someone in there with them.

*

Kate sat on the chair and watched Malcolm from the corner of her eye. She spun round and nearly fell off. 'I feel sick.'

'You'll be okay.'

'What's going on?'

He pointed to the frequency dial on the machine. She tried to read the numbers on it.

He turned the dial to the right.

At that moment, the door opened. Jodie staggered into the room and stared up at them. She was convulsing.

They turned to her. Malcolm rushed to pick her up before she fell.

'Darling?'

But it was too late.

The room got darker. Jodie looked behind them, and then screamed at the top of her voice.

It was the last she ever saw of them.

2

Hampstead in north London is full of fine Victorian houses, leafy streets and multi-millionaires. Mention the name to anyone in the city and you'll be told it's a quiet, upmarket suburb, not the haunt of serial killers and murderers. That stuff happens in other boroughs further down the hill.

But not that night.

The police were called by one of the neighbours. He'd been walking his dog late along Heath Drive when he heard the screams.

The first thing the officers noticed was the wide open patio doors. The moon cast a pale shadow over the lawn and the long fingers of night pointed towards them. They flashed their torches inside and steeled themselves against the silence.

'Nineteen Heath Drive. Occupier is Malcolm Lawrence.'

The radio static made them jump.

'We're here now. Possible breaking and entering.'

It was then they heard the choking cry. At that moment, they'd have taken any fight in Kentish Town than stay there. They saw the piles of books and magazines on the kitchen table; they saw the covers of a child's bed thrown back and the master bedroom quietly undisturbed. The flat was asleep, yet both of them knew something wasn't.

They made their way slowly past the kitchen towards the basement. Their torches lit up the stone steps. They heard the choking sound again. They could smell something, too, hanging in the air like cooked meat. The door at the bottom was slightly ajar and the choking sound turned into the sound of sobs.

They pushed open the door slowly. What they saw brought them to a sickening halt. The room was painted red: on the ceiling, on the walls and all over the floor. Not just spots, but pools of it everywhere. It took a few seconds to register what it was: blood. The smell hit them with its full force and the rest of the ghastly scene came into focus. Thick globules of fat hung from the ceiling; entrails and intestines slid down the walls like molluscs; limbs were scattered about the floor. The bench at the back was even worse. It resembled a dissection table, the scene of a human sacrifice.

At first, they thought they were looking at animal bones taken from an abattoir, but then they noticed two human heads on the floor, looking up at them in white horror. Kneeling beside them was a small girl, maybe five years old, in a red nightdress. She was shaking.

'Jesus,' one of them said.

He bent down to look at her. She didn't seem to see him.

Then, when he turned her round, she opened her mouth. She screamed so loudly that his ears nearly burst. The sound rattled along his inner ear and his nape hairs stood up. Her fists smashed into his chest. He felt raindrops of blood across his chin and a nail across his cheek. He lost his footing and fell to the floor, found himself staring into the vacant eyes of one of the severed heads.

As he struggled to get up, he noticed bolts and coils and plates of metal lying about. There was also a broken fencing foil. Before he could work out what it all meant, his head grew dizzy and his vision blurred. The last thing he remembered was a shadow looming over him.

*

The little girl sat on the chair in front of the WPC and said nothing. She had straight brown hair and almond-shaped hazel eyes. They looked through the WPC to a remote point on the wall.

An austere lady stood beside her, touching forty but looking older, paralysed with grief. 'Maybe we should call it a day?' she said, glancing at her watch.

It wasn't that the little girl looked upset or displayed any resentment. Quite the opposite, in fact; she showed no emotion at all. She got up when the lady did, put on her red coat and walked out of the station.

The WPC followed them before turning into an operations room at the end of the corridor. Police officers milled around in various states of shock, some consulting a map of Hampstead on the wall. Beside the map were pinned pictures of Malcolm and Kate Lawrence, and the little girl, Jodie. They were on holiday together by the sea. Jodie held a bucket and spade in her hand.

The WPC had pictures like that of her own family. It was

hard to imagine it was the same girl she'd spoken to. She looked at the wall on the other side of the map. There were mugshots of men – men with or without motives for the ghastly murder. It was hard not to leap to conclusions. Red crosses were placed over some of them. The WPC tapped a senior officer on the shoulder.

He looked at her grimly. 'Nothing?'

She shook her head.

'She's the best lead we have.'

'She won't talk. She's too traumatised.'

He nodded. 'Someone breaks into your house at night and murders your parents, who wouldn't be?' He looked at the crime scene photos on the wall. 'What kind of monster would do this?'

The WPC left and sat down on a chair outside the interview room. This time she was the one staring at a remote point on the wall. She tried to imagine what the little girl was going through and what she'd seen. But she kept coming back to the picture of her with the bucket and spade in her hand, and hung her head so no one could see her cry.

3

Jodie sat in the waiting area, staring at the pile of toys on the floor. Now and then, she looked round, as if to make sure she wasn't on her own, but she didn't smile or laugh or otherwise acknowledge anything. Once or twice there was a flicker in her eye, when she looked at the paintings on the wall – they were of Hampstead Heath at twilight – but it didn't last long. She was as closed to the world as one of them, just an exhibit in a gallery, an eerie shadow of a child etched on a canvas.

Aunt Gene looked at her disconsolately. A door opened and a tall, wolf-like man came out. He stood, dark and uncontained, like he'd stepped right out of the paintings. Only his grey eyes betrayed any life, flickering in the wild wood of the evening.

She turned to him. 'William?'

'I'll call Clara,' he said. 'Jodie can play with John. Then

we can talk.'

Presently, a housekeeper came in with a little boy. He was pale, almost jaundiced-looking, with long black hair. He looked at Jodie warily and hid behind the housekeeper's leg.

'Can you keep them occupied, Clara?' the man said.

The housekeeper nodded.

Aunt Gene took a last look at Jodie before they left. She was still as a china doll.

The man led her into the library. 'You look tired, Genevieve.'

'I don't know what to do with her. She won't speak. She won't sleep. She's having nightmares every night.'

'Aren't there things you can give her? Medicines?'

'I don't want to pump her full of drugs. The problem's mental, not physical. It's inside her.' She looked at the bookshelves snaking along the walls. 'Can't you help, William?'

'How?'

'By talking to her. Talking to Kate.'

William Habborlain thought for a moment, 'You want me to hold a séance with her?'

She paused, weighing up what she was about to say. 'Yes.'

'She's too young.'

'She's seen psychiatrists.'

'You think talking to some shrinks in Harley Street compares to talking to the dead? I've been there, Gene, I know what they're like. This is serious, not a matter of writing out a prescription. Things can get disturbed.'

'She's already disturbed.'

He stared at her darkly. 'Have you thought this through, Gene? There's nothing I want more than to help her, but we haven't been able to get hold of Kate, have we? You can't

13

make a spirit come. They have to want to see you.'

'Then why doesn't she?'

He paused. 'Maybe she's frightened.'

Aunt Gene shook her head, frustrated. 'We both want to know what was in the room that night. This is the only way, William. The only way to know what really happened. To know whether Malcolm's stupid experiments killed my sister.'

There was a sudden commotion outside.

Habborlain ran to the library doors and threw them open. He and Gene looked across the waiting room to where Jodie and John were playing. Clara had brought out some more toys. John had a green Godzilla model in his hands and was scratching the air with it, roaring at Jodie. She was chasing after him, lashing out with her hands.

Aunt Gene hadn't seen her so animated since it all happened. Before she could intervene, the room was split by a scream. It brought them all to a standstill and caused John to drop the model. He ran to Clara, buried himself in her waist, and burst into tears.

William Habborlain watched the children carefully. Jodie was standing in the centre of the room, oblivious to everything except the green Godzilla model. She picked it up and threw it on the floor, then stamped on it. First, its long, sinuous tail came off, then a leg. Then she brought her foot down on its head. There was a loud crack and Godzilla was vanquished, broken into pieces.

John sobbed. 'Make her stop, Clara.'

Habborlain walked across the room and picked up the pieces of the broken model. He towered over Jodie. Aunt Gene half expected him to strike her, but he held his hand out and led her away. In the grey light, and with the pictures

14

of the heath so life-like and sinister, she thought of the wolf leading Little Red Riding Hood, and followed them to the library to make sure she was okay.

*

Jodie swung her legs on the chair.

'Does she understand everything you say to her?' Habborlain said.

Aunt Gene nodded.

They were sitting at a long brown bureau with an ornate, mahogany mirror on it. The room opened up behind them. Long shadows grew in the corners.

Jodie kept her eyes averted. She was staring at the broken pieces of the Godzilla toy.

William reached over and picked them up. 'Has she got a toy like this in the house?'

'Not that I know of. I saved everything I could from Kate's.'

He turned to Jodie. 'What's so special about this, Jodie? Why don't you like it?'

She didn't move.

'Shall we throw it away?' He got up and threw the pieces into a wicker basket. 'It's gone now, hasn't it?'

She stared at him like a cat, silently.

'Have they tried to work out what she saw?'

'Of course. But she wouldn't say anything.'

He looked at Jodie in the mirror. 'Her unconscious is where the answers are. The key is how to get access to it.'

He went to the shelves, took down an encyclopaedic-looking book, and opened it on the bureau.

'I last used this technique some years ago. It's a tried and tested method. But I warn you, it can have very powerful results.'

Gene nodded. On the thick vellum pages were pictures of fabulous-looking animals, some drawn, some painted, all of them strange and exotic: dragons and unicorns and griffins and centaurs, creatures of nightmare and dream.

'I'd like you to look at these with me, Jodie. I want you to tell me if you recognise anything.'

Jodie's eyes scanned the pages with a glazed look.

'Children quickly associate objects with things they've seen. They project feelings they have no control over. She saw her parents killed in a most terrible way. It's natural she would associate their attacker with something.'

Aunt Gene put her hand on Jodie's shoulder, reassuring her. 'How long will she be like this?'

'For years she may forget but, just as quickly, it may come back. Anything can trigger it. Stress, something she's seen, emotional changes, particularly as she's growing up. She's always at risk.'

Aunt Gene looked at Jodie and felt her future disappear into a long, dark tunnel.

After a few minutes, William led them back out into the waiting area.

John was still sitting on Clara's lap. He looked at Jodie and held on tighter.

*

When they'd gone, William Habborlain went back inside and put John on his knee. 'I'll get you a new toy, John. One that won't break.'

He gave him back to Clara and disappeared into the library. He picked up the pieces of the Godzilla toy from the wicker basket and laid them on the bureau. He assembled what he could and stared at it, then glanced down at the book he'd left out. Jodie had turned a few more pages with-

16

out him noticing. He looked at the last page and stopped. It was a picture of a medieval demon with a face just like Godzilla's.

PART TWO: THE SOUND OF THE UNDERGROUND

TWELVE YEARS LATER

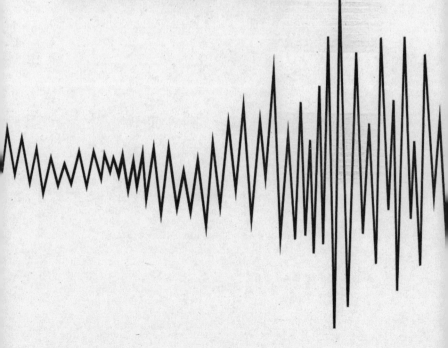

1

The railway sidings could just be seen over the high brick wall. Power lines hung like grey gibbets over the West Coast mainline, sending twenty-five thousand volt charges down the tracks. Trains thundered by, drowning out the sound of the skateboard. Morrisons' car park was the perfect place to practise: ramps and bollards were a natural obstacle course. The rumble of tiny wheels and gleeful shouts when he executed a move punctuated the deep, blue stillness.

Jodie looked through the railings at the train lines. Kamran was beside her, holding on to the bars.

'Don't you want to join in?' he said.

'I leave the athletic stuff to Luca.'

She smiled at him and turned round. Juniper Crescent glowed eerily in the evening light. The place sounded more exotic than it was, but tonight the trees and bollards made it look like a lunar landscape.

Luca raced towards her. At a speed bump, he did a kick-flip and stopped a few paces from her. He looked at her with a big smile on his face. 'What do you reckon?'

'I'd stick to your Ollie.'

He picked up the board. 'Cheers.' Then the smile faded from his face. 'Looks like we've got company.'

She followed his gaze. A group of goths were headed their way – the school psychos. The boys' drainpipe trousers and billowing coats made them look like a flock of rooks.

A top hat stuck up from the middle of them like a bent chimney. It was Trent's.

'I think we should go,' said Kamran.

She looked at the dark cloud approaching. Laura was in there, too, with Bethany and Cheryl and all the other weirdoes. She could hear their mocking laughter already. 'Maybe you're right.'

They hurried down Juniper Crescent, but had only gone a few yards when a stone landed in front of them.

'Hey, Luca?' Trent shouted. 'You wanna show us some of your moves?'

There was more laughter. The goths filed out around them. Jodie could see their black wings unfurling on either side.

Trent stepped in front of them like a giant black scare-crow. 'Come on, buddy. It won't take long.'

Jodie tried to push past him. 'We have to go.'

Laura came out of the shadows and looked at her intently. Her face was a spider's web of mascara, beautiful and complicated. 'Too late for you, Jodie?'

Trent grinned. 'Come on, Luca. Five minutes. You give us

your best, I'll give you mine. The winner gets the board.'

'And who's going to judge that?' Luca said.

Trent's eyes flitted from Laura to Jodie. 'The girls can.'

A Virgin train thundered by, splitting the air down to Euston.

Jodie looked at Luca and knew he was going to say yes. He couldn't say no to competition. She watched him take the board down the road. The goths stood in a line like a firing squad.

'What do you want? A drum roll?' Trent shouted.

Luca sped towards them. She'd seen him do this a hundred times, knew what to expect. He popped the back of the board and pointed it into the sky. Lift off. He glided for a few seconds, then came down to earth in a textbook landing.

The goths went quiet.

'Nice,' Trent said.

'Very,' said Laura, and looked at Jodie.

Luca gave Trent the board. There were some half-hearted cheers. Everyone watched as he made the same run up and, at the same point, brought his foot down. Jodie measured the height in her head. Luca had gone further and higher. Trent hit the ground to a burst of catcalling and ironic applause.

'Whoa, Trent, watch the seagulls.'

Trent stared disgustedly at the board. 'Well, it's a devil to ride.'

As he handed it back to Luca, Laura stuck out a bangled arm.

'I thought we were deciding this?'

Trent shrugged. 'There's nothing to decide. I lost.'

Laura shook her head. 'No, you didn't. He cheated. You can't let him do that. Why don't you play something else?'

'Like?'

'Chicken.'

The word stopped him dead. The other goths went quiet, too.

"Cause it's gonna get someone killed,' Trent said slowly.

Another train passed and the overhead lines hummed with electricity. Sparks lit up the sky.

'Isn't Chicken for kids?' Luca asked.

Trent eyed him quietly. 'Not where we play it.'

Jodie tugged at Luca's arm. 'Come on.'

But he held his ground. 'Where?'

'The Underground, man. We ride the trains.'

'Doesn't everyone?' Luca said.

There were some smiles from the other goths.

'Not on the outside,' Trent said. 'We wait for the train to come in. Hold on as long as we can. You wanna try?'

Jodie interrupted. 'No, he doesn't. His brain's not fried.'

She grabbed Luca's hand and dragged him down Juniper Crescent.

'What is it with those guys?' Kamran asked.

She stared at Luca. 'What did you want to encourage them for?'

He shrugged. 'I didn't believe them.'

They turned on to Chalk Farm Road and waited at the bus stop by the Tube station. It was quiet. The sky had slipped into a comatose blue twilight. She looked down the road and saw Trent and the goths following them at a distance. She saw pinpricks of orange light up the air around them like fireflies as they drew on their spliffs. Little by little, they got nearer and nearer.

She prayed for a bus, but none came.

The goths were level with them now.

24

Laura crossed the road and walked up to Luca like he had her on a string. 'You sure you don't want to try it, Luca? It's a big thrill.'

He glanced at Jodie and shook his head.

Jodie watched Laura coil round him seductively. Her black hair hung down her back, sleek and sharp. She wore a purple taffeta dress that pinched her waist like a whalebone corset and left nothing to the imagination. That was Laura through and through.

She looked at Jodie and her laugh floated on the summer night. 'I don't think he gets it, do you, Jodie?'

A red 168 appeared round the corner of Camden High Street. Trent and the other goths had crossed the road and joined them. Their weed wove an invisible net of gauze around them and sent strange signals into Jodie's brain. Her nostrils dilated.

Laura took out a small mirror and looked at herself in the misty light. Jodie was reminded of the Wicked Queen in *Snow White*. She saw the spark of Laura's lighter and watched the end of her cigarette burn the tail of the sky.

Jodie stuck her hand out. The 168 pulled up with a squeal and hiss of air brakes.

'We're not going down,' she said.

Laura turned to her, mockingly. 'Why not, Jodie?'

Luca stood on the top step of the bus. 'She doesn't like the Underground.'

At the words, Jodie felt a small sense of betrayal.

Laura smiled. She stared at Jodie through the window. 'You'll be with Edward, Bella!' she shouted. 'You can hold his hand if you get scared.'

She put her face to the window and banged on it. The other goths did, too. The vibrations sounded like thunder.

2

The house in Belsize Park was left to Jodie's mother and aunt by their parents. For many years, Aunt Gene and her mother lived there together, but when Kate left to marry Malcolm, Gene was left on her own.

There was a strange, sombre air about the place and an eerie sense of abandonment, quite at odds with the other laughter-filled houses on the street. It wasn't like it needed any physical work doing on it – the structure was, like all Victorian houses, built to last – but rather that it felt like there was something missing. There were three floors – four, if you counted the attic – and the rooms were big. It would have suited a well-to-do suburban family very well, but Gene De Dulin had no family. She had Jodie and she had God.

Some of the rooms were left empty, without even a bed or a chest of drawers. When Kate died, Gene took the furniture and stored it in the room next to hers. She didn't want reminding. Whenever Jodie asked why the room was always locked, Aunt Gene told her she'd lost the key. It would have been easy to force the lock and get a new one made, but that would have been to change things and Aunt Gene wanted things left as they were.

As Jodie grew up, she forgot about the room. She had, by that time, found her own special place: the attic. She loved to wander up there on her own and hide in the built-in wardrobes. She'd take a book up and read by torchlight on the floor, or draw pictures and stick them up on the wall. Some were quite weird and disturbing and Aunt Gene was tempted to take them down, but the doctors and psychiatrists said it was important that Jodie be allowed to get her demons out; it would help her recovery.

They were proved right. After a few years, Jodie's drawings took on more familiar shapes: castles and valleys and mountains and, most importantly, herself. They weren't the usual representations a child had of themselves: a melange of colours and triangle bodies and arms that stuck out like spider's legs. Jodie's pictures of herself were lifelike. Aunt Gene had to pinch herself she was so young.

When Jodie was bored, she'd take down the ones she didn't like and put other ones up. The doctors said it would be possible to work out how she was feeling from them, but Aunt Gene was just happy when the nightmares stopped, and when Jodie went to school and started talking again. She didn't like the idea of her being up in the attic on her own, but she didn't stop her. She knew she had no one else in the world. Neither of them did.

*

The night before it all started again, there had been a storm over Haverstock Hill which turned the air electric and lit up

27

the houses with a ghostly hue. Jodie closed the window and switched her laptop off. She'd left it on to download a film and the screen was flashing at her. She hadn't remembered falling asleep. She pulled her dressing gown tightly around her and looked at the time. It was well past 3 a.m.

Thunder rumbled ominously overhead. Rain lashed against the rooftop and water cascaded down the guttering. There had been plenty of storms before, but this one was so powerful it seemed to get inside her and make her head feel heavy.

The wardrobe doors behind the bed rattled on their runners. They were sliding ones that opened horizontally. She never quite got used to sleeping next to them. She always imagined they would open up in the night and swallow her, or that there was something behind them waiting for her.

There was another crash of thunder, then a thud on the roof above. Her heart jumped. She ran to the window and looked out. All she could see was the rain lashing down and the distant lights of the hospital. She opened the window a fraction and the wind nearly took it out of her hands. Rain arrowed in on to the dressing table and paper wrappers flew across the floor like confetti. She pulled it to, quickly.

As she did, she heard a scratching on the roof, like something was being dragged along it. She froze. Something was out there. Maybe a bird had been buffeted against the slates and was struggling to stay upright?

She heard it down by the gutter now. Another bolt of lightning electrified the room, then the scratching stopped. The rain beat harder on the roof. Jodie put her hands over her ears. She wished it would go away. She sat on her bed and wondered if she should wake Aunt Gene and tell her.

The thunder rumbled into the distance, but the rain continued unabated. It seemed like heaven and earth were in some diabolic union, the pregnant sky in labour with their child. Then, as quick as it had come, the rain relented. When it became a pitter-patter, she took her hands away. The sliding doors stopped their rattling and the wind died down. The storm had passed. She was so intent on listening to it, she hadn't heard the footsteps outside her door. The knock made her jump.

'Are you okay?'

It was Aunt Gene.

'Yes. The storm woke me.'

'Do you need anything?'

'No. I'm fine.'

'You're sure? You're not frightened?'

She paused. 'No. Not tonight.'

She heard the footsteps wind down the stairs and the door to Aunt Gene's room close. She lay on her bed in her dressing gown and stared out of the dormer window. The clouds broke to reveal a clear sky. She half expected to hear another thud, then the scratching to start again. Every sense was on a trip-wire, ready to send alarm bells ringing. But she heard nothing.

Her head was still heavy and she couldn't sleep. She took out her sketch book and tried to draw, but she was distracted. Her eyes were drawn to the wardrobe doors. They hadn't moved, but she had that feeling again that there was something behind them, and that the reason the scratching had stopped was that something was in the attic with her.

*

She woke in a second and reached for the radio. She wondered why the alarm hadn't woken her. There were no red lights flashing when she turned it on, so there hadn't been a power cut. She looked at her phone and saw the time: 8.17. She was late for school and late for Luca. He usually called about now and she was nowhere near ready. She lay on top of her bed in her dressing gown and looked out of the dormer window. The sky was a clear blue.

She got up and walked straight into a damp patch on the floor. Her feet recoiled. She noticed the water on the dressing table. It had watermarked her revision notes. She groaned. She looked in her mirror and wiped the brown fringe from her eyes. They had shadows under them like black bananas. Then she heard the knock and it all came back.

She went to the window and tried to look over the apex.

Rat-a-tat.

Again, more insistently.

It was the front door. She pulled the dressing gown tightly around her and ran down the stairs. Sunlight sheered through the Victorian stained glass but she could see the familiar shadow behind it, and the two eyes peering through the letterbox. She opened it.

'Why do you always do that?'

Luca shrugged.

'It's annoying.'

'I'll stop.' He followed her up the stairs.

'Wait on the landing.' She felt better he was there. 'Did you hear the storm last night?'

'Yeah, my mum said a few Hail Marys. She thought the world was ending.'

Jodie threw a t-shirt and some jeans on. She covered the shadows under her eyes with foundation and ran a comb through her hair. 'You can come up now.'

She finished her makeup with a line of mascara. Her hazel eyes glinted. Luca sat on the bed. His short black hair was spiked at the front. He pulled at the nascent lines of his goatee.

'Something weird happened last night,' she said, standing on tiptoes and looking out of the window.

He stared at her legs. 'What, other than us nearly having our necks bitten by Trent and Laura?'

'Something hit the roof during the storm.'

'Maybe it was a meteor?'

'I thought it was a bird.'

'Birds can't fly during storms.'

'There was a loud bang and some scratching. It woke me up.'

He got up and squeezed beside her. 'Let me look.' He turned his body to the side and hung out over the roof. 'I think I see the problem.'

'What?'

'There's a hole there. Some slates have fallen off.'

'Where?'

'Above your bed.'

'That's where the scratching came from.'

'Well, there's your answer.'

She opened the wardrobe doors. 'What should I do?'

Luca looked at his watch. 'Nothing. We're gonna be late.'

'Something fell in, I'm sure.'

'So am I. But we have an exam. Mr Green's laid this mock on especially. *Great Expectations*, remember? You know what he says about missing revision classes.'

She started taking her clothes off the rail. 'Yeah, and I need to find out what happened to the roof. Don't just stand there. Help me.'

He rolled his eyes. 'Okay.' He took the clothes from her in one big bundle and dropped them on to the floor. 'All these houses have big attics. The wall at the back is just a divider. If the builders were sensible, they'd have left an opening to get into the rest of the roof.' He picked some boxes up and threw her shoes and rubbish out. 'What is all this stuff? Don't you throw anything out?'

'I'd forgotten it was there.'

His hands searched the wall. 'You're gonna have to move your bed out the way.'

She yanked it back and watched as he cleared a path. There were two wooden panels propped up against the interior wall.

'That's strange,' he said.

'What?'

'Someone's tacked these on.'

He stuck his fingers into the plaster and pulled. The panels came away. Dust puffed up in a cloud.

'God.'

'What?'

She looked down and saw a small door, about three feet by two. 'Does it open?'

He pulled at it and, after a few tugs, it gave way. There was a cold greyish light coming from inside. He bent down to look.

'Can you see anything?'

He took off his jacket, now covered in wood and dust. 'You got a torch?'

'I have candles.'

'They'll do.'

He got on his knees and stuck his head in the hole. She started to feel funny about him going in. A deep sense of unease crept up from the pit of her stomach as she watched his legs disappear.

'Well?'

He didn't reply.

'Luca?'

She heard his feet on the floorboards and the scratching again.

'Yeah. There's a hole in your roof.'

'Anything else?'

'It's too dark. Pass me one of the candles.'

She picked one up from the dressing table, lit it, and took it to the hole. She got on her knees and put her head through. Cold, damp air rushed into her lungs.

'Here.'

A shadow moved above her. Luca took it and held it above his head. She coughed the smoke back.

'Well?'

There was more scratching.

'You were right. There is something here.'

Her heart beat faster. She crawled through the gap.

*

Jodie didn't think she'd seen so many cobwebs in her life. In every corner, there were thick curtains of them, with big black spiders hiding in the funnels. She pitied any stray fly or moth that wound up there. They didn't seem to bother Luca. He was kneeling down, staring at something on the floor.

'What is it?' Jodie asked.

'I don't know. Looks like some kind of electronic equipment.'

'Maybe it's a satellite?'

He pulled a sarcastic face. 'Yeah, maybe you should

33

check your Sky box, see if you're still getting a signal.'

'Well, where did it come from?'

'Not through the roof. The hole's not big enough.'

Jodie could see it now. Two or three tiles had come loose; one had completely come away. Sunlight struggled through the damp lagging. Luca moved a tile to the side and it made a scratching sound.

'Is that the noise you heard?'

She nodded.

Luca got on his hands and knees and crawled to the far side. The angle of the roof was against him now. There were boxes piled up in the corner. He dragged one to the middle of the floor.

Jodie knelt beside him. She had a strange sense of déjà vu. She turned the box round and examined it. There was something written on the side.

Imperial College, London.

The name stopped her dead.

'What's up?' Luca asked.

She said nothing, just looked at the faded red letters. 'I'm not sure.'

She tore open the box. Inside were coils of metal and circuit boards.

'Is your aunt into building TVs?'

'I don't think they're hers.'

He held the candle up. It coughed and spluttered in the damp air. Jodie held something in her hand. It looked like a large calculator.

'Nice phone,' he said.

She pressed some of the buttons but it didn't come on. Like everything in the attic, it was dead. She took the candle off him, crawled to the corner from where he'd got the box and tried to grab another. The spiders took refuge in their funnels.

The box was heavy and perched on one of the beams; no one had put any boards down.

'Be careful,' he said.

It was too late. It fell with a heavy thud and reverberated along the beams. A few of them buckled. She stumbled and felt her knee go through the fibreglass floor.

'You'll go through the ceiling.'

She stared at him, embarrassed. 'How come you know so much about building, anyway?'

'My dad's a DIY freak.'

He offered his hand but she waved it away.

'Just help me with the box, will you?'

They managed to lever it back on to the beam and then slide it along the boards, but not without effort.

'Why did you choose this one?'

'It's the only one that says what's in it.'

She pointed to the side. There was a white sticker with the words *Research Papers* typed on it. She tore it open like it was a birthday present. Inside were documents, so many they would have covered her dressing table. Most was technical stuff – diagrams and graphs and numerical data she didn't understand – but others seemed to be essays and articles from magazines and journals. She picked one up at random and read the front, pausing to let the words sink in:

An Investigation into Paranormal Activity on the London Underground

Malcolm Lawrence (Imperial College, London)

Journal of the Society for Psychical Research 1996

*

A shadow covered her. 'It's my dad's.'

Luca looked over her shoulder as she flicked through the pages.

'It's about ghosts. Brilliant.'

Jodie looked at him. 'Is it?'

'Yeah, I mean, it's not what everyone's dad does, is it?'

The candle spluttered again.

'You mean *did*. I'd rather he'd been good at DIY.' She blew out the candle. 'Come on.'

She crawled through the gap in the wall and he followed her. When they were back in the room, they were covered in dust and plaster and cobwebs. After they'd cleaned themselves up, Jodie opened the window wider to get rid of the smell of damp. The sun was shining. Luca re-spiked his hair in the mirror. Reality wound its way back.

'If my mum finds out I missed the exam, she's gonna kill me,' he said.

'It's not that late. We can say we missed the bus.'

She took the two wooden panels off the bed.

'You're not putting them back now?'

'If my aunt finds I've been in there, *she'll* kill me.'

'You can tell her about the hole in the roof.'

'She blocked this up for a reason, don't you think?'

He helped her put her clothes back and watched her close the wardrobe doors. They ran down the stairs into the hall. As she locked the front door, she saw the panels in her mind and thought of what lay behind them and she realised how blocking them off would do no good.

Her father had come out.

*

They ran for the 168 bus, swung themselves on board and climbed the stairs to the top deck. Tree-lined Haverstock Hill was bathed in early morning sunshine. The road was an eclectic mix of old Victorian pubs, chic restaurants with names like Ikura and Chez Nous, cheap kebab places run by Mediterraneans, corner shops run by Asians, and arty design shops – all strung along cheek by jowl.

Luca sat down and looked at Jodie. 'You've never told me . . . '

'What happened? I only know what my aunt said. I don't remember my parents at all.' She paused as if trying to summon up the strength. 'They were driving back late from a restaurant. My dad lost control on a bend and ploughed straight into a wall. The crash killed both of them instantly.'

She said it in a monotone, like she was reading a news report.

Luca shook his head. 'That's horrible.'

'It happened a long time ago. It would have been worse if I'd known them.' She looked out of the window. 'I sometimes think I do, but I don't know whether I've invented it . . . '

And she lapsed into a long silence.

3

Luca sat on the bed, flicking through Jodie's battered copy of *Great Expectations*. 'You sure this is more important than Green's bollocking?'

Jodie opened the window wider. 'Positive. I don't want my aunt knowing I've been in there.'

She finished throwing the bits of plaster out, then turned the music up on her iPod.

Luca peered over the edge of the book. 'Who is this?'

'Starsailor.'

'Never heard of them.'

She turned the volume up some more. The speakers, balanced on the edge of the dressing table, started to rattle and distort. 'I hate it when they do that.'

'It's 'cause your cones have split. You need bigger ones if you're gonna play it that loud.'

'What?'

'You're losing your bottom end. The low frequencies are distorting.'

She looked at him like *he'd* lost something.

He put the book down, picked up one of the speakers, and rattled it. 'It's all woofers and tweeters inside. The woofers produce the low frequency sounds. The tweeters produce the high ones. Without them vibrating a little, you wouldn't be able to hear anything. I can fix them for you, if you like?'

'I'd rather we just listen to the song.'

He shrugged.

She shut the door and sat on the bed.

'I thought your aunt wanted that left open.'

'She's not back for a bit. I think we'll be safe. And you seem to have found something more interesting than me to play with.'

He weighed the speaker in his hands. 'Sorry.'

As soon as he put it down, the distortion began again.

She lay on her side. 'I guess it's not just DIY you know about.'

He sat on the bed by her feet. 'When my dad's not in the shop, he's in his shed. He's taken apart everything in the house.'

'Why?'

Luca shrugged. 'So he knows how things work. One of his things is TVs and hi-fis. He used to repair them.'

Jodie stared at the speakers and then looked out of the window. Outside, it was warm and bright. She heard the shouts of children playing. Luca droned on about woofers and tweeters and top ends and bottom ends, but she'd given up listening to him.

She reached over and picked up the paper she'd taken from the attic that morning. It was typed out, with a few red pen marks at the side: numbers, mainly, although now and again a word was decipherable. Her father had bad handwriting, too. She imagined him at a desk somewhere, hunched over a typewriter, peering at it carefully and crossing things out.

She read the first page, felt the music fade into the background.

The Effects of Infrasound on the Human Vestibular System.

As she read, she began to feel light-headed. The words on the page blurred and became indistinct. Luca did, too. One minute he was there, the next she was looking down a long tunnel. The words lit it up like flares of light, giving glimpses of the past, remote and unknowable, yet close, too.

They pulsed in her head.

Luca had thrown *Great Expectations* away. 'Well, what's it like?'

His voice broke the spell.

'What?'

'Your father's paper.'

'Freaky.'

'How?'

She looked up. 'It's like he's talking to me.' She pointed to a paragraph. 'What do you make of that?'

He read it out: 'Like a lot of people, I have been fascinated with the supernatural since I was a child, and have often wondered what people meant when they said they felt the presence of ghosts, or saw spirits and fairies playing at the bottom of the garden. Were they seeing real objects or was their mind playing tricks on them? A year ago, during the course of my research, I stumbled across something that left me wondering whether both could be true.'

He stopped.

'Well?' she said.

'A bit like Dickens. Creepy.'

'You don't believe in ghosts?'

'Not the spirits of dead people, no. When you're gone, you're gone.' His voice trailed away. 'Sorry.'

She took the paper off him. 'It's okay. I agree.' But she thought of Pip in the lonely churchyard, by the graves of his parents, and felt a kinship with him.

Malcolm Lawrence: late of this Parish. Also, Kate.

She put the paper away in her dressing table drawer.

The speakers rattled in front of her, louder than before. One of her favourite songs came on.

'I can't see myself when I look in the mirror . . . '

'What do you think of this?' she said.

He looked at her, curiously. 'Cool, but I can't understand why he can't see himself, unless the glass has no reflective coating.'

'Probably the same reason Wilshere couldn't see Walcott the other week. He was standing unmarked in front of goal and he didn't pass to him. Walcott should have been wearing his reflective shorts.'

He nodded appreciatively. 'For someone who hates football, that was actually very impressive.'

The speakers rattled again. It was like there was an angry insect caught in them. She went back to the bed, lay her head on the pillow, and put her feet out. She felt his hands touch her soles.

'How many times have I said don't tickle them? I don't like it.'

'Sorry.'

'Don't try to make me feel bad, either.'

He went quiet and she knew she'd hurt him. When he spoke again, his tone had changed. The carefree banter was gone and a serious undercurrent flowed between them.

'What's up with you today, Jodie? Ever since you came out of that cupboard, you've been acting funny.'

'Nothing.'

'You're being spiky now.'

She closed her eyes. 'No, I'm not.'

She sighed and tried to sit up. As she did, she lost her balance and fell off the bed. Her head jolted back. She looked up at the window and tried to get her bearings. For a second, everything swam in front of her eyes.

He jumped to her side. 'You okay?'

'I don't know. Didn't you feel something?'

'What?'

'Like the room vibrating?'

He looked around. 'No.'

He helped her up. Her brain righted itself but the dizziness continued. The music sounded even louder and the rattling now seemed to be coming from inside her ear.

'My ears feel like there's something in them.'

'It's quite loud. Shall I turn it down?'

There was another Starsailor song playing. The words insinuated themselves into her brain:

Get out while you can, it's set to blow.

She nodded. The rattling stopped immediately. She felt a vague tremor of unease, then the noise of children playing outside returned. The faint choral buzzing of bees replaced the insects in the speakers.

'What's this one called?'

'What?'

'The song.'

'"Get Out While You Can".'

'Maybe there's a message in there?'

'Like?'

'Like your aunt will be back soon.'

He put his jacket on and flicked his hair back. He had a Gunners t-shirt on underneath. The red looked like dried blood and she felt sick.

*

Half an hour after he'd gone, she tried to get off the bed and fell down again. This time the dizziness lasted longer and she felt sicker. She wanted to ring him and let him know, but knew he'd be stuck in the shop and felt guilty. She *had* been spiky, and now it was too late. She lay on her bed and watched the sun crawl round the dormer window. The children had all gone in for tea. She put her hand out and touched the wardrobe doors. They were cold.

At half past four, she heard the front door go. Aunt Gene was back. She shouted up to let her know she was in. Jodie looked out. A full moon peered in through the dormer window like a peeping tom. It looked so beautiful, hanging in the blue sea of the sky. Like her, it was waiting for darkness to fall.

4

Aunt Gene was in the kitchen when Jodie came down. She had a copy of *The Times* spread across the table like a map of London. She had a pen in her hand and her reading glasses on. Her eyes flicked over the rims, but she didn't say anything. It was obvious something was wrong. When she was annoyed, her face would go all drawn and her lips would purse as if saying what was on her mind was too much for them.

Jodie swallowed. 'What's the matter?'

'Nothing.'

'You're acting like there is.'

The lips pursed even tighter. 'How did your exam go?'

Jodie tried to keep herself calm but inside she was thinking the worst. 'Fine.'

Aunt Gene nodded. 'It was a morning exam, wasn't it?'

'Yes.'

'Nine o'clock?'

She was a stickler for details.

'Yes.'

The lips were free now. Disappointment had prised them apart. 'You were seen leaving the house after nine again.'

'Who told you that?'

'I hardly think it matters, do you?'

Jodie guessed it was Mr Merriman. He had one hand on his curtains all day, the other on his grave. Her aunt was always making him food and taking him things.

'I was a *little* late.'

'So you couldn't have got there on time?'

'Well, I did. It was on *Great Expectations*.'

'One of my favourites.'

Jodie knew the storm clouds were brewing. Aunt Gene was just taking her time to strike.

'I had a call from the school before. From Mr Green. Apparently, you *missed* your exam. Which would tie in with you leaving the house late with Luca. And you apparently missed a meeting with him afterwards? He was very cross. I spent fifteen minutes trying to calm him down. I can't say I blame him. I'd be cross if someone wasn't listening when I was trying to help them.'

Jodie said nothing.

Aunt Gene stared at her. 'Jodie, you and Luca . . . You're not seeing each other, are you? I mean, you're just . . . friends?'

She felt the blood rushing to her cheeks. 'Of course.'

'I know you're nearly eighteen, but I wouldn't want things to develop. This is an important time for you. Not just exams.'

The cheeks got hotter. She wished she could hide them

behind her hair. 'He's a devout Christian.'

'He's also a boy,' said Aunt Gene. 'I'm just saying it for your own good. It's what your mum would have said, I'm sure.'

She brought Mum up whenever she wanted to *emphasise* something. You couldn't argue with the dead.

'We're just friends,' Jodie reiterated.

'He *was* here this morning, wasn't he?' It wasn't a question. It was a statement of fact. 'I said he wasn't allowed in. Not without me here.'

Jodie nodded.

'If I can't trust you, Jodie, I'll have to change things. You have plenty of time to do what you want when you're older. There are far more important things than boys right now. I suggest you think about them.'

Jodie looked at her and wondered if she knew about Luca being round in the afternoon, too. She'd put a brick through Mr Merriman's window for that.

She went upstairs with the words ringing in her ears and threw her books on the dressing table. Letting Mr Green down was one thing, but Aunt Gene, quite another. She tried to concentrate on the pages in front of her, but the notes she'd taken over the last two years read like hieroglyphics. She couldn't remember anything.

She got up, put the radio on, and lay on her bed. She slid the wardrobe doors back and stared at the clothes on the hangers. She moved them surreptitiously aside to look at the wooden panels. She could feel a cold draft coming from them, and thought of what lay behind.

About 10 p.m., Aunt Gene shouted up and said she was going to bed. Normally, Jodie just shouted down, but not this time. She went to the top of the stairs and saw her aunt looking up. There was something fragile about her tonight, something old, and Jodie didn't like thinking of her that way. Aunt Gene was all she had. She wondered how she could live the way she did, with just the newspaper and her work at the hospice to keep her going. It wasn't as if she had a boyfriend or was in communion with the devil, or something exciting – unless you counted the weird spiritualist church meetings she went to. When she was young, she must have been quite pretty, Jodie thought. Even now, she kept herself trim. But recently she had been distracted, and grey hairs were beginning to appear.

'Don't stay up too late, Jodie.'

'I won't.'

Aunt Gene pursed her lips and, in the semi-darkness, they seemed to tremble. 'I'm telling you things for your own good, darling. Not because I want to. I don't want you to make . . . mistakes.'

She disappeared into her room. There was a portion of it directly underneath the attic and Jodie was careful not to step on the creaking floorboards.

She got undressed and put her dressing gown on. She felt the soft material on her skin and traced the nascent line of hairs on her legs. She didn't know whether it was from the cold, but they'd pricked up. She opened more books and tried to force herself to read, but it was no good. The wardrobe doors beckoned her. She wondered if she should try Luca's revision technique.

He said he put books under his pillow at night so the information would seep into his head through osmosis. He said a lot of things like that. She didn't feel confident about any of her A-levels except art. She turned the light off and lit some candles. In the half-light, the pictures on the walls of rooftops black and bent, seemed to come to life. She thought of Mary Poppins being blown across the skyline and a chimney sweep with a black face.

She looked through the dormer window at the clear sky. Everything was quiet. The candles cast long shadows on the walls and her eyes started to close.

Scratch.

Her eyes went wide as buttons.

The candles were still flickering. The radio was still on. She looked at the clock. It was past midnight. For a few seconds, she just lay there and waited.

Scratch.

She hadn't imagined it. It was coming from behind the wardrobe doors.

She sat on her bed and took her clothes off the rail. She laid them out and moved her shoes and junk carefully aside; she didn't want to wake Aunt Gene.

Her hands gripped the wooden panels. They were cold and clammy. She imagined spiders scuttling away behind them. She looked at the small cupboard door. For some reason, it was open. She got on her knees and peered inside. The attic smelt of damp.

She should tell Aunt Gene about the hole in the roof. It would only get worse. In the dark, it looked like a grey moonlit eye. She went back and got one of the candles. It gave out a meagre light.

She held it in front of her and crawled through the opening.

The scratching seemed to have stopped. She shuffled carefully along the joists, back to the *Research Papers* box they'd opened that morning. There was more stuff in there about ghosts and paranormal sightings on the Underground.

She couldn't believe it was all her father's. She was worrying about writing a few essays and he'd written all this. She wondered why Aunt Gene hadn't mentioned it. Then she thought of the panels and how they'd been nailed on.

She stood up and the candle spluttered. She took out some of the books. Most of them seemed scientific but a few others were about the supernatural. There was a large volume at the bottom about witchcraft and demonology. She didn't know why but the cover seemed vaguely familiar. She wondered if she'd seen a picture like it in art class. The pictures were in colour and looked like they'd been painted by Brueghel or Bosch. Some were medieval friezes and woodcuts. In the dark, the colours seemed even richer and the faces more grotesque.

As she flicked through, she had another feeling of déjà vu. The pictures flashed by in a kaleidoscope of colours; reds and browns and ochres blurred into one. Then she stopped. Something was looking at her from within the book: a pair of lopsided eyes. She thumbed through the pages again. Back and forth she went, but she couldn't find it. Then she saw the green wings and the face. Her throat constricted and her mouth felt dry. The darkness grew and the candle shrank to nothing. Her fingers were wet with fear. She *had* been here before.

The picture was near the middle of the book. She turned the leaves slowly and they made soft footfalls on her memory: the witch with the wrinkled nose, the gargoyles on the church wall, the sprites at play. Then came the woodcuts of beasts, half-men and demons. The pages of her memory turned slowly in the darkness.

There it was. She could hardly breathe. It stared out at her as if it knew her and pulled her into the page. She felt her hand touch the cool sheet and crawl towards it. Her eyes were wide with preternatural fear. Her nape hairs stuck on end. Something was wrong. She shook her head to get rid of the feeling but it insinuated itself into her. Her hand was covering it now, tracing its outline.

It was humanoid with brown antlers and green scaly wings. Its back was ribbed, its limbs taut and its face comprised of two sections, with reptilian red eyes and curved boar tusks emerging from a red melon of a mouth. Eyes and a mouth were stuck on its buttocks. It was a demon of nightmare, a devil in her attic. She shut the book with a start. Her heart was beating like a train. She tried to get up, but her foot hit the floor between the joists and the noise echoed through the attic. As it did, the candle and book slipped from her hand.

Thud. She was plunged into darkness. *Beat, beat.* She stifled a cry. Her hands reached out in the dark and touched something metallic. It sent her recoiling across the floor. Cobwebs strung across her face and a shadow reared up before her. This time she couldn't keep quiet. She cried out. Then silence came rushing in like chloroform over her open mouth. *Beat, beat.*

Aunt Gene's room was directly below. Had she woken her? She kept still, listening for her door or a footfall on the stairs. But there was nothing. She waited in the darkness like a fly in a web, knowing any movement would bring the spider. Gradually, her eyes took in the grey light, and the shadow in front of her face became the electronic device they'd seen that morning. She touched its cool surface again and this time the cold seemed to wake her up. She brushed the cobwebs from her hair and felt something crawl down her neck. Her hands struck out like windscreen wipers across the wooden boards. She found her father's book.

She weighed it in her hand. Falling had broken its spell, but now all she could think of was opening it again. She put it back in the box but the voice in her head told her to take it out.

Her fingers reached for the pages. Just one more look wouldn't do any harm. Then she heard footsteps and panic set in. Aunt Gene was up. She put the book back and laid the others on top like tombstones. She crawled back through the hole.

'Jodie? Are you okay?'

She struggled through just in time. 'Yes.'

'Did you hear anything?'

'All my books fell off the bed. I was studying. I'm sorry.'

'I told you not to stay up too late. You need to sleep.'

'I'm going now.'

She heard Aunt Gene's footsteps recede and the door close. She put the wooden panels back over the hole. For the first time all day, she actually wanted them there. She wanted to block out whatever was inside. She put her clothes back quickly and closed the wardrobe doors. Her heart was still beating fast. The voices on the radio sailed over her. They were talking about the war in Afghanistan.

She went to the dressing table and opened the drawer. She looked at her father's paper: *An Investigation into Paranormal Activity on the London Underground*. She wondered what he was doing down there and what it all meant. She had another image of a man in glasses working at a desk. She wished she could remember something of him. It all stopped when she was five. Other kids could remember their childhood. All she had were the old photographs. Aunt Gene said everything had gone. It happened sometimes after a trauma.

She shut the drawer and turned the light out. She tried to sleep but her mind was electrified with other thoughts. She didn't want to sleep with her back to the wardrobe. She couldn't stop thinking of the thing that was in there. It was at the bottom of a pile of books, sandwiched between a thousand pages, yet somehow it seemed to have slid out of her imagination. She saw it as clearly in her mind's eye as if the page was open in front of her.

She tossed and turned and began to drift into an uneasy twilight. She saw her dad in his glasses, and Tube trains, and then nothing. She was walking somewhere, down a long, dark tunnel. Something was following her, dragging its feet and catching up with her.

*

She was in the attic again, the wardrobe doors wide open, and the hole in the wall much bigger. Something had got out. The book was on the floor. She leafed through it. Her fingers came to the page with the demon on. But it wasn't there. She looked round into the corner and saw two red eyes staring at her. She screamed so loud she thought her throat would tear. She didn't stop until she felt the hands on her shoulders and saw Aunt Gene's face.

'Jodie, what's the matter?'

Jodie grabbed hold of her. 'Where am I?'

'In bed, darling. You've had a nightmare.'

She looked over Aunt Gene's shoulders around the room. Everything was the same. There were no holes in the wall and nothing on the floor.

'I'm sorry, Aunt Gene.'

'What for?'

'Waking you up.'

'You did it enough when you were little. One more time won't hurt, will it?'

Jodie looked at her. 'I suppose not.'

Aunt Gene swept the fringe from her eyes. 'You need to get that cut.'

'I like it long.'

The fringe fell back into place. Jodie watched Aunt Gene through the curtain of hair and thought of all the other times she'd come up to see her when she was small.

'You never told me I had nightmares.'

'Didn't I?'

'No. What were they about?'

Aunt Gene's lips pursed, not from anger this time, but from concern. She glanced round the room as if she was checking something.

'Nothing, darling. Every child has nightmares. Try to sleep now.'

She gave her a kiss and went downstairs. The last Jodie heard was the door closing.

Thud.

5

The next day, the grey clouds made an ominous thumbprint on the sky. Jodie skittered out of the drizzle, her jeans trailing along the wet tarmac, and clutching a purple Maylee bag to her side. She hurried through the main school building and went to the photocopier room. She took a purple plastic wallet out of her bag and put some sheets on the glass. There was a low hum and a flash of light as they scanned. When she came out, she headed for the science block.

There were a few lab technicians in white coats and glasses putting equipment away, but otherwise it was deserted. She looked out of the window and saw the workmen on the road. The sound of drilling made the glass vibrate. She put her hands on it and felt it shake.

'Are you looking for anyone?' said one of the technicians.

'Yes, I came to see Mr Cronin.'

'He's holding a revision class in his lab. If you rush, you'll just make it.'

'Thank you.'

She hurried down the corridor. At the end were two science laboratories. She looked through their narrow glass windows and saw him. He was sitting on his desk, his legs crossed. The lab was, unsurprisingly, full. Mr Cronin was good-looking and popular, especially with the girls.

She glanced behind and saw Laura and Trent following her. She had no choice but to go in.

She knocked. Everyone turned to look. Even Mr Cronin wore a puzzled expression. 'Jodie?'

'Hello, Mr Cronin.'

'What have we done to deserve this?'

'I was wondering if I could have a word.'

'It'll have to be later, I'm afraid.'

'Well, would you mind if I sat in?'

'Not at all. Are you going to draw pictures of us?'

She smiled, a little embarrassed, and wondered if he was still disappointed with her. When she told him she was doing English, Art and Psychology at A-level, he said it was a great loss to science – and a good way to become unemployed.

She saw Kamran at one of the tables. He was on his own, blinking at her through his glasses. Drops of perspiration clung to his spotty forehead. She sat down next to him.

'Hi,' he said. 'You in the wrong place?'

'Not now,' she said.

Trent and Laura came through the door.

'Well, this *is* my lucky day,' said Mr Cronin, looking at the lab clock. 'The return of the living dead. You know it's Chemistry today, guys, not Biology?'

'Yeah,' said Laura, looking at Jodie. 'But you said it's all connected, didn't you? With all the lessons we missed, we thought we'd better come along. We have some catching up to do.'

Mr Cronin nodded sceptically.

Jodie watched as they walked over and sat on the other side of the table. She avoided their looks and brought out the photocopied sheets. They were of her father's paper. She'd been reading it all morning. The technical stuff was beyond her, but the imaginative stuff about ghosts and the Underground and demons made the hairs on the back of her neck sit up. Her father's words brought things so compellingly to life, it was as if she was there with him.

She felt a sudden rush of heat and saw the Bunsen burners on the table had been lit. They looked like birthday candles. She looked out of the window. It was open and, through it, she heard the sound of drilling. The Bunsen burners roared and tripods were set like Martian legs. Kamran's forehead was sweating profusely now, his spots inflamed and protesting angrily. He laid some gauze on the tripod and it glowed yellow and orange.

'What are you burning? It stinks.'

'Phosphorus,' he said. 'It's meant to.'

She went to the window to get some air. Her hands touched the glass and she felt the vibrations again. She stood there for a minute and began to feel dizzy. It was the heat, she thought. Or the smell. It scoured her nostrils like claws. Something moved behind her and she jumped, still twitchy from last night's dreams.

'Don't worry, Bella. It's only me.'

She whirled round and saw Laura. Her skin was so white and her eyes so black she looked dead. The smell of her perfume or hairspray overpowered the phosphorus.

'What do you want?'

'I just came to say hello.'

'Haven't you anything better to do?'

'Yeah, lots. But I thought we should have a talk. About that game on the Underground. Why don't you come back to the table?'

Jodie looked over to where Trent was sitting. His tongue flicked out and he licked his lips slowly. Laura wasn't dumb. Beneath the makeup and jewellery and pincushion rings she wore, you could sense that. But she seemed hell-bent on proving it, and having a boyfriend like Trent was good cover.

'I'm fine where I am.'

The drilling intensified outside. Diggers broke up the ground and littered it with slabs of concrete. It started to rain harder.

'Can you shut the window, Jodie? I can't hear myself think!' Mr Cronin shouted over to her.

Laura smiled at her. Her mouth seemed to metamorphose. 'He won't be around all the time.'

Jodie went back to the table and stared at her father's paper. Maybe she should come back later? The phosphorus and hairspray had made her nauseous. Kamran was burning something on the gauze. It had a green tinge to it.

'Phosphorus undergoes spontaneous combustion in air and burns with a brilliant flame. It yields the toxic chemical compound diphosphorus pentoxide,' Mr Cronin went on.

Jodie didn't really hear the words at all. There was something in her head. A throbbing. No, not a throbbing: a rushing. A rushing like wind. She could see Laura and Trent looking over. They seemed to be pointing their Bunsen burner at her. There were brilliant flames on the other

57

tables now as the phosphorus ignited, more green tinges and tiny explosions of small stars. Then there was the drilling, like it was coming up through the earth.

'Are you okay, Jodie?'

She couldn't hear Kamran properly. It was as if he was talking through glass.

'You're shaking.'

She watched her hands vibrate on the table.

They'll think I'm scared, she thought. But she couldn't stop.

Laura was staring at her. Her black hair stood on end like she'd grown antlers. From out of her mouth, her teeth emerged like tusks. The room seemed to get very dark. Jodie was back in the attic and looking through the book. She felt herself spinning and falling. The Bunsen burners crackled like fireworks and flames shot into the air. They were all Jodie could see. The rushing grew louder in her ears. Then, from the corner of her eyes, she saw something move.

It crept up the classroom wall and cast a darker shadow over the tables. The drilling was incessant now. It was all she could hear. The ground seemed to open up as she fell towards it. The wind roared past her and the Bunsen burner candles were blown out. She hit the floor with a thump, and for a second everything went black. The shadow lifted.

'Don't touch anything!'

It was Mr Cronin. He checked the mains gas supply behind his desk, then ran to her. He checked the valves on the tables. From every one, the fizz of escaping gas could be heard.

'Whatever you do, don't . . . '

But it was too late. Someone flicked a switch.

A tongue of flame licked across the room and ignited the air. It shot past Kamran and went straight for Laura. She let out a scream and crashed off her stool. For a second, there was a silence like an intake of breath; then her hair caught fire. She shot up, ran round like she was possessed, batting it wildly with her hands. But the flames kept shooting from her head like it was a beacon on a hill. Jodie flitted in and out of consciousness. Laura's face seemed to melt in front of her, like a witch's burnt at the stake.

Mr Cronin got a fire blanket and tried to put it over her. He told her to hold still but she wouldn't listen. It was only when he threw water over her that she calmed down. The fire went out as quickly as the Bunsen burners had.

There was a horrible silence. Mr Cronin ran to his desk and shut the mains supply off.

'Open the windows!' he shouted.

The smell of gas and phosphorus hung in the air. He grabbed a first aid kit and rushed back to Laura. Trent was holding her and trying to stop her shaking.

'Are you okay?' he said.

'She tried to kill me.'

'What?'

Laura pointed to Jodie. 'She tried to kill me. She lit the gas valve on the table. I saw her do it.'

'We need to get you to sick bay, Laura. Trent, call the nurse.'

He looked unsure.

'Now, Trent!'

Mr Cronin dismissed the rest of the class. He went to Jodie, knelt beside her and put her in the recovery position. She was already waking. Her eyes were on him, transfixed.

'What happened?'

*

Jodie watched him pack his case away. A few years ago,

she'd have welcomed the proximity to him, but now she just felt numb.

'It wasn't me. I didn't make the Bunsen burners go off.'

'I know. The gas was still on.'

'So what happened?'

'There must have been an interruption in the supply. Enough to knock them out.'

'You couldn't blow them out?'

He smiled. 'Not unless you were much bigger.' He paused. 'You wanted to have a word with me?'

'Yes,' she said.

'What about?'

She took the photocopied sheets out of her bag and handed them to him.

'Infrasound.'

He stared at her as if he'd misheard.

'My father was working on it before he died. There's lots of it I don't understand.'

He looked at the first page. 'He was a scientist?'

'A lecturer.'

'On the paranormal?'

'I think so. Have you time to read it?'

'I haven't, Jodie. Not now.'

'Please, Mr Cronin.'

He stared at the sheets, then at her, and put them in his case. 'I'll see what I can do. In the meantime, you may want to check out London Zoo.'

'The zoo?'

He shut his case. 'Yes. I think you'll find elephants use infrasound.'

She followed him out, tried to keep up with him. 'What for?'

'As a warning.'

They walked down the long corridor together. It was raining and the drilling had stopped.

'Has it happened before?' he asked.

'What?'

'The epilepsy.'

'I don't remember. Maybe it was the gas?'

'Maybe.'

They stopped in the reception area.

'I should really take you to sick bay, too, let the nurse look you over.'

'I'm okay. Really.'

'The Head Teacher might not see it that way.'

'Please, Mr Cronin.'

He nodded to the doors. 'Scram, then.'

As they slid open, she turned back.

'What about Laura? Will she be okay?'

'I'll go and check on her now. Looked like superficial burns to me, but I'm no expert.'

She felt his eyes on her. She thought of Laura screaming and everybody looking. Mr Cronin had saved her from a lynching. The shaking had stopped and the dizziness had cleared, but something was left, walking behind her. She knew the gas hadn't cut out. Something had come into the lab with her. And followed her out.

6

Jodie lay on her bed and stared at her phone. There were twenty-one missed calls. She watched the light flash as another one came in. Laura had been ringing her all evening, leaving voicemail after voicemail: *You've burnt my hair. You're gonna pay.* Jodie didn't know why she was blaming her, but the thought of going into school next day sickened her. She imagined Laura in bandages waiting for her in the common room with Trent. No one was going to stick up for her.

She got up and sat at her dressing table. The mirror on it was one of those old-fashioned ones, divided into three, with side panels that could be angled inwards. It belonged to her grandmother and Aunt Gene said it was French and very valuable. She tilted the sections back and forth and saw the endless reflections of herself disappearing into a long tunnel.

There was a splashing noise from her laptop.

Adriano41: hey, r u up?

It was Luca.

IHateBella: Just.
Adriano41: r u ok?
IHateBella: Yeah.
Adriano41: Laura just MSN'd me.
IHateBella: What did she want? Watch you skateboard again?
Adriano41: Not exactly. She said she wants to kill u for what u did.
IHateBella: Thanks.
Adriano41: What the hell happened?
IHateBella: There was a fire in the lab. She thinks I tried to burn her face off.
Adriano41: I bet there's plenty of others who'd want to do that.
IHateBella: Yeah, well someone's done it for them.
Adriano41: Someone?
IHateBella: I can't explain.
Adriano41: Try me.

The tunnel in the mirror seemed to grow darker.

IHateBella: Something wasn't right in there. Before she got burned there was this awful smell. Then all of a sudden the Bunsen burners went out and the room went dark. The next thing I know this flame shoots across the room and Laura's screaming. I nearly passed out.
Adriano41: Sounds like a power cut.

IHateBella: That's what Mr Cronin said.
Adriano41: What are u going to do?
IHateBella: What can I do? You know any knights in shining armour?
Adriano41: ☹
IHateBella: I don't want you to speak to her again.
Adriano41: I won't. I promise.

The computer went quiet. She pushed the sides of the mirror back and picked up one of her psychology textbooks. It wasn't just work that was piling up. A creeping paranoia was spreading through her. The room felt weird, like it was vibrating again. She thumbed through a few pages and came to a black-and-white drawing called 'The Anatomy of the Human Brain'.

It showed a brain divided into small sections, with brief descriptions of what went on in each. There were four lobes, a couple of cortices, and weird structures like the hypothalamus, the hippocampus and the amygdale. Every neuron and nerve cell had its purpose. They affected your senses, your memory, and your emotions. It made her think of her father's paper and what had happened in the lab.

IHateBella: I need to go to the zoo tomorrow.
Adriano41: The zoo?
IHateBella: I need to find out about infrasound.
Adriano41: What about ur revision?
IHateBella: I'll say I'm at yours.
Adriano41: What will I say?
IHateBella: Say you're at football.
Adriano41: I *am* at football.
IHateBella: No, you're not. You're coming with me.

The computer went quiet again.

IHateBella: You owe me one, Luca.

Another splash.

Adriano41: I guess. This infrasound stuff's really got to u, hasn't it?
IHateBella: Yes. Amongst other things.

She looked at the purity ring he'd bought her in Camden market. It was plain and unadorned like the One Ring. She'd never even put it on.

IHateBella: Goodnight.
Adriano41: Goodnight Jodie x

She shut the laptop down and took the psychology book to bed. She tried reading but most of the time just looked at the pictures. The human brain was so complicated and yet so beautiful. Each piece had a function, everything fitted in somewhere, yet the little pieces couldn't explain the whole.

She closed the book and turned the light off, and the grey mist of a clear north London night, no longer hemmed in by the light inside, passed through the gap in the curtains. She looked at her phone and saw there had been another missed call. She deleted the voicemails and turned towards the wardrobe doors. She put her hand out and made sure they were closed. As she closed her eyes, she thought of the things behind them and felt herself being sucked through the hole into the attic.

She felt the dead air and cobwebs on her face and the books in her hands. She was kneeling down, leafing through the one on witchcraft and demonology. She didn't want to look but the pages kept turning. She started to shake and her head lowered. She tried to draw it away but it was as inexorable as time. Bit by bit, the picture came into view, only this time something was wrong. Something was missing. The background was still there, but the green horned demon was gone. In its place was a black silhouette. She threw the book down and looked round. Something was in the attic with her. She felt herself crying and heard laughter in the shadows.

'Please stop.'

'Not till you drop,' a voice came whispering back.

'Just leave me alone.'

'You'll never go home.'

'Who are you?'

A light flickered and twenty-one candles flared like Bunsen burners.

'Who do you think, Bella?'

Laura's head had antlers and red eyes, and from her mouth melon seeds dropped like flies. Jodie shot up from her bed and screamed. Her dressing gown clung to her wet skin. Her heart thundered in her chest. She heard a door open somewhere and looked round. Aunt Gene was standing there. She didn't need to say anything. The look on her face said it all.

7

They sat in their usual seat on the top deck of the 168. As it passed school, Jodie thought of Laura and Trent inside, waiting with Bunsen burners in their hands, ready for revenge. Unconsciously, she gripped Luca's hand tighter. He gave her a half-smile but there was something doleful about his expression, as if he had other things on his mind.

They got off at the start of Camden High Street, crossed the road, and walked down Parkway. The famous Jazz Cafe was on the left. It was one of the few remaining links she had to her dad. Aunt Gene said he used to take her mum there. Somewhere in the house was his record collection. She remembered seeing it once. Names like Charlie Parker and Dizzy Gillespie blew out of the dusty vinyl like smoky memories. At the time, she hadn't bothered. Dizzee Rascal was more the scene.

She felt dizzy now. The heat had got to her. There were men drinking outside The Dublin Castle and a group of women on the opposite side of the road, outside Pizza Express. They had sunglasses perched on their heads and wore flimsy, summery dresses. The clink of glass chimed in the soft, evening air.

They approached Prince Albert Road. She noticed the jagged lines on the junction like giant spider's webs. They reminded her of the tattoos on Laura's face. Above Regent's Park, a line of pink clouds gave the sky a lip-gloss smile. She wished she'd brought her sketch pad.

They turned right and passed large, imposing white houses that looked like the homes of famous actors and pop stars. The clamour of Camden gradually faded. Ahead, on their left, the Feng Shang Princess floating restaurant emerged from the canvas of greenery. They crossed the footbridge. Barges nestled on the banks of the canal. Some looked like dragon boats with demon heads on the prows, their tongues lolling in the water. They stared at her over the water margin.

They came to Outer Circle and headed towards the zoo. Strange cries could now be heard, the exotic calls of birds and animals. She tried to put flesh on them, imagine which animal was calling which.

A long line of tourists snaked down the road towards them.

Luca's expression got more doleful. 'That's a *long* queue.'

'Don't worry. We've got till ten. They do late opening on Fridays.'

He gave that smile again and she wondered if it was really worth dragging him from his football. But the queue whittled down quicker than they thought and, in ten minutes, they were at the entrance. A large, child-friendly picture of a lion, a tiger, a giraffe and some monkeys emerging from the undergrowth greeted them.

An attendant in a green ZSL London Zoo top stared at them as they approached the turnstile. He gave them the once-over. 'No under-sixteens on Zoo Lates, I'm afraid.'

Luca held up his school ID card. 'I'm eighteen.'

The man turned to her.

'Me, too,' she said.

He nodded doubtfully but gave them their tickets.

Luca whispered in her ear as they went through. 'You mean *nearly* eighteen.'

She stopped in front of a large map of the zoo. Names like Gorilla Kingdom, Bug House and Penguin Beach gave the whole place a cartoon feel. She half expected characters from *Madagascar* to leap out of it.

'So, where are we going?' Luca said.

She pointed to a strange-looking building in the centre. 'There. To see the elephants.'

*

The elephant and rhino house looked more like a medieval fort. It had imposing grey walls and conical copper roofs like ship funnels. It reminded Jodie slightly of the Roundhouse music venue. She had a dim recollection of Aunt Gene taking her there when she was small. A sad-looking elephant statue stood outside, but there didn't seem to be any real ones, just a few camels and pigs.

They went inside.

The smell of dung hit them immediately.

'Christ,' said Luca. 'It's worse than the boys' toilets.'

Jodie looked around. 'Except the animals have an excuse.'

He pulled a face at her.

There was a grizzled, grey-haired ZSL attendant nearby, clearing straw from the pens with a pitchfork.

She went over to him. 'Excuse me. Where are the elephants?'

He stuck the pitchfork into a bale of hay. 'Elephants?'

'Yeah. This is where they live, isn't it?'

'We haven't had an elephant since 2001, luv.'

'What happened to them?' she said.

He looked at her curiously like she should have known. 'One of the keepers got crushed. They all got moved to Whipsnade.'

She looked round the empty chambers. 'That's horrible.'

'Yeah,' he said. 'It was.'

'I'm doing a school project. You wouldn't be able to help, would you?'

'Depends what it's about. The only thing I know much about is elephants.'

'Do you know anything about infrasound?'

He stopped and kicked some straw off his boots. 'Infrasound?'

'Yeah, my teacher said they use it.'

He stuck his pitchfork into another bale, letting it rest there like Neptune's trident. 'Well, your teacher's right. This place would be full of it now if the elephants were here.' He looked round the pens as if they still were. 'Especially at mating times. Females let the males know when they're receptive, ya know?'

Luca flashed her a knowing look.

'Not bad, is it?' said the attendant. 'They don't need phones to fix up a date.'

He pulled his pitchfork out.

'So what is it?' she said. 'Where does it come from?'

70

'It's a sound, luv. Only one you can't hear. But they can. Elephants let out a rumble from here.' He pointed to the sides of his nose as if an invisible trunk was hanging from it. 'It can travel several kilometres. The infrasound passes through the ground and is picked up by the others in the herd.'

'How?'

'Vibrations. The sound vibrates their bodies.'

Before she had time to reply, he made for the other pens. She followed him. 'Is it just elephants that give it off?'

'No. Giraffes, any of the big land animals. Even big cats.'

'Lions?'

'Tigers, mainly. I'm not exactly sure, but their growls mix infrasound with stuff we *can* hear.' He stopped to look at her. 'They use it to paralyse their prey, y'know. Some of the keepers here have noticed it. It's like a great force coming at you. It shakes you up. By the time you've righted yourself, the tiger is on you.'

Jodie felt her nape hairs rise. 'It scares you stiff?'

'Yeah,' he said. 'That's exactly it. As if seeing them isn't scary enough already.'

She looked round the walls and imagined tigers leaping from the enclosures.

The attendant smiled. 'But you're safe enough here. The animals are all locked up.'

She gave him a half-smile. 'I suppose.'

He walked off with his pitchfork.

Luca put his hand on her back. 'We finished now?'

She nodded.

When they got out, the pink lines in the sky had turned red. She thought about her dad, and ghosts and elephants calling to each other.

Luca took his phone out. He seemed anxious to get off.

They passed the Meet the Monkeys enclosure. Squirrel monkeys jabbered and swung in the evening sunshine. They chased each other along the vines, turning somersaults and doing cartwheels. Their faces reminded her of clowns, with white eye makeup and big black mouths. A few seemed tamer than the others and clung to the fence, gazing at the tourists, occasionally pulling back their gums in rictus smiles.

A little one appeared from behind the bars. Jodie put her face close to the fence and watched it. It swung amiably for a few moments like it hadn't got a care in the world. She made a clicking noise and tapped the fence gently. It stopped swinging and looked at her.

Luca stood beside her, fidgeting. 'You've made another friend.'

'Another?'

'You know, apart from me?'

'Maybe if we threw a football in there it would make it more interesting?'

She walked off to the indoor part of the enclosure. The little squirrel monkey clambered down from his perch and followed her.

It was warmer inside and the noise levels of the monkeys increased. There seemed to be an altercation on the far side: two chimps were squaring off against each other, their mouths pulled back in anger. It reminded Jodie of the boys at school, gathering round for a fight.

The little squirrel monkey came to the window and climbed on the sill next to her. It turned its head to the side and pawed at the glass. She stared at its tiny fingers and placed hers on the glass over them. It chirped. As it did, two others came scuttling across the fake arboreal floor. They hit the window with a thump. She stepped back, shocked. There were some Japanese tourists beside her. They smiled at her surprise and took pictures. There were small flashes of light in the glass.

Luca grinned at her but she felt a vague sense of unease. From the corner of her eye she saw flurries of movement like grey rain. There were more knocks on the window. When she turned, there were two, three, four squirrel monkeys staring at her.

'He's brought the fan club,' said Luca.

'What are they looking at?'

'You, I think.'

'I don't like it.'

The din in the enclosure had died down.

'C'mon. Let's get going,' Luca said.

As they walked back to the entrance, more of the monkeys started looking at her. A terrible silence had now come over the enclosure. Jodie felt her eyes twitch and a growing nausea creep up her insides.

Before they could reach the door, there was a deafening scream from inside the pen and a large black object flew against one of the windows next to her. She staggered back as if it had hit her. A chimp was pressed against the glass, its teeth set maniacally, gnashing and screaming.

'Jesus!' said Luca. 'What's up with him?'

Smash. The chimp threw its body into the glass again.

'He's trying to get out,' she said, panicking. The nausea spread up her stomach and reached into her throat.

Another chimp launched itself against the glass. Then the squirrel monkeys threw themselves against it. There were screams of panic from the tourists. The Japanese group were no longer smiling but rushing to the exit.

Luca grabbed her arm and tugged at her. But she felt something else dragging her back, a shadow in her mind. She was shaking at the thought of it.

Smash. Another chimp threw itself against the glass.

They weren't trying to escape. They were trying to get her.

The squirrel monkeys launched themselves repeatedly against the glass like miniature catapults. The little one she had befriended was still there. He was no longer staring amiably, but doing what the rest were doing. Desperation and anger contorted his face.

The shaking inside her got worse. Luca's hand was the only thing that kept her from falling. With a last tug, he pulled her through the door and fresh air rushed through her. Her head cleared and the nausea dissipated. The monkeys followed them outside, heading for the high trees in their enclosure like they were running from something. After a few minutes they settled and the panic and hysteria ebbed away. All that was left was a curious jabbering, as the sun slowly sank behind the trees.

'What was that all about?' Jodie said.

Luca shook his head. 'God knows. It was like something from a film.'

'They were after me, Luca.'

'I'm sure they weren't. Maybe you shouldn't have been so friendly?'

But she could tell he'd noticed, too.

*

On the way out, they passed the big cats' pens and she remembered what the attendant had said about them. She stopped to look. A Sumatran tiger stood on its hind legs,

74

sniffing at a branch of a tree. Its massive claws scratched the bark, revealing the white wood beneath.

'Tyger, tyger, burning bright,' she whispered.

Luca stared at her. 'Don't start anything, yeah?'

'It's beautiful.'

'And dangerous. You know what that guy said.'

'It can't get through the bars, though, can it?'

As if on cue, the tiger opened its jaws and gave a loud growl. A large piece of meat that had been dangling from the branch fell to the ground. The tiger sank its teeth into it.

'Let's hope not,' said Luca.

The tiger slipped sinuously through the long grass, its stripes the perfect camouflage for evening. For a brief, uncomfortable second, Jodie imagined something else in the enclosure.

'Well?' said Luca.

'Well, what?'

'Have we seen enough now?'

The smaller, female tiger came out from behind a rock. She stalked the perimeter slowly, sniffing the ground. For a brief moment, she raised her head. The black stripes on her face looked like mascara lines, Jodie thought. They'd been put there for a reason. To scare, to chill. The amber eyes glistened from within, deep and impenetrable. She moved slower now, examining the ground, then lay down in the thick grass not far from them.

'I guess so.'

As they passed through the turnstile on the way out, the strange, exotic calls she'd heard before started up again. They seemed clearer now, as if her ears had been syringed.

Soon, the roar of the tiger and the chatter of monkeys were lost in the distant rumble of traffic on Prince Albert and

Marylebone Road.

Luca held her hand. 'Well, what do you think?'

'About?'

'You came here to find out about infrasound, didn't you?'

'I'm not sure,' she said.

His phone rang. He looked down at the display but didn't answer. 'So, you want to get back?'

She thought of the attic and the things behind the cupboard. 'No.'

'What, then?'

'Can we stay in the park for a bit?'

He nodded understandingly, but she knew he had other things on his mind.

They turned down Broad Walk and walked by the side of the zoo. There were men, stripped to the waist with bronzed and tattooed torsos, playing football, and courting couples lying on the grass, and lonely cyclists making their way home.

They sat under a tree. Luca watched the footballers. She put her head on his lap, felt his fingers tap quickly on the phone.

She looked out. Regent's Park didn't have the wide open spaces of the heath. Or the rolling hills. It was too contained, too flat, too predictable.

'Aunt Gene doesn't want us to see each other,' she said finally. 'She knows you came round the other day.'

'I knew I should have gone earlier.'

With her ear so close to his body, the sound of his voice took on a different pitch and resonance. The tapping of his fingers vibrated in her chest and spread through her. She thought of what the attendant had said about infrasound passing through the ground and elephants calling to each other.

'She thinks boys are dangerous.'

The tapping stopped. 'We are.'

'I think she's been hurt somewhere down the line. A bit like Miss Havisham.'

There was a long silence, the slow intake of the evening air.

She looked up. His face was framed by the azure sky. She took out her own phone and pressed a button before he could move. There was a click and a small explosion of light. Behind the photo was a small flashing envelope icon. A message. And another. And another.

Missed call. Missed call. Text.

She opened one. *Ur gna pay Bella. U w8.*

She closed her eyes. It was from Laura. They all were.

'Does she think we're doing it?' he said.

'I dunno. I think she'd be madder if she thought we were.'

'Do you want me to talk to her?'

'And tell her what? That we're not?'

There was a commotion inside the zoo: a loud screeching and caterwauling from one of the pens, then a roar that cut it dead. She closed her eyes and felt the ground opening up beneath her. She felt the horrible sense of falling she sometimes had before waking, but more intense. There was a dull thud coming from somewhere. Then the nausea came back. Maybe she was coming down with something?

8

It was nearly half past ten when she got back to the house. Luca waited at the gate while she let herself in. There was no chance of him coming in now. She waved goodbye and put her back against the door. The house was quiet. She could hear the metronomic ticking of the kitchen clock. The only light downstairs was from the hall.

She breathed deeply, then made to climb the stairs. But, when she looked up, she saw Aunt Gene on the top step, in her dressing gown. She swallowed. 'I'm back.'

'So I can see.'

'I'm sorry I'm late.'

'I know what it's like when you're revising. You lose all track of time.'

Jodie nodded. The full weight of Aunt Gene's displeasure bore down on her.

'I suspect Luca was with you?'

The question caught her unawares. She paused guiltily and knew there was no point lying. 'For a bit, yes.'

'His mum wanted to know where he was.'

'You rang her?'

'I had things to discuss. Like where you were. *She* thought Luca was here.'

Jodie felt a wave of anger sweep through her. On top of Laura, her father, and the nightmares, she had this. She couldn't breathe without Aunt Gene knowing.

'We *were* revising.'

'I told you before I didn't want you to get involved, darling. Or I'd have to change things. You remember that?'

'Yes.'

'You're too young, Jodie.'

The unfairness of the statement stung her. *Young?* She would be eighteen in a few days.

She climbed the stairs to the attic, sullen and humiliated. She wanted to tell Aunt Gene she was old enough to look after herself, but tiredness and worry robbed her of the strength. She closed the door silently behind her.

*

An hour later, she lay on her bed and looked out of the dormer window. The sky was now a deep black. The curtains rippled gently in the breeze. She felt it on her skin, cool and close, like the breathing of a secret lover.

She looked at her father's paper and turned on her side. 'I hope you're okay, Dad. Wherever you are.'

She put her dressing gown on and took the paper back to its drawer, then shut the window and the night away.

She lay down and turned to face the wardrobe doors. Old fears came back to join the new: the hand from under the bed reaching out and grabbing her; the demon in the attic.

They were part of the same thing: an imagination gone wild. She had them as a child. Now they'd come back. But that's all they were. She was just stressed and tired. She didn't need a doctor for that, did she?

She closed her eyes and thought about the animals in the zoo, the little squirrel monkey and the chimps. She saw the imposing grey walls and copper roofs of the elephant house. Then she saw the trees and the red sky over Regent's Park, and finally the flashing lights of the police cars as they were leaving.

Pad.

She was falling, spinning to the ground. A whirlpool was round her and she was being sucked into its eye. She tried to reach out, but this time Luca's hand didn't save her.

Then everything went black.

She was pushing through thick undergrowth. Branches scratched and tore at her, but she kept going. There was a light ahead, and cages and pens, and the copper funnels of the elephant house. She was inside the zoo. All the tourists were gone. She passed the monkeys' enclosure. They looked out of the twilight at her like she was a ghost. She could tell they were on edge. They clung to the fences, gibbering and jabbing. The lions were up, too, circling restlessly. She ghosted past red-faced spider monkeys and night-black macaques. They were swinging wildly, clutching at anything, as if the ground would open up and swallow them.

Pad.

She turned quickly and stared into the darkness. There was a low, ominous growling coming from the tiger pen. She made her way slowly towards it. She knew something was wrong. The smaller female was on her haunches, staring at something, now backing away, frightened.

She was suddenly aware of the smell, like phosphorus and sulphur. Was something on fire? She walked round the pen to see what the female was looking at, but the rocks blocked her view.

There was a sudden commotion behind them, and a huge, angry roar. She guessed it must be the male. There was a flurry of movement, then a sickening thud like a huge object being thrown against a wall. Then there was silence. She ran round to the other side of the pen, tried to see what was going on. Through the foliage, she could see an orange glow in the darkness. The tiger was there, lying on a slab of stone. Its body jerked a little, then a little more. Horribly, she realised something was pulling it.

She crouched down, peered through a gap, caught a glimpse of something else. The sight of it set the whirlpool spinning again. There was a flash of green: a tail and two beating wings.

She tried to run but her limbs wouldn't move. The tiger was pulled off its feet. She saw its tail dangling uselessly. Then, after a few moments, the whole body came back to earth, lifeless.

The moment it did, she ran. She heard a wind behind her, sensed movement and something coming after her. Its hot breath burnt her neck. She couldn't look back; knew that, if she did, she would never come out. She'd be like Eurydice, dragged into the Underworld.

She tried to scream but no sound came out. Then she saw the eye of the whirlpool and made for it. It was amber with a black slit in it but, just as she dived in, it turned reptilian red.

'Go away!' she screamed. 'Go away!'

Her face hit a wall. Something wrapped itself round her

and she felt herself being pushed backwards. She expected to feel the ground any moment, but instead she landed on something soft.

'Jodie!'

The voice cut though the darkness. She opened her eyes wide.

'Jodie!'

There was no tiger, no demon, no nightmare. Just Aunt Gene.

Jodie felt like crying. 'I'm sorry, Aunt Gene.'

Aunt Gene took her in her arms. 'So am I, darling.' She pressed her lips to her forehead. 'So am I.'

*

Half an hour later, Jodie's fever finally abated and she settled into an uneasy sleep. Aunt Gene got up and paced the room and looked at the pictures on the walls. She picked up Jodie's psychology books from the floor and put them on the dressing table. The drawer was half open. Her fingers touched the handle. She knew Jodie kept a diary. Little by little, she pulled at it. Jodie stirred a little and she stopped. When the breathing resumed, she opened it fully. There was no diary. There was something much worse. Her fingers curled round the edges of the white sheets as she read the front.

Malcolm Lawrence. Infrasound.

She took the paper out and closed the drawer.

9

Aunt Gene left the house early, gripping the steering wheel as if it was a rubber ring and she was adrift at sea. She hadn't slept the rest of the night. She thought of the long, silent vigils she'd kept when Jodie was small, and hoped it was just coincidence the nightmares had started again; maybe she was stressed about her exams, or leaving school, or what she'd said about Luca. But in her heart, she knew it wasn't. The long shadows of the past were creeping back.

She drove up Rosslyn Hill and down Downshire Hill till she got to East Heath Road. In the distance, she saw the kites flying over Parliament Hill. Jodie had drawn some beautiful pictures of them a few years ago. She had one framed and hung on her bedroom wall. If only life had been so serene. She wondered if she should have left her this morning. Jodie was still a girl, still vulnerable. She drove past work and continued across the tops of the heath, along Hampstead Lane, to Highgate. The sun had drawn a haze across the city all the way down to Canary Wharf.

She didn't go all the way into the village but took the Swain's Lane turning, pulling up next to a large house overlooking the cemetery and the church she attended every Sunday. It was set back from the main road and surrounded by trees. On top of the gateposts were two stone owls. There was a silver plaque on one of the gateposts. It said *Highgate Spiritualist Circle* in neat letters.

Anxiety and fear of what she was about to do ate at her. There was still time to go back. She fingered the paper in her bag and scanned the pages. Nothing good had come of Malcolm Lawrence; William had warned him often enough. It was his fault what happened.

She got out, pressed the intercom button beneath the plaque, and watched the black gates open. Sunlight filtered through the trees but they couldn't dispel the shadows that had gathered over her.

The front door was opened by Habborlain's son, a young man about Jodie's age, dressed formally in a black suit. He was very pale, with sharp cheekbones and sunken eyes. He looked like he'd never seen the light of day.

'Hello, Ms De Dulin.'

'John, how are you today?'

'I'm fine. Thank you.'

'Is your father around?'

'Yes, he's about to start a reading.'

'I'm sorry. I hadn't realised.'

'It's okay. I'll tell him you're here.'

He led her into a large atrium with brown leather sofas facing each other and pictures on the wall of their church, the heath and the cemetery. They hadn't changed for years.

John disappeared through some large double doors. After a few minutes, he came out with his father, a tall, sturdily built man, also dressed in a black suit. William Habborlain's long, silver-grey hair was thrown back over his shoulders and his handsome bronzed face had a strained look about it. He took Aunt Gene's hand and kissed it. With his grey eyes and chiselled features, he had a dashing air about him, a touch of the Mr Rochester.

'Gene, are you sitting with us today?'

She looked into his grey eyes. 'I can't, William.'

'Something is the matter?'

She looked over at John.

Habborlain nodded and John left. He led her through the double doors and shut them quietly to behind them.

They were on their own. A fire was lit in the hearth along the far wall. She could hear it spitting in the grate and felt its warmth on her arms as he took her coat.

It seemed to quell her fear.

'I think it's starting again,' she said.

He paused. 'You know?'

'She's been having nightmares. Not normal ones. The ones she had when she was little.'

'It could be coincidence.'

'It could. But I found this.'

She handed him the paper she'd found in Jodie's room.

Habborlain looked down and his eyes glowered darkly. 'Malcolm's research papers from the Society?'

'I don't know where she got it. I hid everything.'

'You think it's disturbed her?'

'I know it has.'

'So what do you want me to do?'

'I want you to see her, as you promised. She's old enough to cope. She'll be eighteen soon.'

He went to the fireplace and looked into the great mirror above it. The fire crackled loudly.

'I've waited twelve years for this chance, William. I need to know what happened. You said we should act if the dreams started again. You said she would need your support—'

'Have you told her anything?' he interrupted.

'No. She thinks they died in a car crash.'

'It's going to be quite a shock.'

'It was quite a shock.'

He turned to her. 'You know we've never been able to call Kate. Even if she agrees, what's the chance Kate will come this time?'

'Jodie knows something.'

'Drawing such things from her might be very dangerous.'

'She deserves to know the truth, William.'

The fire flickered, sending ghosts of light out into the room.

'She's our only hope. Unless she wakes up one day and remembers everything, we will never know what killed her parents. It's your Christian duty to find out . . .'

He stared into the mirror, beckoned her to join him. The bookshelves stretched along the wall behind them.

'Look into the mirror, Gene. Tell me what you see.'

'Us, William. The bookshelves, the room.'

'Anything else?'

She searched the shadowy corners. 'No.'

He turned her round so her back was to the mirror. 'Now, what do you see?'

'The same, of course.'

'No, you don't. You see things the other way round.'

She felt his hands on her shoulders. 'I don't understand.'

'What if I told you your reflection was still there, staring at you?'

'Then I wouldn't believe you.'

He spun her round quickly. 'But it is, Gene.' The flames leapt up and hissed like angry cats. In the half-light, her reflection was there, staring back at her, confused and angry. 'Dealing with the paranormal, you're always looking at two different things. What you see and what you don't.'

'What do you mean?' she asked.

'That all this is your damned brother-in-law's fault. He was hell-bent on discrediting me and my profession. All those inflammatory articles he kept churning out. Science has the answer, science has the answer! Then that convention sponsored by the people he wrote this paper for.' He held it up to the light. 'The Society for Psychical Research. Turning up with his fancy gadgets, ready to wipe away two thousand years of *superstition*. No more ghosts, no more spirits, no more demons of the mind. Everything could be explained by infrasound.' He stared into the glass as if reliving the moment.

The fire spat beneath him, as if possessed with its own anger.

'He failed, of course. Or, rather, his equipment did. He leapt about the stage, pointing his fingers at people. He thought someone had sabotaged it. I told him there'd be a price to pay for it. The supernatural has a way of protecting itself. Something from behind the mirror.'

She looked at him, spellbound. 'I know, William. It was all Malcolm's fault. If he'd listened . . . if he'd stopped his experiments, Kate might be here now.'

87

'I went to investigate his infrasound ideas soon after he died, you know? I saw his Walkers. None of them believed in his sounds you couldn't hear. They all thought what I always did. Something was disturbed down there. Something that should have been left undisturbed.'

'And you think it came after him?'

He looked into the fire. '*Like one that on a lonesome road doth walk in fear and dread, because he knows a frightful fiend doth close behind him tread.* What could be more chilling?'

The fire dimmed and she looked round the room.

'What about Jodie?'

He paused. 'She needs to be careful. Very careful.'

Behind them, the double doors opened silently and John came in.

'I have to go, Gene. Think about it. There's no knowing what we'll let loose if we bring her in.'

10

Jodie woke with a start and looked out of the dormer window. The house was quiet and still, but her heart was thudding. She listened for Aunt Gene downstairs but heard nothing. The silence wound its way upstairs like a heavy mist and settled on the room. It felt late. She reached over to turn the radio on but found herself stuck to the sheets. There were damp patches underneath her and stray pages stuck to the covers. She pushed them off and they slid off the side of the bed like an avalanche. Flashes of last night's dreams rolled with them.

She saw the enclosure and a grey slab of rock with a tiger lying on it. Then there was a train with a light on coming down a tunnel. Laura was strapped to the front like a figure-head on a ship, her hair alight, her long fingers reaching out. Behind her, something was moving.

She turned the dial on the radio and a shadow fell across

the dormer window.

Scratch.

She looked round quickly. A rook with beady yellow eyes was perched on the ledge. It stared at her for a second like it was looking for her, then twisted its head and flew off with a cry.

A newscaster's voice cut in. 'Police are still unclear about the motives for the attack.'

She went to her dressing table and looked in the mirror. The bags round her eyes had got bigger.

'I've been working here twenty years and I've seen nothing like it,' a man said.

The words only dimly registered.

'They've always got on.'

Another domestic, another mugging, another night in London. She was about to change station when the newscaster came back.

'We're joined now by animal behaviour psychologist, Professor Neal McGuiness, from Imperial College.'

On hearing the name of her father's university, her ears pricked up.

'So, Professor, what might have prompted this, do you think?'

'At the moment, it's impossible to say,' the professor said. 'In the wild, female tigers will attack a male to defend their cubs or territory, but generally they stay far away. In this instance, in the confines of a zoo where there are no cubs, it's baffling. Tigers are essentially solitary animals and prefer *not* to fight each other. The only thing consistent with a tiger kill here is the timing. They do tend to hunt at night.'

Jodie turned the sound up.

'Reports from the zoo say the male appeared to be slashed?'

'Well, that's another puzzle. Tigers normally attack from the rear and go for the nape of the neck. This, really, does not have the hallmarks of a tiger kill.'

There was a short silence. 'You're suggesting another animal, then?'

'Well, I'm not party to the police report, but from the people I've spoken to, I gather the wounds and lacerations are more consistent with a blade than a tiger's claws and teeth.'

'You mean some*one*, then?'

'That would be my guess.'

There was another pause, as if the newscaster couldn't digest the information. 'Well, who'd do that? Who'd be *able* to do that?'

'I really can't speculate,' said the professor. 'It's quite baffling and a most terrible thing to happen.'

Jodie stared at the radio, incredulous. She felt sick.

She looked quickly round for her phone but couldn't find it anywhere. She looked under the bed sheets, under the bed, found it wedged between the side of the mattress and the wardrobe doors.

She tried Luca but his phone was switched off.

She threw on some clothes and raced down the stairs.

'I'm off!' she called out, but Aunt Gene was nowhere to be found.

She was all alone.

*

The delicatessen on Haverstock Hill had been in the Adriano family for years, far longer than Jodie had been alive. It was one of those shops that seemed to survive

91

the ravages of time, with all the old windows and furnishings still inside. The bell rang as she went in, and Mrs Adriano, normally so maternal towards her, gave her a cold look.

Jodie felt its draft. 'Is Luca in?'

Mrs Adriano splayed her hands on the counter like a martial arts expert. 'He's doing some revision.'

The emphasis on the last word told her all she needed to know. She thought of Aunt Gene's phone call and twigged. He was in trouble for missing the English exam and she was being blamed. 'It'll only be for a second.'

Before Mrs Adriano could reply, Mr Adriano came out of the back of the shop wearing his string vest. His chest hair sprouted from the top and spread like a forest across his back and arms. Behind him was Maria, Luca's sister, carrying a large vat of hummus.

'You coming to help, Jodie?' Mr Adriano smiled.

'Not really. I came to see Luca.'

He glanced at his wife and the smile turned sour. 'Right, well he's busy at the moment. Perhaps, if you come back later?'

He gave her a quick, conspiratorial wink.

Jodie nodded. He'd pulled this trick for her before.

She left the shop and walked up Haverstock Hill, looking back to make sure she wasn't being followed, then turned down a narrow alleyway at the end of the row. It was full of empty crates, newspapers and discarded takeaway cartons. The smell of half-eaten pizzas and putrefying kebabs was everywhere. She pinched her nose, picked her way carefully down the alley, then turned left again. There was broken glass, beer cans and cigarette butts on the ground, and 18-rated graffiti on the backyard walls. She kept walking until she was directly behind the shop.

She peered over the back gate. She could see Luca's room at the top, his Arsenal shirt hanging up in the window. The yard was full of stacked up crates and lines of clear, plastic bags with leftover cakes and pastries inside. The sun beat down and squadrons of flies buzzed round them, dive-bombing the cellophane.

She tried his phone again. It was still switched off.

She looked up at the window. 'Luca!' she called.

No response. He probably had his headphones on.

She vaulted over the back gate, looked round for something to throw at the window. She tore open one of the plastic bags, weighed up a hefty pastry in her hand, then settled on a small currant bun. She took a few steps back and threw it. It hit the wall a few feet beneath his window and broke up.

'Crumbs,' she said, looking at the mess. 'Luca!' she called again.

She found a large roll, took a few more steps back, and threw it harder. It smacked his window right in the centre and bounced back down. For a second, nothing happened, then the Arsenal shirt was pulled back and his face appeared at the window.

She waved her arms.

He hung out of the window in just his boxers. 'Are you insane?'

'We need to talk.'

'I can't come out.'

'It's important.'

He disappeared from view.

She dropped the roll into a wheelie bin, jumped back over the gate into the alley, and peered over the top like a sniper.

After a few minutes, the back door opened and he came out.

'Here,' she said.

'Where?'

'Behind the gate.'

He made his way over to her, looking warily back at the door. 'I've only got a few minutes. My mum's furious.'

'More with me than you, I think.'

'I wouldn't bet on it. What's up?'

'Did you hear the news this morning?'

'No. I've been revising.'

'One of those tigers was attacked last night.'

'Which tigers?'

'The zoo ones, you dummy.'

He paused. 'So?'

'So it was killed. It had its throat slashed.'

'Christ,' he said.

'I had a dream about it last night.'

'A dream?'

'Yeah. Something was in there with the tiger. It got in and killed it.'

The back door opened and Mr Adriano came out. He gesticulated for them to hurry up.

'I can't talk now, Jodie. Really.'

'You have to, Luca. Something's wrong.'

'Look, I'll be out in a bit,' he said. 'I need to get my phone off my mum first.'

'So how do we get in touch? Where do we see—'

'I'll see you at Stables. Give me an hour.'

'Luca . . .'

He squeezed her hand and ran inside.

Mr Adriano looked over at her. He didn't look cross or judgemental. He looked like he understood everything.

If only she did.

11

The 168 passed school and the Roundhouse and arrived at Camden Lock. Jodie felt the warm sun on her neck and the magnetic pull of the market. Every esoteric, bric-a-brac stallholder in London had one there. Designer clothes at magic mushroom inflated prices, Wiccan charms and candles – you could buy anything. There were world-famous palmists and mystical tarot readers and goth witches wearing pentagram cloaks. No one was out of place at Camden market. Every loser and weirdo had a place to go. That's what made it seem like home. Even Aunt Gene ventured down. She'd browsed the antiques at Stables and taken Jodie on one of the narrow boats to Little Venice.

Inside the main building, the smell of incense and perfume and exotic food piqued Jodie's nostrils. The Saturday crowds were already growing. The air became suffocating and full of clamour. She passed racks of designer printed t-shirts and vintage rings that sparkled on tables. In her hurry to get out, she knocked over a display of trinkets and postcards and found herself on the concrete floor, staring at one with a London Underground sign on it.

An old woman with a wrinkled face came out. 'Watch where you're going!'

'I'm sorry,' Jodie said.

She helped the woman pick her cards up but felt suddenly dizzy, noticing beads like man o' war tentacles rippling over a nearby door. Someone was looking at her through them. He was dark and swarthy and had a long ponytail. He reminded her of a gypsy. Behind him was a New Age picture of the planets surrounding an orange sun like a medieval astrolabe. In the middle were the words 'Reiki Master/Palmist'.

'You want a hand?' he said, coming to the door.

She shook her head. 'No. Thank you.'

He handed her a card. It was written in spidery handwriting. 'You looked as though you were in a hurry. You running from something?'

The words floored her. *Was it that obvious?*

'I was waiting for my boyfriend.'

'Lucky boy.'

She swallowed, tried to appear grown up. 'You tell fortunes?'

'Take your pick. Palmistry, Reiki or hypnotherapy.'

'You're like Uri Geller?'

'Better, I think.'

She thought of the demon and her father and the dead tiger in the zoo. 'Could you tell me mine?'

'If you wanted me to.'

An unseen hand seemed to propel her forward. The old woman gave her a look of warning but she ignored it. He showed her the door and she followed him through. The beads dangled down behind them.

'You read the notice?' He pointed to a handwritten sign behind him. *Readings may only be carried out on adults. You must be 18 or over.*

'Yes,' she said, and wondered if he knew she was lying.

'Does this really work?'

He shuffled a deck of Tarot cards. 'Well, that's an interesting question. There's a quote from the Book of Job I really like. It says God caused signs or seals on the hands of all the sons of men, that the sons of men might know their works. What do you think?'

Jodie thought of Aunt Gene and the Bible beside her bed. She held her palms out. 'I can only afford ten minutes.'

He put the cards down, reached out, and took them.

The first thing she noticed was the warmth. His hands seemed to light her up.

'Palmists were once seen as witches and devil worshippers, weren't they?'

'Yes, the practice was banned for many years. But, you know, what was witchcraft one century is the next century's science.'

He turned her hands over.

'Well?'

'Hands have the potential to reveal a person's character, health and psychological state. Some are clearer than others.'

'Meaning you can't see anything?'

'No. Quite the opposite. You came in here because you're running from something. What that is, I can't clearly see, but you're frightened of it. Very frightened. You have a very unusual psychic alignment. One might almost call it an out of alignment. You're intelligent, sensitive and careful. Yet you are wilful when you want to be, and destructive.'

The words shocked her. How could he read her so well?

He picked up her right hand. 'This is your dominant hand. It is the face you show the world, your consciousness.' He picked up the left. 'This is your subconscious, your instincts, what goes on inside. The two are very different.'

'I don't understand.'

'You're two different people.'

'You got that from my palms?'

'Yes.'

'Is that bad?'

'It's not anything. It's just what I see.'

'What about my future? What does that hold for me?'

He paused and his eyes glinted. It made her feel uncomfortable. 'You're at school.' It wasn't a question. 'Taking exams.'

She nodded.

'That's all I can see.'

'Aren't you meant to tell me if I'll get married, or if I'll be successful, or what's going to happen to me?'

'If I saw it, I'd tell you.'

She was suddenly beset with a greater fear. 'You mean I'm going to die? You can't see anything because I'm not there?'

A half-smile appeared on his face. 'No, I don't see that, and I didn't say it. Hands change over time. Life lines, heart lines, head lines tell us of the person now. They tell me what your past is, who you are, and what you may become. Tomorrow, next year, that may all change. In your case, the present is unclear. I'm not someone who's going to concoct a future for you and take your money. I'm telling you what I can see.'

'Well, there must be more than that?'

He paused again. 'Give me your left hand.'

He stared at her for a moment, then his eyes winked out. She studied the wrinkles on his face and tried to read *his* future. Moisture collected between their hands. After a few seconds, he suddenly jolted and his eyes opened.

'It's still dark. I don't know why.' Their hands parted. 'You're looking for something. Or something's looking for you.'

'What?'

'I don't know. It's like a tunnel that has no end.'

She thought of the tunnel in her dream.

'What kind of tunnel?'

'It's too dark, I'm afraid. But there's a smell.'

'What of?'

His nose wrinkled. 'Trains. The Underground, maybe.'

She looked at him. 'The Underground?'

'Yes, it's something down there.'

'But I never go there.'

He looked at her and didn't say anything.

She took a ten-pound note out of her bag. Deep down, she hoped he'd let her off. It was annoying to think she'd spent so much on so little. But he took it from her, folded it up, and put it in his pocket.

He led her back to the beads and she half imagined his hand on her back, but when she looked round, he was sitting down again.

*

The crowd was now three or four deep beside the stalls, a

100

broad church of humanity. It was impossible to make her way through without a struggle. She looked at her phone to see if Luca had got in touch, but there were no messages and no calls.

She tried him. His phone was still switched off.

Then, above the din, she heard her name being called. Her eyes came to rest on an Asian takeaway. Two men were serving kebabs and samosas over steaming grills. The skewers were black with oil. Beside them, and through the smoke, someone was waving at her. It was Kamran. He said something to the two men, then waded his way through the crowd towards her.

'Jodie!' Drops of perspiration clung to his spotty forehead. The steam from the tandoor left his pores wide open. 'What are you up to?'

'I'm looking for Luca.'

'I've just seen him,' he said.

'You have?'

'Yeah. He ran right past me.'

'When? Which way?'

He pointed towards Stables.

One of the men at the tandoor shouted over. 'Kamran, *ider ao*!'

He looked embarrassedly at her. 'I've got to go, Jodie. Sorry.'

She didn't wait to say goodbye. She ran as fast as she could. As she turned on to High Street, she passed a newspaper vendor.

'Standard. Early edition!' the man shouted, waving a paper.

On the cover was a picture of the tiger. She recognised its face and pulled up quickly. The headline screamed *Zoo*

Horror. It cut right through her. She grabbed a copy, opened her bag to put it in, then noticed something.

Her folded-up ten-pound note was back inside.

12

Stables market was once a Victorian horse hospital, built beside the arches of the old North Western Railway Company. An endless maze of cobbled alleys and stalls, it was the part of Camden market Jodie loved best. But not right then. All she could think of was Luca. How come he hadn't rung? How come he hadn't turned up?

She searched the shops they normally went to, but couldn't find him anywhere. She ran down the winding alleys and Dickensian pathways, through catacombs of art, clothing and furniture, and eventually stopped outside the entrance to the Horse Tunnel market. She tried his phone again. There was a little click, then the inevitable: *The mobile phone you have called is switched off. Please try again later.* Well, it *was* later.

She hurried to the old catacombs. She knew he liked going to Cyberdog, the wildest and most futuristic of all the shops in the area, maybe in all of London. Two giant Metropolis robots stood sentry outside. Inside, it was an LED-flashing, mind-expanding, ear-imploding drug. You could hear it long before you saw it. The cyber-electro, trance, techno music made the floor shudder. The noise and the flashing lights gave her a headache.

Her eyes quickly adjusted to the science-fiction setting. Most of the shop was underground and lit by fluorescent strip lights. Purple ones scored the brick ceiling like road marks. She followed them through the arches till she got to the cavernous cybercafe. 'Axle Grinder' was booming from the huge stack speakers on the wall. The drums beat her ears till she couldn't hear herself think. It was like shopping in a nightclub.

She ran down the aisles, mesmerised by the pink and blue strips along the walls. She began to feel queasy. Everything was UV and bright fluorescent. Even the t-shirts had *Matrix*-style flashing lights. She stared at the designs and the letters on them jumbled up. Her eyes flickered. She shook her head and they cleared momentarily, but the sense of unease was still there. She passed robot memory sticks, robot moneyboxes, plasma balls and colour changing alarm clocks, and saw rows of cyber-robots on the walls, all glowing in different colours. Their eyes lit up red, green and indigo.

The music was drilling in her head. From the corner of her eye, something leapt out at her. She spun round quickly but couldn't see anything, just the blank-faced robots. She looked up at the ceiling and the purple strip lights beamed back coldly. She put the plasma ball she was holding down. Then she froze. There was a boy watching her from the shadow of one of the arches. He had long dark hair and was so thin he looked almost anorexic. Something about him made her feel as though she'd seen him before. She shook her head again.

She went the other way and pretended she hadn't seen him. She tried to lose herself in the labyrinth of rooms, but he appeared to be following her. She cut left, right, left again, then looked about. Her heart was going faster than the music. She made for the exit. She could see it up ahead. Then she felt something on her arm, cold and fleshy, and she turned. It was Laura's Belladonna Bratz: Bethany and Cheryl. She had been so caught up with the strange boy that she'd walked right into them.

They seemed to be shouting at her. She couldn't hear them but she could lip-read their words.

'Laura's looking for you.'

'Why? I haven't done anything.'

'She wants to see you.'

'I'm meeting someone.'

They smiled. 'No, you're not.'

Jodie looked down. Something was glinting in the dark. At first, she thought it was the buckle on Bethany's coat; then she realised.

'What are you doing?'

'Laura wants to see you *now*.'

She stared at the knife. Her eardrums rattled and her body shook. She felt herself falling, losing control again.

'Help me.'

The witches were momentarily confused. Then Jodie's body righted itself and her mind cleared. It was all the time she needed. She pushed past them and ran. Even when she got outside, she didn't stop. She hurried through the crowds and lost herself in the iron press of humanity. She ran past

Gilgamesh restaurant until she was on Chalk Farm Road. She knew where to go. The Roundhouse was a haven from all that was bad, a sanctuary for artists, a place for outsiders like her. She made for its turret like it was her last refuge on Earth. It was only when she'd got there that she looked back. Bethany and Cheryl were nowhere to be seen, and neither was the odd-looking boy.

She hurried to the upstairs gallery and slunk against a wall. The posters of Andy Warhol and photographs of famous past productions still hung on the bare brickwork, and a press clipping of the Living Theatre from the 1960s. She looked over the rails into the foyer. There were no witches. She wondered if she'd imagined the knife and Bethany had held something else in her hand. Seeing people relaxing in the cafe bar, living their ordinary lives, made her think so.

She went down, sat by the window, and got out the sketchbook Luca had bought her. She felt like ripping it up. She drew one of the cyber-robots with a knife in its hand, then tore it out. As she did, her phone rang.

It was Luca.

'Hello?'

There was a pause.

'Jodie, where are you?'

She didn't say anything. He sounded strange.

'Jodie?'

'Where have you been? I've rung loads.'

'I can't talk.' He sounded hoarse, as if straining to speak.

'Why not? What's the matter?'

'Don't go out . . . Stay where you are. Laura and her friends are after you.'

'I've already seen them.'

There was another pause and the sound of shuffling feet. It sounded like someone was talking to him now.

'Let me come and get you.'

'Where have you been, Luca? Who's there with you?' She was growing more desperate.

'Jodie, listen to me. You're in trouble. Just tell me where you are.'

There was a small click.

Something was up.

'I'm at home.'

'No, you're not. I've rung there.'

'I'm at the Roundhouse.'

'I'll be there in a bit. Think of Starsailor, yeah?'

'What?'

'The song you played me.'

'What about it?'

The line went dead.

'Luca?'

She rang him back but there was no reply. What the hell was going on? Why did he ask her to think of that?

She caught her reflection in the glass and ran the lyrics round in her head. *I can't see myself when I look in the mirror.* It couldn't be that one. She racked her brain, all the while unable to shake the feeling of approaching doom. Then she stopped. It wasn't that one. She'd played him another. Suddenly it made sense. *Oh God.* He *was* trying to tell her something. She grabbed her bag and ran for the exit.

Get out while you can, it's set to blow

She ran to the bus stop by Chalk Farm Tube station, the one where Laura and Trent had caught them.

You should just be glad I let you know

She was, but it was too late. There was shouting down the

road. She could see Laura and Bethany and Cheryl running towards her. Others were coming from the council estate behind Chalk Farm Grill. She was trapped. Why hadn't he just told her? She made for the Underground. It was her only hope. A car screamed to a halt as she crossed the road and a horn blared. It looked like one of Trent's friends inside. He looked at her quizzically like a snake feeling the air with its tongue.

She ran round the station corner and hoped he hadn't recognised her. She entered the concourse and tried to buy a ticket. The pound coins kept going through the machine. Trent's friend disappeared into the Food and Wine shop. The shouts were louder now. They knew where she'd gone. She left the change and pushed past the guard, clutching her ticket.

The air was thick with heat. She ran down the tunnels to the lifts. The noise of footsteps above her grew. The lift doors closed before she got there. There was only one thing left to do: take the stairs. She took several steps down, pressed herself against the wall, and hoped they'd pass her. She could hear them now. She looked down and saw the staircase winding round. It was a long way down. The Northern Line had some of the deepest tunnels on the network. The corners receded as she walked, just like they did in her mirror.

She heard Bethany's voice. 'She has to be around here some place.'

She took another few steps down.

We don't like your kind here

'Have you seen her?'

Then one cut through, louder than the rest. It was Laura's.

'She won't have gone down to the platforms. The bitch doesn't like the Underground. Try the stairs.'

She heard footsteps at the top and began to run. The air was warm from the trains. She could hear them roaring through the tunnels like minotaurs. She pulled out her mobile phone and tears streamed from her eyes. Who was going to save her now? Not Aunt Gene, not Luca, not even the guard. She was on her own.

She took one step, two, then three at a time, all the while listening behind her. Just as she thought she'd got away, she tripped and the phone skittered down the stairs in front of her. The sound echoed up the tiled walls. Instantly, there was a reply from the top. The ghouls started running down after her. She grabbed the phone, held her arms out like a plane and ran, using the walls for balance. She could hear them catching her, took the steps three and four at a time, nearly fell. The walls were narrow; she didn't have a chance to look back. Then, she felt a buffet of air billow up the stairs and knew she was nearly there. Another train had come.

The roar got louder. She raced down the tunnel towards the platforms, but it was too late. The train pulled out and warm air was sucked back. She had seconds to hide. A few stray passengers took detours as she passed. They looked at her like she'd lost her mind. There was a narrow barrier with yellow danger signs stuck on it. She looked at the train display and the letters were all askew.

1 Egdwrae 5 msni

She looked at the posters on the Tube wall, but their letters had moved, too: *SkyS Strops HD We knwo you hwo fell, becse we fel the same*; *Del Eat yorslf*. At the end of the platform was the long-haired boy she'd seen in the market. Who was he? He beckoned to her, then leapt down on to the tracks and into the tunnel mouth. She had no choice. It was that or be cut up by Laura and her gang. She jumped over the barrier on to the line and ran into the tunnel.

Darkness enveloped her like a thick black cloud. The musty smell of oil rose up from the tracks. Behind her, she heard voices. She turned and saw the ghouls running down the platform to the other exit. She recognised Bethany and Cheryl but Laura was nowhere to be seen.

'We've got just over four minutes to get out,' came a voice from the dark. It was the boy. He was in there with her.

The train display turned to *4*.

She edged back into the darkness and wondered if there was somewhere else she could hide.

It was then that Laura came into view. She was wearing a long black leather coat with chains on it, which rattled as she walked. Her platform shoes elevated her several inches and her hair stuck up from her head like antennae. Trent was beside her in a gothic top hat. They looked like the King and Queen of some fairy tale ball. Despite her fear of her, there was fascination, too. There was something beautiful and chilling about Laura. She seemed so composed. Or decomposed. Jodie shook her head, began to feel dizzy.

1 Egdwrae 3 msni

'She must have caught the train.'

Bethany was coming back down the platform.

'She can't have.'

Laura's eye sockets were painted like spider's webs. Her purple lips receded from her gums. She stared into the train tunnel. Jodie shrank back against the wall. She felt the boy brush against her and began to feel nauseous. What did he want? The train was coming. She had to get out. Her fingertips dug into the walls. They were shaking, desperate to hold on to something.

'I know she's here.'

Jodie closed her eyes. She was going to throw up.

Please go. Please go.

The wind was strong enough to blow her hair.

'I told you, she's gone.'

Laura took a last look into the tunnel. She seemed to be mouthing something.

1 Egdwrae 2 msni

Jodie looked behind her and her eyes flickered. There was a rush of air like a river and a sound louder than any minotaur. It bellowed down the tracks. There was something down there.

Laura vanished. Jodie waited a few seconds, then ran to the tunnel mouth. Any second now, it would pass her.

1 Egdwrae 1 mni

She put her hands on to the platform edge and felt a shove from below. The boy was helping her up. She could see the light of the train now. It was right behind them. Something appeared to block its way for a second, but there was enough time to see what it was.

Wings flapped, a tail curled, and red eyes bored down the tracks. It was coming for her. This wasn't a nightmare. It was real. If the train didn't cut her in two, the demon would. She scrambled on to the platform and turned to offer her hand to the boy. She caught his skinny wrist and pulled, but his legs seemed to dangle over the side for an eternity, the wind trying to blow them both back on to the track. She grabbed hold of the barrier and pulled again. This time he made it, sprawling on to the platform just in time.

The train blew past them like a whirlwind, the demon clinging to the top, its green-fingered claws outstretched.

The carriages rattled and the station shook. She closed her eyes. When she opened them, there was nothing. No sound. No wind. No boy. The platform was empty. She looked at the train display.

1 Edgware 8 mins

The letters on the posters righted themselves, too. *We know how you feel, because we feel the same.*

She crawled to the edge of the track and threw up. They bloody didn't.

13

Aunt Gene sat at the kitchen table with an unopened copy of *The Times*. Her reading glasses were perched on the end of her nose, but she wasn't reading. She was looking at a silver mortise key. She turned it over in her hand several times. The past was the key to unlocking so many things, but with this, there was more a sense of trepidation. Who knew what would come out? She laid it on the table and waited.

At 6 p.m. there was a knock at the door. It wasn't who she was expecting. Jodie had brought two visitors with her: police officers.

'Mrs De Dulin?'

She was too shocked to correct them.

'May we come in?'

Jodie was as pale as moonlight.

'What's happened?'

'It's better we speak inside.'

She led them into the kitchen and invited them to sit down. There was such a seriousness about them, she thought someone had died.

'Has she been arrested?'

'No. She was found at Chalk Farm Tube station.'

'Found?'

The officer hesitated. 'Yes. A member of the public alerted station staff. She had her head over the side of the northbound platform.'

'What are you saying?'

Had all her years bringing Jodie up led to this? She wanted to kill herself?

'She was delirious. We're not sure if it was attempted suicide or she'd been taking something. We had a paramedic look her over.'

Aunt Gene began to think it was a dream. Jodie was now a drug addict? She turned to her.

Jodie kept her head down. Her hair hung over her face like a shroud and she said nothing.

Aunt Gene looked at the police officers. 'She's not being charged with anything?'

They looked at her sympathetically. 'No.'

She led them down the hall.

At the door, the officer turned. 'We have a support line if you need someone to talk to.'

'No,' she said. 'But thank you.'

She closed the door behind them. It was still warm from the afternoon sun but inside it was cold. Her body cast a shadow on the wooden floor. It shimmered like a memory. She went back into the kitchen and sat down. Jodie hadn't moved at all. The kitchen clock ticked slowly. She pursed her lips and looked at the key.

'Jodie, we need to talk. I need you to tell me what's wrong. If you're bothered by something, if you're cross with me, you need to say.'

'I'm fine.'

'You call trying to kill yourself fine?'

'I don't remember doing it.'

'What were you doing down there?'

'I don't remember.'

'Jodie, you have to.'

She kept her head down.

'Will you look at me when I'm talking to you?'

Aunt Gene reached across the table and drew the curtain of hair from her eyes. They were sunken and red.

'I want you to tell me what happened.'

'I don't remember, Aunt Gene. Really I don't.'

Aunt Gene looked down at the table. She wondered if it was really the right time to force the moment when Jodie was so upset, or if there would ever be a good moment.

She paused. 'When I was in your room last night, I found something.'

Jodie's eyes flickered.

'I don't know whether it's got anything to do with how you've been, or how you came by it, but I'd like you to tell me.' She lifted the copy of *The Times* and brought out her father's paper on infrasound. 'Where did you find it?'

Jodie stirred. 'In the attic.'

'The attic?'

'Behind the wardrobe.'

'What were you doing in there?'

'Something hit the roof a few nights ago. I went to see what it was.'

115

Aunt Gene paused. 'Did you find anything else?'

'Just Dad's books. You didn't tell me he had all that stuff.' Her tone was defensive.

'I packed it away when he died. I was going to show you.'

'When?'

'When the time was right.'

'I'm eighteen in a few days.'

'Is that what all this is about?'

'All what?'

'Putting your head on Tube lines, Luca coming round, not sleeping.'

Aunt Gene wondered if she already knew the truth about her mother and father. 'Jodie, I want you to be quite honest with me now. Did you find anything else up there?'

She held her breath and waited for the knockout blow. In a sense, she'd have welcomed it. It would have spared her telling the truth.

'Yes. There was a machine. Most of it was packed in boxes. My dad was working on something, wasn't he?'

Aunt Gene paused. 'Yes,' she said. 'Something terrible.'

14

Jodie knew Aunt Gene would take it badly, the way she took anything antisocial badly. It was a reflection on her and all the things she stood for. She couldn't remember much of what happened when the police came. She was just glad they did.

The boy who'd saved her had gone but Laura, Bethany and Cheryl were at the station exit. They looked less like ghouls in broad daylight and more like stupid kids; their expressions had changed from anger to anxiety. Even Trent seemed to look sorry for her. Maybe they were all worried she'd tell the police? But when she caught her reflection in the rear view mirror, she saw the real reason. She looked dead. Actually, she looked *undead*, more of a ghoul than they'd ever be. She'd thrown half her guts up and her head spun.

Just as it was doing now.

She sensed Aunt Gene's anxiety and the feeling spread to her. *Terrible?* What could be that terrible?

'Your father was a clever man, Jodie. It was one of the reasons your mother fell in love with him. He was very passionate and committed. He worked at a university and spent a good deal of time on his research. Often, he brought it home. Your mum was very supportive of him. She had her own work but I think recognised she would have to sacrifice it, especially when you came along.'

Jodie listened. It was like a diary being opened. Each sentence Aunt Gene spoke seemed to wake dormant memories. She started to see her mum and dad as flesh and blood, not as figures in photographs. Every now and again, Aunt Gene paused and Jodie knew she was choking back thoughts and reliving things.

'Things like this aren't easy for me to talk about. I loved your mum. We were very close. She was more than a sister to me.' She brought out a white handkerchief from her pocket and dabbed her eyes. 'Your father had some pretty unconventional ideas. He described himself as a ghost hunter.'

Jodie thought of the papers in the attic. 'A what?'

'He tracked them down, tried to explain them away. Spirits, poltergeists, every type you could think of. He thought he had the answer to everything,' she said bitterly.

Jodie picked up the paper on the table. 'Infrasound,' she said.

Aunt Gene stared at her. 'Yes. I didn't understand, at first. It seemed so far-fetched. But Kate believed in it. Or rather, she believed in him. She watched it consume him and did what most loyal wives would. She stood by him.'

'You didn't approve?'

'No. But it wasn't any of my business. Not until a friend of mine became involved, anyway.'

'Were they happy?'

Aunt Gene shook her head. 'What's happiness? They had plans like every other couple, before life gets in the way. I know you brought them happiness. Your father doted on you. He may have been distracted and taken off when he shouldn't, but he always had time for you, and his work, of course, even when he had none for Kate.'

She dabbed her eyes again. Jodie felt tears well in her own.

'I wish I remembered more of them. The machine in the attic – was that part of his work?'

'Yes. He was working on it before he died.'

'Why is it in so many pieces?'

Aunt Gene paused. 'I don't know.'

Jodie looked at the paper on the table and ghosts seemed to rise up out of it. 'Why didn't you believe him?'

'I thought his theory was nonsense, but he was driven by it, even when his health failed. He had a pacemaker fitted before he died, but it didn't stop him. At the end, work was the only thing he could see or hear. He wouldn't listen to anyone else.'

Jodie thought of the other things she'd seen in the attic. 'I believe in ghosts and spirits.'

'So does anyone sane and God-fearing.'

'I think I've seen one here, in the house.'

Aunt Gene stared at her. 'What do you mean?'

Jodie wondered if there was still time to go back. 'The last few nights, I haven't felt right, ever since I looked in the attic. I felt there was something in there. A presence, a thing.'

'What thing?'

'You won't believe me.'

'Tell me, Jodie.'

Jodie swallowed. 'There's one of dad's books up there, about witchcraft. I think I've seen it before. When I looked through it, I seemed to recognise the pictures. When I got to a certain place, it's like I knew what was coming up.'

'What did you see?'

'I told you, you'll think it's daft.'

'Tell me.'

Jodie paused. 'It's a picture of a demon.'

'A demon?'

'It's green with horns and tusks, and its face is split in two.'

With each detail, Aunt Gene seemed to shrink into her chair.

'And a red mouth?'

'Yes.'

Aunt Gene trembled. Jodie sensed something terrible was about to break inside her. The world outside had ceased to be, just as it had in the tunnel. Maybe the bad thing hadn't happened yet? Maybe it was building up to it?

'I've always told you about the importance of telling the truth, haven't I, Jodie? How you can't live without it, and how I always expect it of you?'

Jodie felt the dread creep up her insides.

'I want you to forgive me for what I'm about to do.'

'What is it?'

Aunt Gene picked up the silver mortise key. She seemed to age in front of Jodie's eyes. 'I need to show you something.'

*

When Aunt Gene led her out of the kitchen, Jodie felt like she was discovering the house for the first time. She noticed cornices and doorframes that were never there before, and marks on the walls where the paint had frayed and scuffed. She thought they were going to the cellar. All the houses on the road had them. You could see flowers sticking out of their grates and hear children playing in them in the summer. But Aunt Gene laid a hand on the balustrade and took her upstairs. She wondered if she was going to take her up to the attic. Maybe there was another part of it she hadn't seen, with more secrets?

Aunt Gene paused on the landing beside her bedroom. Then Jodie understood. The key was for the room next to it. She'd been told it was an airing cupboard when she was little, full of junk and rubbish. It didn't sound like Aunt Gene even then; she had the contents of cupboards and the food in the fridge neatly laid out.

Jodie stared at the key and felt the past reach out to her. She saw her mother and father arguing and a little girl playing on her own.

'I've always kept this room locked. It was my way of coping,' Aunt Gene said.

'With what?'

Aunt Gene didn't reply, just turned the key in the lock. At first it didn't move, then, all of a sudden, there was a small crack and the door opened. Grey light and a dank, musty smell seeped out. It wasn't an airing cupboard at all, but a small bedroom. Aunt Gene went in and drew the curtains back. The red evening sun slewed in like a bleary, bloodshot eye and gave the room an orange glow.

Jodie looked around. It was full of furniture – period pieces, mainly. There were mirrors and figurines and a couple of chests of drawers that looked hundreds of years old. There was also a mahogany chair, which reminded her of Miss Havisham's in *Great Expectations*. It was quite a treasure trove and must have been worth thousands of pounds.

'Whose are these?'

Aunt Gene looked round. 'Originally, your grand-mother's. She was quite a collector. Your mother took them with her when she got married. I never thought they'd come back.'

'Why have you left them here?'

'Because I didn't want reminding.' She opened the top drawer of one of the chests and took out some papers. 'Not all memories are pleasant.'

Jodie wiped the dust off a porcelain mirror and saw her reflection. The red sun gave her a tinge of rouge. She imagined her mother doing the same thing long ago. Trepidation gave way to sadness. 'Why didn't you show me before?'

'I didn't think the time was right. For either of us.'

She stared at her and it seemed to Jodie as if she was apologising for something.

'Is this what you wanted to show me?'

Aunt Gene's hands trembled. 'After your mother and father died, you were quite poorly. It was difficult looking after you. You had nightmares and fainting episodes. The doctors thought you might be epileptic. I kept everything for you in this. It's a log of what happened to you. When the doctors had finished, you were sent to a psychologist. Several, actually. They said you were suffering from a trauma. They couldn't really help you and hoped time would sort you out. They said children were very resilient.'

After each sentence, Aunt Gene took a small breath. It

122

was like she was measuring the words against her reaction. With each revelation, the past came slowly into focus.

'They asked me to keep a record of things that you did and said, and the drawings that you made. They said problems were often worked out that way, in the subconscious. They thought they may be able to diagnose you through them.'

She flicked through the papers and brought out a plastic wallet with some drawings in. Jodie glimpsed the slapdash colours of paints and crayons.

'You were a very sophisticated artist when you were little. It's amazing what details you picked out. Your school thought you were a prodigy. You were drawing objects before most children were learning to write their alphabet.' She took the drawings out and laid them on a round table. 'Some of the pictures are quite frightening.'

Jodie picked them up. Some of the scenes looked like they'd been painted by Bosch. To think any child had drawn them would have made her uneasy. But to know the child was her?

Some of them looked vaguely familiar, too. Then she realised why. They were stills, approximations of the pictures in her father's book. Every picture she saw was like turning a page. She knew what was coming before she even got to it. The green sinuous limbs, the mouth in two halves, even the red melon mouth, it was in every one. She'd known it since she was a child. She clutched the drawers and let Aunt Gene help her into Miss Havisham's chair.

'It's the demon in the book.'

'I know. So did the psychiatrists. They said it was your way of shifting blame.'

'For what?'

Aunt Gene paused. 'For what happened.'

'To Mum and Dad? They were killed in a car crash. How would that shift blame?'

Jodie stopped. It was as if she was walking down a corridor towards a door. It was dark, save for a narrow cleft of light. She felt a punch to her chest.

'I was with them, wasn't I? I was with them in the car?'

She felt hysteria clutching at her throat and panic in her lungs. Aunt Gene held on to her hands and wouldn't let go.

'No, Jodie.' She put her arms round her. 'It wasn't like that.'

'I don't understand. How would I be traumatised if I didn't see them die?'

She choked out sobs. The events of the day had finally caught up with her.

'I asked you to forgive me, Jodie.'

'For what?'

'For lying.'

Lying?

'I always wanted to tell you, but I couldn't bring myself to. It was all so horrid.'

Aunt Gene's measure and composure had gone. The trembling had turned to shaking.

'As the years went by, I hoped you'd just forget, the same way I wanted to. I hid the furniture and your father's things and hoped the whole thing would just go. But it hasn't. It's been lying here, waiting. Waiting just like I have. Well, now I have to account for it and I only hope you'll understand.'

'Understand what?'

Jodie could hardly breathe.

'Your parents weren't killed in a car crash.' There was a sickening pause. 'I made it up.'

The words rushed through Jodie's head like a wind, running from corner to corner, upturning the anatomy of her mind.

'I don't understand.'

Aunt Gene picked the papers from the chest of drawers and gave them to her. The topmost was a newspaper article from the *Evening Standard*. Jodie looked at the headline.

Couple Slaughtered In Their Home

She saw the picture below. It was of a couple by the beach. With them was a little girl. It was her. The words below were a jigsaw. Everything in her life seemed to fall into and out of place at the same time. The way she was, and who she was, changed in an instant. Her mother and father looked so happy. She was standing between them with a smile on her face. Her fringe was in her eyes and she carried a bucket and spade. There was nothing special about the picture other than its ordinariness, but the ordinariness was what made it so difficult to comprehend.

'What are you saying?'

'They were killed, Jodie.'

'Killed?'

A different kind of panic set in: not the fear of anticipation any more, but the fear of coping.

'How?'

Aunt Gene was crying. Her face was a stricken vessel too far out at sea. She held out more clippings and an official-looking file. 'It's all in here. I saved what I could.'

Jodie looked at them. There were more tragic headlines and the same terrible photograph.

The file was a police report with a case number on the front. Her hands trembled as they touched it.

She couldn't read it.

'Tell me,' she whispered.

Aunt Gene looked at her as if she was asking for forgiveness. 'They were murdered. The police thought someone had come into the house and stabbed them, but they couldn't find a motive.'

Jodie lay back in the chair.

'It's best you read it.'

'I can't.'

Aunt Gene wiped her eyes. 'The police said they'd seen nothing like it. It was . . . horrible.'

Jodie felt an icy chill course through her. *Slaughtered*.

'Who did it?'

Aunt Gene shook her head. 'No one knows. There was a big search. There was forensics. There were investigations. But the killer just vanished. I've been trying for the last twelve years to find out.'

Her words drifted to the back of Jodie's mind. She stopped hearing them and looked out at the red sun. The dread feeling crept up inside her again. There was the narrow cleft of light and another punch to her chest.

'What about eyewitnesses?'

She knew Aunt Gene was looking at her and knew from the grip on her hand what it meant.

'I was there, wasn't I?'

'Yes, darling. They found you in the room. You were their only lead. But you wouldn't talk.'

'The doctors and psychiatrists, they couldn't find anything?'

Aunt Gene shook her head. 'You were so young and vulnerable, they thought it dangerous to push. Whatever you saw or knew was locked up for good.'

Jodie looked at the picture of herself on the beach. What a

126

gap there was between the two of them. One had every-thing, the other had . . . what?

'Why have you told me this?'

'I'm sorry, Jodie.'

'Just because you couldn't live without the truth doesn't mean I couldn't.'

Aunt Gene looked like she'd been slapped. 'There's no need to talk like that.'

Jodie shook her hands off. 'Why not? You didn't need to tell me.'

'You'd have found out one day and hated me even more. You're having those dreams again. Something's happening. I couldn't keep it from you any more. You need help. You need to face this.'

Aunt Gene extended arms of solace but Jodie shrugged them away. She went to the window. 'You're a hypocrite. Don't ever talk to me about truth.'

'Jodie, please. You asked me to.'

Jodie's anger reached its zenith. 'I didn't ask for anything.'

The anger was unstoppable. She pushed past Aunt Gene to the door.

'Where are you going?'

'Out.'

Aunt Gene followed her to the top of the stairs. 'Where?'

Jodie ran down them. There were long shadows in the hall. They hid the tears and guilt and pain. Her mother and father had been ripped from inside her. She opened the door and ran to the one place she knew could contain her. It had to be big to match the gulf left in her heart.

15

Jodie made her way in the fading light over Parliament Hill Fields. There were joggers out and people making their way home after a day out. She could hear dogs and children and the distant traffic along East Heath Road, but most of all she could hear the voices in her head. Aunt Gene's was there, telling her to come home; and Mum's and Dad's, telling her they loved her.

She ran over the long grass to Kite Hill. It had always been her refuge, far from anyone, a place to think about herself and the world. She stumbled several times but she wouldn't rest till she was there. At last, her chest heaving and her body aching from the ordeal, she collapsed on top of the hill and lay down, looking up at the twilight. The orange glow was now no more than a flickering ember in the west.

The view over London was spectacular. Kite Hill was three hundred feet high. The lights on top of Canary Wharf could be seen for miles and the dome of St Paul's Cathedral was all lit up. She took in all its vast detail. It always made her and her problems seem smaller somehow. There were millions of people in London and only one her. Maybe there were people out there who'd been through what she had; maybe people who understood; maybe there was also someone out there who knew what had happened to her mum and dad, roaming the streets of Camden or Archway or Gospel Oak?

She lay back on the grass and sobbed. The pain was like nothing she'd ever known. Before, it was something she'd grown up with and got used to. Now, it was different. There were other kids who had no mother or father, kids whose parents had been killed; but how many had parents who'd been murdered? That happened in books, in *Great Expectations* and *Macbeth*, not in real life.

She lay, tearful and angry and guilty. She watched a fleet of summer-white clouds drift by. There was no point crying. It wouldn't bring them back. But there was no other way to express how she felt.

She made her way down Kite Hill to Highgate Ponds. It was dark now and the only light seemed to come from the city. There were still some late night walkers out with their dogs, but mostly it was quiet.

The ponds used to be reservoirs but were now used for bathing and boating. There was one for men and one for women. The ladies' pond was screened, although you could see it from the hill, but the men weren't so lucky. Jodie made her way to the water's edge. The warm, evening air washed over it and sent waves lapping against the sides. All the swimmers had gone. The dark shadows of the treeline hung like low-lying clouds across the horizon. There were

129

no kingfishers or jackdaws at night, just the fine lines of pipistrelles flitting through the trees.

She walked towards the jetty. Its tall, still poles emerged from the water like a wicker fence and stuck out into the pond perhaps twenty yards. She was about to get on when she noticed someone at the end hanging over the rails, looking into the water. Her feet on the wood made too much noise and the figure turned. It was the boy from the Underground station. What was *he* doing there? Following her? Aunt Gene was right – she shouldn't be wandering around in the dark on her own. She felt the phone in her pocket. There was still time to ring her.

'Hello,' he said.

She said nothing.

He turned down the jetty and walked towards her. She thought of running, then thought how stupid that would be. He'd helped her in the Underground, hadn't he? And where would she get to in the dark? She was pretty sure he'd catch her. She caught a glimpse of his face. He didn't seem much older than her. In the moonlight, his skin glowed white, making his cheekbones stand out.

'I don't often see people here at this time of night.'

He spoke well.

'I don't normally come here.'

'I can't say I blame you. There've been loads of suicides in these ponds. Swimmers say you can hear their footsteps on the pier. I thought you were one.'

She looked at the chill, silent water. It was easy to imagine some ghostly apparition walking along.

He smiled cryptically and walked past her. 'Well, I'm on my way back. Don't stay out too late.'

She turned round. 'Why not?'

'There are some nutters round here. You've got to be careful.'

The water chopped against the bank. It seemed more forbidding now, and eerily black.

'Thanks for the warning.'

He walked off up the hill. 'If you're scared, you can walk with me.'

'What?'

He hadn't broken step.

'How do I know *you're* not a nutter?' she called up.

'Good question. I saved you, didn't I? Would a nutter do that?'

She ran up the hill after him. There was something faintly comical about him; he seemed so lost in his own world.

'Sorry. I didn't get a chance to thank you. I must have passed out on the platform. What were you doing there? What are you doing here?'

'I saw those girls were after you. You looked like you needed some help. And I'm thinking.'

'Thinking?'

'Yes. I find looking into the water helps.' He walked quickly. His long legs ate up the ground. He didn't offer to say more and she hesitated from asking.

'You're not following me?'

'No,' he said. '*You're* following *me*. Where do you need to go?'

She pointed over Parliament Hill towards Hampstead.

'Right, we'll go there straight away.' He paused. 'Actually, do you mind if I check something first?'

It was impossible to take him seriously.

'It won't take a second.'

'Sure.'

He took gangly strides up the hill and she followed as fast as she could.

'Where are we going?'

'Boudicca's Mound.'

'Where?'

He pointed to a copse of trees on a raised hill. 'There.'

Walking with him was a respite from the storm. She found herself thinking more about him than the pain she'd left behind. There was definitely something familiar about him, as if he was family, a kindred spirit on the heath. He led her along a silver trickle of a footpath between tall trees. It seemed to Jodie like she'd seen it in a picture in one of her art books at home. There was something serene and detached about the trees that hung over it. They were solitary even with others around them. Eventually, they came to the top of a small hill. The boy paced around, taking measurements with his feet.

'What is this place?'

'It's a tumulus. It's meant to be the burial place of Queen Boudicca.'

'Right.'

The shades seemed to gather on the hollow mound.

'But it's not. She's buried under platform ten of King's Cross Station.'

'So why do they call it Boudicca's Mound?'

'I guess they haven't got round to changing the name.'

He continued his pacing.

'What are you doing?'

'Trying to find a ley line.'

He was a nutter, just not the bad kind.

'Do you need any help?'

He stopped to look at her. 'What kind of help? Do

you think I'm mad?'

'No, quite the opposite. I think you're rather . . . sweet.'

He showed no sign he'd registered it. 'Hampstead Heath is very old. It's written in the Domesday Book. This place is meant to be a part of a ley line which runs across the city to Horseferry Road.'

He pointed somewhere over Hampstead Ponds to the south.

'What's so special about that?'

'I'm not sure. London is divided up into lots of sacred triangles. They were important for pagans and druids. Some people reckon they have psychic or mystical energy; others think they were just travel lines for the ancients to mark out.'

'What do you think?'

He stopped. His black hair blew in the breeze. Once again, his face seemed vaguely familiar. 'I think it's nonsense.'

'You don't believe it?'

'Not at all.'

'So why are you here?'

'I'm not sure. Maybe because other people do. I like to debunk theories. You know, banish ghosts, sweep away people's superstitions.'

She stared at him, suddenly unable to move. That's just what Aunt Gene said her father did. The synchronicity of the words made her shiver. She felt she was looking at a ghost. What fate had brought her here at this time? Was Dad trying to send her a message? The time on the hill, she must have fallen asleep. She was dreaming this and would soon wake up.

'I'm sorry,' she said. 'I have to go.'

'Yes,' he said. 'Quite.'

He led her down the hill towards Hampstead. Every now and again, she would check if he was beside her and every time she expected him not to be. She felt she was walking through a dream. When they were in sight of East Heath Road, she stopped.

'I can get back on my own from here.'

'Are you sure?'

'Yes. Thank you.'

He looked at her briefly. 'Well, I'll be going, then.'

He turned on his heels and headed off without saying anything.

'Hey,' she shouted. 'What's your name?'

He didn't seem to hear her. He continued walking. But, at the top of the hill, she saw him stop and heard his voice rolling down the breeze.

'*John.*'

She turned it over in her mind and made her way quickly to the road. As she did, she felt the phone in her pocket and turned it on. The moment she did, it rang. It was Aunt Gene.

She was back in the real world.

16

It was nearly midnight when she got back. The key slipped in the lock and turned without a sound. She thought Aunt Gene would be up, but the hall light was off and the house was quiet. There was a narrow strip of light under the kitchen door. She pushed it open and looked inside. Aunt Gene was at the table. She looked frail and old. There was a half empty cup of coffee beside her and a sheet of paper. The moment she saw Jodie, her eyes lit up and she pushed the chair back. There was a look of almost exultation on her face. Jodie was at a loss as to what to say. She felt guilty for leaving.

Aunt Gene tried to get up, but her movements were unsteady. 'I've been worried sick, Jodie. I had to call the police again.'

She went to put her arm round her but Jodie backed away. The rejection smarted across Aunt Gene's face.

'Why?'

'You didn't pick up, darling. I didn't know where you were.'

'I told you I was on the heath.'

'At eleven o'clock?'

'I can look after myself.'

'It's a dangerous place at night. Especially for a girl. I don't want you going there again.'

Jodie let the words wash over her. She thought of John and what he'd said: there were nutters round there. When the lecture finished, she couldn't think of anything to say.

'Well?'

'I'm sorry.'

Aunt Gene tried to sit her down. 'I think you need to see someone, darling.'

'About what?'

'About you.'

Aunt Gene looked at the paper. There was a list of telephone numbers on it. She picked it up and showed Jodie. 'There are people who can help us.'

'Doctors?'

'No, darling. We've seen enough of them.'

'Then who?'

'An old friend of mine. I think it would be a good idea if we went to see him.'

'What does he do?'

'He's a psychic. He helps people sort out their problems.'

'You're kidding?'

Aunt Gene shook her head. 'No, darling. I know you're mad with me. But I just want what's best for you.'

She walked unsteadily to the door and turned. 'I love you, Jodie. Always.'

The words brought tears to Jodie's eyes. She put her head on the table. She'd be eighteen soon and could take charge of her own life, yet she seemed as powerless to do so as ever. *A psychic?*

She picked up the cup of coffee Aunt Gene had left. It smelled of alcohol. *Her* life was spinning out of control, too. It was hard to imagine her with any vices; she kept everything so well hidden. She poured the spirit down the sink and washed the cup. She didn't want Aunt Gene knowing she knew. She had a duty to both of them, for all the years she'd looked after her.

She climbed the stairs and passed the secret room where the furniture was. The door was closed again. She went silently up to the attic and lay on her bed. She was still crying when sleep took her.

*

She awoke with a start, breathless and cold. It was dark outside. A gentle rain buffeted the dormer window. She got up and closed the curtains. As she did, something scuttled along the window ledge. The sound made her jump. She peered through the gap. All she could see were the dark slates and the silhouettes of the rooftops.

She opened the window and felt the rain spot her face. Had she imagined it? She waited a few moments but there was nothing there. She sat on her bed and looked out, her ears straining, but all she heard was the rain come down. She put her head on her pillow, alive to everything, every sense on alert. Then, unmistakeably, there was a knocking. This time it seemed to come from inside. It began softly, but gradually got louder until it sounded like someone banging nails out of a piece of wood. She turned and faced the wardrobe doors, put her hands on them to stop them shaking.

'Who is it?' she said.

The banging stopped. She slid the wardrobe doors back and looked at the panels. They were halfway off the wall. Something was trying to get out. She kicked them closed, not caring if Aunt Gene heard. Then she rammed the nails back into the wall, pushed everything she could in front, and sat down with her back against them.

Suddenly, the room got darker. She looked up at the window and the curtains bulged with a black presence. There was a fetid odour and the acrid smell of smoke. She'd left the window open. She ran to close it but, before she was halfway across, something emerged from it: a clawed green finger.

She screamed, threw a book at it, tried to beat it back, but it was useless. Inexorably, limb by limb, the thing unknotted itself from the curtains. The shadow of its antlers covered the room like a dense thicket of trees. Reptilian red eyes and curved boar tusks gleamed in the dark. This time there was no escape.

Jodie reached for the door. 'Aunt Gene, help me!'

Her hands fumbled at the handle but it wouldn't turn. The cold reached her neck. It was breathing on her. Still the door wouldn't open. It laid its hands on her, turned her round. She kept her eyes closed, unable to look.

'Leave me alone, leave me alone.'

It slapped her hard and her head jolted to the side. This was it. She was going to die. It turned her head the other way. She could hear it now, calling her. It shook her so violently she thought her insides would break.

'Leave me alone!'

The last slap was the hardest. She screamed again and again, tried to get it off her. But it didn't let go.

'Jodie!'

At the mention of her name, the spell broke. The fetid air dispelled, the green limbs became arms, the horns became hair. Aunt Gene was holding her, rocking her. She felt her lips on her forehead.

'What are we going to do?'

Jodie looked round the room. The light was on, the curtains were drawn. A gentle rain fell against the dormer window. Everything was as it should be. Only it wasn't. It was more a case of how it used to be. One thing was for sure, she realised. Neither of them could go on like this.

17

Jodie's birthdays were always quiet affairs. She'd had parties in the past when she was small, but nothing grandiose; no bouncy castles or loud music and games in the garden. Aunt Gene would pick four or five of her classmates, always the most sensible ones, and invite them round. She'd take them all to a museum and get them to play pass the parcel or pin the tail on the donkey or, if she was feeling very ambitious, charades. As Jodie got older, even that stopped. Birthdays were something you didn't mention, especially at school; you didn't want the attention and you didn't want the practical jokes.

She looked at her phone. There were no Happy Birthday texts, not even from Luca. She wasn't as hurt as she thought she would be. Everything seemed trivial now compared with what was happening. She put the phone back in her bag and looked out of the car window. The kites were out over the heath.

'How far is it?'

'Just to Highgate, near church.' Aunt Gene said.

'It won't work.'

'You don't know that.'

'What can he do?'

'He can help you remember things. I've seen him do it.'

'What, drag people back from the grave?'

'It's not like that. Some of them want to come.'

Jodie thought of the picture by the beach and how it was gone for good. 'They don't come. It's all made up.'

It hurt her quite as much to say it.

Aunt Gene stared at her. 'You're the only person alive who has a clue what happened, darling.'

The kites had disappeared and trees pressed in on either side.

'Suppose I do. Do you think I'm ready to talk to my dead mother and father?'

'None of us has ever been ready, Jodie.'

Jodie said nothing. The nightmare was a blink away. When she closed her eyes, it was there in front of her. Events in the tunnel had shown her that. Wings beat behind the flight of jackdaws, shadows extended beyond the shadow of the trees. Things were no longer confined to the cupboard, or the attic, or even the house. She was carrying the demon with her wherever she went. Was there any chance her mind would just correct itself and she could live a normal life again?

After what Aunt Gene showed her, it seemed as remote as bringing her mum and dad back. She didn't believe she would ever see them, never mind save them, but maybe there was a chance to find out what she'd seen. Was that not the most important thing? To lay them to rest, to give them peace? It was what Aunt Gene wanted. She'd lived with it all these years, waiting for a time when the killer would be brought to trial. Could she refuse her that?

'How do you know him?'

'He's been a friend since you were small.'

'You've never mentioned him before.'

'I've never needed to.'

Jodie felt the seeds of paranoia germinating again. There was something hurried and clipped about her answers. Twelve years seemed a long time to have a male *friend*.

'How long has he been doing this?'

'I'm not sure.'

'Is he married?'

Aunt Gene paused. 'He was.'

They were on top of the heath now, going along Hampstead Lane. A knot in her stomach tightened with each turn in the road. The signs to Highgate became more frequent. Gradually, the open spaces began to thin and large Victorian houses sprinkled the landscape. Roads thickened with traffic. Through the trees on her right, she could see the cemetery. As the car slowed, her sense of trepidation grew.

Aunt Gene drove down a wide, private road and pulled up beside a house with two large gateposts. There were two stone owls on top of them. 'Listen to what he has to say, Jodie. If you don't want to go through with it, you don't have to. We can always go back.'

Go back? Jodie thought. *To what?* Her old life in the attic, sheltered from everything, was gone. Her only option was to face things.

They got out of the car and walked up the gravel drive. She noticed the plaque on the gate: *Highgate Spiritualist*

Circle. Spiritualist was one of those words that conjured up images of old horror films and men holding pendulum watches in front of your face, saying 'Look into my eyes'. It was hard to believe Aunt Gene set such store by it. Then again, it was hard to believe anything that had happened to them.

Her feet crunched on the stones. The front door was large and wooden and looked more like the entrance to a keep than a house.

Aunt Gene gave her a last look. 'You're sure about this, Jodie?'

Jodie nodded.

A tall man in a black suit came to the door. He smiled at Aunt Gene and took her hand. The physicality of the gesture took Jodie by surprise. He turned to her. 'You must be Jodie?'

He stuck his giant hand out. Her small white one disappeared inside. He held it gently and then let it go. The warmth of it tingled up her arm.

'I'm William Habborlain. Please come inside.'

He led them through a large waiting area to a pair of double doors. She could hardly imagine anything more imposing. They were dark oak, with gold plated handles and engravings of wolves, stags, eagles and bears, with Latin script underneath.

'Can I get you a drink?'

Before they could say no, he rang a bell. There was the noise of footsteps from an adjoining room.

Jodie looked round, then stopped. It was John, the boy on the heath, wearing a suit that was too big for him.

'John, could you bring drinks for us?'

He recognised her instantly but didn't say anything.

Again, she had the notion something was going on, just beyond her understanding. Things felt too familiar, even the room. She shuddered. Why had she agreed to come?

Habborlain opened the doors and invited them inside. If the doors were impressive, what lay within was even more so. It reminded her of the reading room at the British Museum. There was a heavy atmosphere, like up on the heath before a storm. In the ceiling was a small dome through which narrow beams of sunlight streamed down. Six giant candelabra were set on a polished, brown table with decorated edges.

Filling every wall was a vast library. There were rows and rows of leather spines divided into subjects she'd barely heard of – occultism, spiritism, scrying – with exotic titles like *The Golden Bough* and *The Goat Foot God*. She wondered how long they'd taken to collect.

In the corners were big brown sofas like those in the waiting area. Some were occupied. There was a middle-aged couple and an older man with a walking stick who sat on his own.

'Let me introduce our other sitters, Jodie.'

She felt like an exhibit at the museum. If it wasn't for Aunt Gene next to her, she would have run away. The middle-aged couple smiled pleasantly but the old man just stared. Their names went through her. She felt disorientated and unsure. Habborlain seemed to sense this and led her into a corner.

'This must seem very strange. Please don't be worried. Let me show you around. I have the most valuable collection of first editions outside the British Museum. Some might say, more valuable. I have copies of *Malleus Maleficarum* and *Compendium Maleficarum* and every grimoire from the

Middle Ages. That's a book of spells to you. People from all over the world ask to come here.'

Magic seemed to leap off the shelves. She looked into his grey eyes. She thought there was something cold about him, something of the heath, even when he was being friendly.

She turned to the table in the centre of the room. At one side was a small stand with a purple cloth draped over it. On it was set a large black ball. Anywhere else, she would have seen it just as an ornament, but here it seemed real and already to possess supernatural powers.

Habborlain noticed her looking. 'What do you see, Jodie?'

'Nothing,' she murmured.

'You were expecting a crystal ball to be translucent?'

'Yes, I suppose.'

'It is a copy of John Dee's magic mirror, obtained by Cortés in Mexico in the 1520s. It is made from black obsidian.'

She felt her hands fumbling. 'Will we be looking in it?'

'Not if you don't want to.'

He invited her and the others to sit down. Aunt Gene sat on one side of her, the middle-aged lady on the other. Next to her were her partner and the old man with the walking stick. Habborlain was at the head of the table. John slunk around in the shadows by the double doors. She watched him from the corner of her eye. He set glasses of water down from a tray.

'John, will you light the candles, please?'

There was a deadly seriousness about Habborlain that made her heart fade. She heard the flick of matches and smelt sulphur. It reminded her of the phosphorus in the laboratory at school. Flames spluttered into life and shadows began dancing round the room.

'Thank you, John. Shut the doors on your way out.'

John bowed his head and glanced quickly at her. It wasn't a conspiratorial look. It was more a *be careful*. When the double doors closed, she felt utterly alone.

'We light the candles to attract the spirits, Jodie.'

Habborlain pressed a switch on the far wall and mechanised blinds closed like eyelids across the dome. At the same instant, two dormant ceiling fans began to turn. A gentle breeze touched her face and beneath it she could feel the soft vibrations of the blades.

'Jodie, I want to ask you one last time if you're okay with this.'

She turned to Aunt Gene, but her face was half hidden in shadow. It was her choice now, but it didn't feel like it. She nodded, unable to say no.

The candlelight left the barren reaches of the séance room black. All she could pick out were the shadows. She felt like she was in a trance already and her ears on standby, waiting for the mad charade to begin.

'Do you believe in the spirit world?'

'I didn't till a few days ago.'

'Séances work best when everyone is receptive.'

'I'll do my best,' she said.

'I want you to put aside all the things you've heard or seen in films. People make good careers debunking spiritualism, and poor mediums let them. You won't see tables being picked up or drinks being spilt, or ectoplasm being thrown out of spirit boxes. Those are the theatrics of the past. Real mediums produce communication between the living and the dead. We are like lighthouses, attracting spirits like ships at sea.'

Jodie looked round the room for a sight of them. The vibrations had spread to her fingers.

'Your Aunt says you've been having nightmares again?'

'Yes.'

'The same ones?'

'Yes.'

'Would you describe to us what you saw?'

Jodie looked at Aunt Gene again. She was out of her depth. 'It was a demon. I saw it in a book when I was small.'

She took the book out of her bag and gave it to him.

'Your book?'

'My father's.'

Habborlain flashed a look at Aunt Gene. Jodie caught the communication and felt the rush of paranoia again.

'It's on page sixty-eight.'

He turned the pages slowly and then stopped, like a shadow had come over him. 'Saint Wolfgang and the Devil?'

Jodie nodded.

'The Medieval Church's most disturbing dialogue. It is the back of the Altarpiece of the Church Fathers by Michael Pacher. I can well imagine the horror this would invoke in a small child. Here, St Wolfgang compels the devil to hold the Gospel and share the worship of God.'

He showed the picture to the middle-aged couple and the old man. The woman looked at Jodie intently. She had fine, brown hair and an aquiline nose. She reminded Jodie of a bird.

'It's more than a dream. I've seen it.'

'I'm sure. Every man and woman usually experiences two or three instances of magic in their lives, things that could not normally be explained by the cold reality of reason. But the witchcraft of sleep harbours more than sorcery. Sometimes, the forgotten companions of childhood reappear. They haunt us, delight us, tease us, then vanish. Dreams are jealous of being remembered, Jodie. They do not like you to hold on to them. They are a menagerie of the mind, a place where souls and demons walk, where fabulous animals and exotic worlds reside. To some people, as with the ancients, such worlds and phantasmagoria are real. There are people in our world who have the power, or I should say the facility, to reach those worlds, which have been relegated to the subconscious.'

'You mean me?'

'Maybe. Goethe once said dreams have an analogy with our whole life and fate. Science can predict our future health in the womb, it can read the anatomy of our mind, it can diagnose our spirit. Yet the lines in a man's hand, or the lines on his face, it maintains, are as meaningless as a child's scribble. Signs and prophecies are there if only we would look. Only now, when we realise how a butterfly's wings can cause a hurricane on the other side of the world, does science take note. Nature makes as much demand on our faith as superstition. *Everything* is connected. The gossamer threads of life run in all directions.'

Jodie glanced at the others as he spoke. They hung on his every word. Aunt Gene's eyes were fixed on him like he was the priest at church.

The wind of the blades stirred her hair.

'Can you get in touch with my mum and dad?'

'We can try.'

'What will happen?'

He paused. 'I don't know. If you keep going back to the doctor because of a pain in your chest, the chances are there is something wrong with you. To ignore the pain would be foolish. Your mind is telling you something is wrong. It is the tendency of today to ignore dreams and omens. We dismiss them as whimsy, as twilights of thought, but a good medium takes heed of them. There are more things in heaven and earth than are dreamt of in science's philosophy. We can but seek the truth.'

Jodie felt herself going faint. She didn't know if it was from the heat in the room, or the hypnotic quality of Habborlain's voice.

'Now, I'd like us to lay our hands on the table and say the Lord's Prayer.'

Jodie found herself slightly behind the pace. She heard her voice like an echo of the others. Words she'd known since childhood stumbled out of her mouth, broken and errant.

Habborlain was watching her closely.

Hallowed be thy name

She looked at the black ball and it seemed to hover in mid-air.

Give us this day

Her eyes began to flicker. She thought it must be the candles creating shadows. Their dying wicks made marionette ghosts on the floor.

For ever and ever

Did she imagine it? Was there a wind blowing in the room?

Amen.

Habborlain's voice stilled her nerves. Beyond the circle was darkness.

'We are looking for Kate and Malcolm Lawrence. If you're there, make yourself known to us. Jodie is here.'

He closed his eyes. Jodie watched his face turn to all

corners of the room like he was smelling for something, picking up a signal. His fingers were pressed to the table. She looked at the others. They also had their eyes closed; all except the bird woman, whose eyes were trained at the ceiling. Jodie followed her gaze and watched the blades turn. They seemed to come down lower and lower. The vibrations spread to her whole body. She found herself shaking and trembling. There was something wrong.

'I can hear something, Jodie.'

Her nape hairs rose like cat's fur.

'I can feel them around us.'

She could, too. It was the wind. It nearly blew the candles out. It blew through her mind. She struggled to stay conscious.

'Kate?'

She sensed Aunt Gene stiffen.

'Kate, Jodie is here.'

It was too late. Jodie looked at the ceiling and saw a shadow move across it. It covered the fans with its wings. From the corner of her eye, she saw the flames shrink. She wanted to get up but Aunt Gene clutched her hand with a dread grasp.

'Mum?'

The voice wasn't her own. It was torn from her throat by someone else.

'Mum, I'm frightened.'

Habborlain's face was moving from left to right, trying to locate her. The bird woman had sensed something, too. Her eyes wouldn't leave the roof. Then came a slow thud on the table.

The old man brought his stick down and beat it like a drum.

'I've never felt anything so powerful,' Habborlain whispered.

Jodie.

It was in her head.

The shadow had moved from the ceiling and crept down the wall. She couldn't understand why she was the only one who could see it. Was it her mum or her dad? Then she saw its silhouette. It caught her breath and made her choke. There was a pair of horns pointing upwards. No human had that profile. It was coming for her.

Again, she struggled to get away, but Aunt Gene wouldn't let her go. The stick came down on the table quicker; it sounded like hooves. The wind blew louder in her ears and her body shook.

'What's wrong with her?'

She could hear Aunt Gene's voice as if in a dream.

'She's possessed.'

The shadow was behind the bird woman now. Jodie tried to scream to warn her, but it caught in her throat. There was a sudden rush of movement. Two of the candles went out and the shadow descended. The woman screamed and it shocked the air. She broke the circle.

Habborlain was up, shouting into the darkness. *'Adjure te, spiritus nequissime, per Deum omnipotentem!'*

He ran to the wall and pressed the switch. Bright sunlight filtered through the dome and the fan's heavy wings came to rest. The moment they did, the shadow disappeared. Jodie felt air rushing into her lungs again.

The bird woman was clutching her face. Blood seeped between her fingers. Her partner gave her a white handkerchief. Habborlain asked her to remove it. Reluctantly, she did so. There was a claw mark on her cheek. Blood dripped on to the table from her eyeball.

Jodie felt all her life drain away. The last she heard was Habborlain's voice. 'Take her home. Something terrible visited us tonight.'

She felt Aunt Gene's arms around her and remembered no more.

*

When Jodie woke, she saw black cemetery gates and head-stones. A host of angels had gathered at her bedside. Gradually, she realised she hadn't died. She was lying on a sofa looking up at a picture. She didn't open her eyes fully; there were voices around her, arguing.

'I'm telling you what I saw, Genevieve. Something clawed her.'

'So you think Jodie released this thing into the room?'

'I can't be sure, but that's the only way I can explain it. Something dreadful was in there.'

Jodie could see Habborlain through the narrow aperture of her eyes. He ran his hand through his silver hair and paced up and down like a wolf.

'Do you know what this could do to my reputation? If I could prove to the world that spirits aren't the imagination of crackpots, but that the hereafter is a real place . . . '

'But it's dangerous, William. If you're right, any one of us in that room could have been killed.'

'Gene, this is more important than any one of us. It's the biggest discovery of all time. Just think how many people would come flocking back to the church. Malcolm was so utterly wrong. How ironic it is that his own daughter has proved it. She has shown us the existence of the afterlife.'

Jodie heard crying. It was Aunt Gene.

'Can't you do anything for her?'

'You want us to go through it again?'

'But I heard Kate.'

At her mum's name, Jodie was still as the graveyard. So she hadn't imagined it.

Habborlain disappeared from view. Jodie guessed they were close but dared not look. She imagined him taking Aunt Gene in her arms.

'If we'd stayed, she would have spoken to us.'

'Maybe.'

'I can't go on not knowing.'

'You have to for the moment. The next time we might let something loose we can't control. I need to learn what's going on inside her before we subject her to it again. Then, next time, we shall find out for certain what it was that killed Kate.'

Jodie felt him sit down next to her. She could feel his warm breath on her face. She tried to keep still, hoped he couldn't see her eyes dancing beneath their lids.

'Strange she should remember that particular picture, don't you think?'

'The one of the demon? Why?'

'The book was mine.'

'What?'

'Her father borrowed it from me.'

'You never told me that.'

'I thought he was returning it the night he died.'

Jodie felt Aunt Gene's shock and the air being sucked into her lungs.

'He came to see you?'

'Yes.'

'William, why did you never tell me that? Why did you never tell the police?'

'And have them bring their grubby investigation to my door? I had things to protect here, Gene. And people.'

'But it could have been important. What did he say?'

'He said he was going to meet someone on the Underground who would settle our argument.'

'The experiments on infrasound?'

'Yes. He was beside himself after the disaster at the convention, desperate to prove I was wrong. He said he was going to tell a poor, unfortunate man that the terrible thing he'd seen down there was a figment of his imagination, that science could explain everything.'

'What thing?' she whispered.

'A monster, Gene. The devil still rides the Underground, you know. He should have taken my advice and stayed away.'

Jodie's heart nearly burst out of her chest.

She'd seen it, too.

18

When they finally left Highgate, the sun was setting over the heath. Neither Gene nor Jodie spoke. Habborlain's words echoed in Jodie's head like the wind down the Underground. She thought of the horrible death of her parents, the demon reaching out its claws to her at Chalk Farm, the shadow in the séance room, and wondered whether the devil was now coming for her.

She opened her bag and felt reassured. The book was gone, back to Habborlain, where it belonged. Maybe that would put an end to the nightmares? For a moment, she felt free. She saw the wide open spaces of the sky and the red twilight and the kites silhouetted against it. She felt like a bird, ready to fly over Parliament Hill. Then the dying sun caught the windscreen and she saw the bird woman's eye, red and bleeding, and the squawks of the pipistrelles echocd like screams over Highgate Ponds.

She looked at Aunt Gene, staring down the road like she was in a trance, shrunken and defeated, the lines on her face etched with worry. She didn't want to add to them, but could no longer contain the questions that burnt inside her. 'How come you didn't tell me about him? That he knew my dad?'

The words stoked the silence. 'Who, darling?'

'Your friend – Habborlain. I heard every word you said to him.'

'When you were unconscious? That's a skill I didn't think you had.' Aunt Gene's words sounded brittle, almost barbed.

'Don't you think you should have? I mean, their argument. It was about infrasound, wasn't it? He seems to know a lot.'

'He knows too much, if that's possible. That's always been his problem.'

'He mentioned a monster . . . '

Aunt Gene flashed a look at her. 'There is no monster. There's nothing, do you understand? Nothing came after your father.'

'What about the woman in the séance? I saw something attack her.'

'You saw nothing, Jodie. Nothing but your imagination. There's a rational explanation for everything.'

The words rang the conversation to an abrupt end.

Jodie stared at the darkening world outside. Perhaps it was just trickery. John had said as much when she'd seen him on the heath. Before, she was sure the demon had attacked the woman, but now she began to doubt it. The scratch on the bird woman could easily have been made by nails. The further they got from the house, the more plausible it seemed. Wasn't that more likely than a shadow coming down and taking a chunk from the woman? Or something coming for her father?

By the time Aunt Gene drove down Hampstead High Street, Jodie had decided what she was going to do. Aunt Gene may not like it, but it was the only thing left to do. She was going to take the attic apart, find things out for herself.

The car pulled up outside the house. She watched Aunt Gene stop at the gate and look at the front door. There was a shadow in the porch. Something, or someone, was there. The palpitations began in her chest again.

'Hello?' said Aunt Gene.

The shadow got up. 'Don't worry, Mrs De Dulin. It's only me.'

He came out of the shadows and into the twilight. It was Luca. 'I was waiting for Jodie.'

Aunt Gene's words were like nails. 'How sweet.'

He held up a small parcel. 'I didn't want to miss her birthday.'

'Well, I suppose you'd better come in. If Jodie doesn't mind?'

Jodie shook her head. She was more than glad to see him.

*

She sat on the bed with his present on her lap. She gave no sign of opening it. Luca sat on the floor in front of her.

'What happened at Stables? How come you didn't show up?'

'I was delayed.'

'Delayed?'

'By Trent and Laura. They wanted to know where you were.'

'You told them?'

'I had no choice. Trent drew a knife, made me ring you.

The only thing I could think of were those bloody Starsailor lyrics to warn you.'

Jodie said nothing. 'You could have rung after? I haven't heard from you since.'

He reached into his jacket pocket and brought out the remains of his Nokia. It looked like someone had taken a hammer to it.

'What the hell happened to that?'

'Trent wanted to play football with it. There's not much left. He took the SIM, too.'

She looked at the bashed-up pieces.

'Look, I knew you wouldn't believe me so I brought you this. I did come looking for you.' He emptied his other pocket and handed her a sheet of paper.

She unfolded it and stared at the picture of the cyber-robot she'd drawn in the café.

He looked at her sadly. 'Did they get you?'

'They were scared away.'

'Laura wanted to kill you. When she spoke, she was mad with jeal—'

At the thought of her, Jodie felt her frustration and anger finally explode. 'Look, I haven't got time, Luca.' She dug her nails into the wrapping paper and slid them down. They made a claw mark. The frayed ends of the paper hung loosely like folds of skin. 'I've got more important things on my mind.'

He looked at her like she'd stolen his lines. 'Okay,' he said.

She stared at the tear. 'I wanted to tell you that day. What happened to that tiger, the fire in the lab. Terrible things have started happening. I think there's something wrong with me.'

'Wrong?' he echoed. 'Like what?'

'I don't know. But I need you to help me find out.'

She put his present on the bed and stared at the wardrobe doors. She slid them back and grabbed the clothes like she was clearing out a warehouse, piling them high till his chest was full of jeans and tops.

'What do I do with these?'

'Whatever you want.'

Next came the shoes and books and CDs. She threw them across the room. After a few minutes, the cupboard was bare and they were staring at the bare plaster wall.

'Very nice,' he said. 'What do we do now?'

'We kick the wall in.'

'Won't your aunt mind?'

'I don't care. I'm not sleeping here with all that stuff behind it.'

'Jodie, do you want to tell me what's going on?'

She stopped and felt the blood coursing through her. For the first time, it felt like she was the one doing the chasing and she felt better. She thought of her dad chasing ghosts and spirits and knew it was infinitely better than waiting for something in the dark.

'You know about DIY. Can we knock this through?'

'You're serious?'

Jodie tore the panels off the wall. 'Watch me.'

She felt cold air come out of the gap and put her hand inside. The wall wasn't thick. She blanked out thoughts of cobwebs and spiders and the things she'd seen. She didn't want any dark places any more. She wanted everything to be out in the open. She aimed her palm at the plaster and it gave a dull thud.

'You'll have to use your feet.' He aimed a kick at the other side and the plaster fell away. 'It's just chipboard. It'll come away but it's gonna be messy.'

He aimed a couple more kicks and the chipboard caved in. Jodie kicked, too. A confetti of chippings sprinkled on the floor. She kicked again and again until the chipboard broke in two. The light in the room illuminated the boxes inside. They were like excavators boring into the earth, the thuds of their feet echoing through the rafters. *Thump*, *thump*.

As the board finally gave way, a creaking sound from the roof reverberated through the house. For a terrible moment, Jodie thought it was going to collapse. Slates slid and dust and fibreglass exploded around her. She fell on top of the board and found herself directly underneath the hole in the roof. Through the narrow aperture, she could see the sky. She thought of the Pharaohs who'd been buried that way, looking up at the heavens, hoping their souls would get out.

She looked round for Luca but he wasn't there. She got up and coughed the dust out of her lungs. The tomb of her father had finally been opened. There seemed to be more boxes now, glinting with electrical parts, copper wires and dials. The large electronic device was covered with plaster.

She swept it clean. 'What do you think?'

There was no answer. She turned and saw the reason why: Aunt Gene was standing next to him. She had a look on her face, half utter incomprehension, half panic.

'What have you done, Jodie?'

'What I should have done before. I'm dealing with things.'

'But the house, darling. What if the roof caves in?'

'I'm not bothered about the roof.'

Aunt Gene stared at the boxes. She went to the plaster wall and tried to build it up again. 'You should have left everything in there. Put it away while you have the chance. We'll take it to the tip tomorrow, give the books to charity.'

'I can't. They're all I have of him.'

'You didn't know you had them till a few days ago.'

'So?'

'So you can be without them again.'

'I can't. If you throw them out, Aunt Gene, you're throwing me out, too.'

'Don't be ridiculous, Jodie.'

'My father knew something. I think he knew what was wrong with me.'

'Darling, you couldn't be more wrong. You were a happy little girl.'

Aunt Gene said the words so simply, it stunned her. The thought of her actually being happy and normal seemed as far away as understanding. She looked at Luca and the dust in the room and it all seemed like madness. The boxes were just boxes, her father's equipment just some old junk. Nothing came out of the attic. There was just a hole in the roof where the slates had slipped.

'Leave this, Jodie. Let's try and get back to how we were. Please.'

Aunt Gene stood in the doorway, covered in dust, then went back down the stairs, crying.

The phrase echoed in Jodie's head: *how we were*.

Luca shuffled. 'Things are bad, yeah?'

'Worse.'

'Shall I go?'

She looked at the mess and did all she could to hold back her own tears. 'I guess.'

She took him down the stairs past Aunt Gene's room. Her door was closed. There were deep shadows in the hall where the moonlight failed to cast its spell. It hid their faces.

Luca turned. 'I'll see you tomorrow, then?'

He touched her hand, opened the door and walked out. As he reached the gate, she called out. 'I'm sorry. Luca.'

He stopped. 'I'm sorry, too.'

She closed the door and put her back to it, then made her way to the attic. She couldn't sleep there now. She took the present off the bed and went downstairs. There were two other bedrooms across from Aunt Gene's. One looked out over the front. From it, she could just make Luca out, walking down the road.

She sat on the bed and tore the wrapping paper off.

She smiled sadly. There was a football card with a drawing of him and her inside. He'd drawn eighteen love hearts and written the words *No Substitute for U*. With it was a book.

Haunted London: A Tourists Guide to the Capital's Spooks.

She opened the cover and looked inside.

4 Jodie. Nothing's a con if you believe it. Luca xxx

19

Jodie didn't dream that night; at least, not that she remembered. She heard Aunt Gene get up at half past six and go to the bathroom, then the sound of cars and the city coming to life. It was weird how much more she heard from the front of the house. Noises from the street, which were inaudible from the attic, took on new perspectives; there were car doors slamming and schoolchildren shouting and people leaving for work. Aunt Gene put her head round just before she left, to wish her good luck.

Jodie went up to the attic to get her things. The window was wide open but the smell of plaster hadn't gone. The space behind the wall looked even smaller in the daylight and much less threatening. She looked at the boxes. Most were full of books, but there was a couple with electrical stuff inside. She picked through the circuit boards and coils of metal curiously and found the calculator-sized object she'd seen before. It had the words *Spectrum Analyser* printed on it.

She thought of her father. The wires were connecting her to him, drawing the circuit together. In another was a battered and charred video cassette. The plastic casing had bubbled like an Aero bar. Jodie picked it up and saw some faded red letters on the side. She read them slowly: *ages*. She didn't know why but the reels seemed to draw her in. She put the spectrum analyser and the tape in her bag and left.

*

There was an air of dread in the common room before the exam. It was as if everybody suddenly realised what they were there for, and how their lives could change because of it. Mr Green was with them, fielding last minute questions. There were copies of *Great Expectations* and *Macbeth* on the tables and pupils frantically looking at things they would soon forget. Jodie sat on her own. Luca was late. She wondered if he'd got home all right.

Bethany and Cheryl walked past and stared at her like she'd killed somebody. Laura was nowhere to be seen. As the minute hand approached ten to, she heard the drinks machine go beside her and a can come rumbling down the chute. It was Trent.

'Mind if I sit down?' he said.

She shrugged and pretended to read.

He sat opposite her. He'd toned down for the exam – more interview for a job than *Interview with the Vampire*. 'How ya feelin'?'

She looked over. The Marilyn Manson lines had gone from his cheeks and left sunken, sallow pits. Razor marks cut his chin.

'Why?'

'Just askin'.'

'It's a bit late now.'

He opened the can. The froth oozed out of the top and covered his fingers. He licked them clean. 'We shouldn't have done what we did. We didn't know how far it had gone.'

'You're not the one who should be apologising.'

'I'm not. I was just saying.' His tongue flicked out and lolled between his lips. 'Didn't you try to kill her?'

'No. It was an accident. A freak one.'

He looked at her weirdly. 'Well, I guess we're all freaks here, aren't we? I mean, you with your telekinetic powers, starting fires, throwing yourself on Tube lines.'

The words stung her. So, everyone at school must know.

'Don't worry,' he said. 'I like a bit of weirdness in a woman.' He finished his drink and looked at the clock. 'Strange, isn't it? After today, we're never going to see each other again.'

'It's devastating.'

He licked his lips. 'Maybe we should say goodbye properly later? You and me?'

The hairs on the back of her neck stood up. 'No thanks.'

'When I'm famous, you'll regret it.'

'Sure.'

He stood up just as the bell sounded and picked his bag up. 'Good luck, yeah?'

He held his hand out. It was long and pale and skeletal. She ignored it. Luca had come through the common room doors.

They filed into the exam room and took their seats. There was an empty seat two places behind her where Laura should have been. Jodie opened the paper and tried to focus on the questions. One of them was about the marshes where Pip met Magwitch. She saw the barren, horizontal flats in her mind and walked along the river. She tried to remember everything Mr Green said about gothic atmosphere and the forbidding churchyard and wrote it down verbatim, but every so often she saw the empty chair behind her and wondered what had become of Laura.

The clock sped to its appointed hour and, at the back of her mind, was the fear she was going to fail. Mr Green paced the floor at the front. She wondered if he was trying to communicate with them, send them answers by telepathy. Once or twice, he looked at her and seemed to be doing just that. *I've seen too many kids your age throw their lives away.*

When the exam had finished, there was an air of expectancy, not the anticipated inquest.

Luca came over. 'How did it go?'

'Not so good. You?'

'Straight A, obviously.'

She looked over his shoulder at Trent. He was making his way out of the room. Something he said stuck in her mind: *your telekinetic powers.*

'I didn't think you were going to make it.'

Luca followed her eyes. 'Neither did I.'

Jodie didn't say anything. She made for the door, then suddenly stopped. She brought the video cassette out of her bag.

'What do you make of this?'

'It's old.'

'I found it in my father's stuff.'

Luca examined it. '*ages?*'

'It's part of a longer word but I can't make it out. Can you get it working?'

'Maybe. If I opened the cover, I could probably get the reels out and spool them on to another tape. But more than likely it's degraded.'

'I want you to try.'

'We'll need a VCR.'

'Where from? I haven't got one.'

'Kamran has.'

She looked at him. 'Can't you do it yourself? I'd rather no one else knew.'

He shook his head. 'Sorry.'

She turned on her heels.

'Hey, where are you going?'

'I have to see Mr Cronin.'

'Why?'

'I've got something to show him, too.'

*

The whole school caught the buoyant mood. Whether it was the Year 11s finishing their exams, or the final whistle abandon of the sixth form spreading through the rank and file, everyone seemed to be smiling. Even the teachers joined in, in their shirtsleeves and jeans.

Jodie hurried to the science block. Luca trailed behind her like a child missing its favourite TV programme.

'I just don't understand why.'

'You don't have to come along.'

The science block was cool inside and smelt of disinfectant. The drilling she'd heard a few days before had gone and there was a calm about the place like a polished table. She walked down the corridor and peered through the narrow glass strips in the door. It was like Mr Cronin hadn't moved. He was sitting on his desk, talking on his phone. From his body language, she thought it must be to his girlfriend.

She waited for him to finish, then knocked.

'Jodie. You're not here to burn my lab down again?'

'Not this time.'

The haze of girlfriend talk was still wafting around him.

'Of course not.' He looked at Luca. 'You're here about *other* things.'

She opened her bag and pulled out the spectrum analyser. 'I brought you this.'

He got up and twisted some of the dials. 'This has seen better days.'

'What does it do?' she asked.

'Technically, it measures signals across the electromagnetic spectrum.'

She looked at him blankly. 'Is it to do with infrasound?'

The haze had evaporated and there was something more guarded about him. 'It can be used to measure it, yes.'

'How?'

'You really want to know?'

She nodded.

He picked up a marker pen and started drawing random up and down lines on the whiteboard. 'Imagine these lines are sound waves. We humans can only hear a fraction of the sound that is made across the spectrum, between twenty hertz at the low end and twenty-two kilohertz at the high end.'

He circled two points.

'Like woofers and tweeters,' Luca whispered to her.

'Yes,' said Mr Cronin. 'The spectrum analyser measures the rest for us. The sound beneath our range of hearing is called infrasound. The sound above it, ultrasound.'

'The stuff they use in hospitals?' she asked.

'Yes,' he said.

She stared at the dials on the metal box. 'Where would I go to find infrasound?'

'It's all around us. It's produced by wind, earthquakes, even drills – anything that disturbs the ground. Infrasonic waves can carry over long distances and are less susceptible to disturbance or interference than higher frequencies.'

'My father thought it had something to do with seeing ghosts and spirits.'

Mr Cronin put the pen down. 'Yes, I know.'

'How come?'

He sat on the desk and picked up the spectrum analyser. 'It's all to do with your little box. They're normally used for testing radio frequency signals. They display the amplitude, or amount of signal, on the vertical axis and the frequency on the horizontal.' He pointed at the screen. 'The signals are measured in decibels. If a signal at a certain strength is emitted at a certain frequency, your father believed you started to feel things, even if you didn't hear anything.'

'Whoa,' said Luca. 'That's crazy.'

'Maybe. Maybe not. Infrasound has a chequered history.'

'You mean it's dangerous?' asked Jodie.

Mr Cronin paused. 'Well, there's no protection against it. It's not absorbed by ordinary matter like walls or concrete or steel. They only amplify its effects. In the animal kingdom, it can be used as a weapon. Whales use it to stun their prey. We've done the same thing. The Germans developed an infrasound gun during the Second World War. They bombarded prisoners with it. Common side effects were nausea, rises in blood pressure and blackouts. High intensity infrasound at certain levels, between three to seven hertz, led to respiratory and organ failure and even death. An attack of infrasound isn't like anything else. There are no bombs going off, or explosions. There's just silence.'

Jodie stared at the spectrum analyser. She imagined empty Tube tunnels and her father walking down them.

'The paper you gave me was about infrasound's effects on the vestibular system. That's our eyes and ears, all our sensory functions, our spatial orientation. Disturb it and you do more than lose your balance. You lose your mind. It can cause nausea, anxiety, panic attacks. At certain levels and at certain frequencies, maybe it triggers other things.'

'Ghosts?'

He nodded. 'NASA was working in the same field. They conducted research on their pilots who reported visual disturbances at high altitudes and in simulators.'

'What kind of visual disturbances?' Jodie asked.

'UFOs.'

Luca grunted. 'Sounds like science fiction.'

She flashed him a look.

'If your father thought infrasound played a part in paranormal activity, Jodie, it makes a certain sense. I remember reading an article a few years ago about why church organs produce shivers down your spine. The long pipes produce extreme bass frequencies beneath the range of human hearing.'

'Infrasound?'

It all started to make sense.

'Churchgoers described it as a religious feeling.'

She felt a calm come over her. 'You said the spectrum analyser measures the levels and frequencies?'

'That's it.'

She looked at the battered dials. 'Can you get it working?'

Mr Cronin knocked it on the back. 'Have you got batteries?'

She shook her head.

He disappeared into the storeroom at the back of the lab.

'I don't believe it,' Luca whispered.

'That's because you're dumb,' she said.

Mr Cronin came out with a box and opened the back of the spectrum analyser with a screwdriver. He stuck a cloth inside and then put in some new batteries. Nothing happened.

'The damp has got to the circuits.'

Jodie felt the past short circuit. The link to her father was broken. 'It's not going to work?'

'Not without replacing the circuitry. It's too badly damaged.'

'Can you fix it?'

Mr Cronin shook his head. 'It's not something I do, Jodie.'

'But I need it.'

Mr Cronin looked out of the window and then back at her. He picked up the box and disappeared into the storeroom again. A few seconds later, he came out with another piece of equipment and put it on the table.

'A new one?' she asked, amazed.

'Notice what it says. *Not to be taken out of the department.*'

'So I can't take it out?'

'Term finishes in a few weeks. Why don't you put this in your bag and bring it back before then?'

'You're joking?'

'You need it?'

She nodded.

'Don't tell anyone you've got it, don't show anyone, don't break it. With any luck, no one will know.'

He put his jacket on.

She exchanged a glance with Luca. 'Thanks, Mr Cronin.'

'Thank me when you've brought it back.'

He ushered them out and locked the lab door. 'Now, I bet you both wish you'd done science?'

'Yes,' she said.

He looked at his phone and smiled. 'Well, I have to go. Teachers have lives, too. Be careful how you use it, won't you?'

She nodded again.

Luca let out a long gasp of air. 'What are we going to do now?'

She looked at the spectrum analyser. 'Find some ghosts.'

'How did I know you were going to say that?'

She walked off down the corridor.

They left school together, one step nearer the end. The loan of the spectrum analyser had given her a deadline more important than any essay or exam. Mr Cronin had given her hope. The sun beat down on Haverstock Hill and the air felt light. She felt herself being carried upwards like a kite over the heath. She clutched her bag to her side and waited for the breeze to blow her home.

20

There was a white builder's van parked outside the house when they got back, and a trail of cement and plaster leading up the path. A man with a red face and blue overalls came out and nodded to them.

Aunt Gene was at the door, staring at the muddy footprints in the hall. 'Have you seen this mess?'

'What's going on?' Jodie asked.

'I'm getting your room sorted.'

At the words, Jodie panicked. 'But I have stuff up there.'

'We also have a hole in the roof.'

Jodie looked at Luca and ran up the stairs. All she could think of was the boxes. If Aunt Gene had thrown them out, she didn't know what she'd do. Kill her, probably. But when she got to the top, she saw them safely piled on one side of the room, along with her dressing table and clothes. A polythene sheet covered them. There was a smell of plaster and cement the open window couldn't mask. The wardrobe doors had been taken off and new boards laid across the joists.

She heard Luca and the builder come up the stairs. The latter was whistling a Britney Spears song.

'Nice room you've got here, luv.'

'It was. Did you move everything?'

'Yeah, I put it over there.'

'You didn't throw anything out?'

'No. Just the rubbish.'

He pointed to some plastic bags with bricks and plaster in.

'How long will you be?'

'A couple of days, most likely.'

'Have you fixed the hole?'

'Yes.'

'Do you know what caused it?'

He scratched his head. 'Actually, it's a bit of a mystery.'

Luca looked at her. 'Maybe it was your satellite?'

She pulled a face.

'How come?'

The builder went to the roof. 'To be honest, I've never seen anything like it.' He showed her where the hole used to be. 'The slats where the slates sat were broken in two.'

'So?'

'Well, normally you'd expect them to be pointing down, like something had fallen through. But here they've been bent upwards.'

'What do you mean?' she asked.

'The hole was made from the inside.'

Jodie felt herself spinning. She heard the thud and the scratching in her head.

'How?'

'To be honest, luv, I don't know. But it's a weird one. It's like something had punched its way out.'

She stumbled and Luca grabbed her.

'What's up?'

She tried to imagine a wholly rational explanation of what the builder had said.

'Jodie, what's the matter?'

She shook her head.

The builder glanced at them and started whistling Britney Spears again. He took the bags of rubbish down the stairs.

'Nothing. I'm okay.'

'You're not. All this stuff about ghosts and spirits and your dad. You said yourself something was wrong. Why don't you tell me?'

She wished she could, but so little of it made sense to her, how could she expect him to understand?

'If I show you something, will you promise never to tell anyone?'

'Of course.'

She drew the cross out from round his neck. 'You swear?'

'I swear.'

She led him down the stairs to the landing and stopped outside the small bedroom next to her aunt's. She looked down the stairs into the hallway. Aunt Gene was outside on the path.

'You won't think any differently about me?'

'Of course not.'

She turned the handle slowly. It wasn't locked.

The room was bright. The mahogany chair and the porcelain mirror had been cleaned and the chests of drawers dusted. There was no need for secrets now. She opened the one with the papers in and took them out. She stared at the headline on the front – *Couple Slaughtered In Their Home* – and her hands shook. Showing him was too much; there'd be nowhere left to hide. But then she thought of coping on her own and her heart called out for help.

She put them in his hands. 'I want you to read them. And never mention anything to anyone in your whole life.'

He sat in the mahogany chair and read. She saw his reflection in the porcelain mirror. Most of the time he was still, but occasionally he looked up as if to check she was still there. He looked suddenly older. His hair had been flattened by the wind. She thought of what Aunt Gene said about honesty. It was the only thing you could rely on. Well, Luca was the only thing she could rely on at the moment. She prayed he wouldn't let her down.

The sun slanted in. He put his head in his hands. 'I can't believe it. All the things that have happened. Not being there for you. It's terrible.'

'Imagine being me.'

There was a sudden thud on the ceiling. It startled her.

'It's the builder,' he said.

'You sure?'

'A hundred per cent.'

There was understanding on his face now. He got up and put the papers on the chest of drawers. 'When you said there was something wrong with you, is this what you meant?'

'Partly.'

There was another thud from upstairs.

'I'm having the same nightmares I had as a kid. It's like something's chasing me. Something horrible. I can feel it near me.'

He listened quietly.

'I felt it in the lab when Laura got burned. I felt it at Chalk

Farm Tube station. There've been other times.'

'Maybe you're feeling it because you're worried?'

'About what?'

'Exams? Laura?'

'I'm not imagining things, Luca.'

'I didn't say you were.'

'Other people have seen things. The burners all going out. Everyone saw that.'

'Someone could have knocked the mains valve off?'

'You don't believe me?'

'I do. I'm just trying to think . . . '

'What, rationally? When I saw you yesterday, I'd just got back from seeing one of my aunt's screwball friends. He held a bloody séance to see if I could speak to my mum and dad and work out what happened to them. During it, the woman next to me got scratched by something. There was blood coming from her eye. Now, tell me how I could have imagined that?'

Luca didn't say anything. He wasn't looking at her; he was staring at her hands. She looked down to see why. They were extended in front of her like claws. Without realising, they'd been scratching the air. She released the tension from her arms and watched them retract slowly.

'I didn't do anything, Luca.'

He held his arms out for her.

'You've got to help me.'

She felt herself weakening, growing dizzy.

The thudding stopped.

Behind them, the door opened quietly. A pair of eyes peered through the crack, then withdrew.

*

It was late when Luca finally left. Aunt Gene hadn't said

anything about him being there. She was too distracted by the builder.

Jodie slept in the room overlooking the front again. She felt cold and lonely. She played with the spectrum analyser. The house registered nothing. She set it down and picked up her father's paper and felt the connection to him grow.

There was a wind outside and the tops of the trees made shadows on the curtains. The windows were much bigger than the dormer window in the attic. She didn't know if it was because of what Mr Cronin said but she seemed to understand more of her father's work now. Words like *infrasound* and *amplitude* and *frequency* made more sense and the implication of them was clear.

Were they seeing real objects or was their mind playing tricks on them? A year ago, during the course of my research, I stumbled across something that left me wondering whether both could be true.

She stared at the spectrum analyser. There wasn't even a flicker. She looked round the room. It was quiet on the landing and quiet outside. She turned on the radio. There were more suicide bombers in Afghanistan and bankers bringing the world to its knees, but all she could think of was her father and ghosts and how he wasn't there any more. She turned on to her stomach.

If you really want to expose yourself to high levels of infrasound, you need do no more than travel the London Underground. At Kennington Loop on the Northern Line, 90-95db has been detected. That's as loud as a lawnmower. When infrasound reaches a frequency of 18.98

Hz, something spectacular happens. Your eyeballs start to shake – they have reached their resonant frequency – and you start to see things. Your survival instinct kicks in, the nape hairs stand up, and you want to run. Who wouldn't? It is probably no coincidence that the London Underground has more reported ghost sightings and paranormal reports than any transport system in the world.

She re-read it again and again. *18.98 hertz.* That was it, the frequency you saw them. She underlined it with a marker pen. She looked between eighteen and nineteen on the spectrum analyser but the bars were flat. She went back to the paper. On the final page, she stopped.

In 1860, the Reverend Doctor Cumming prophetically claimed, 'The forthcoming end of the world would be hastened by the construction of underground railways burrowing into infernal regions and thereby disturbing the devil.' Alas for Doctor Cumming, he was only half right. We did disturb something down there, but it wasn't the devil. It was our imagination.

Her nape hairs rose and Habborlain's words shot through her. *The devil still rides the Underground, you know. He should have taken my advice and stayed away.* If her father were alive, he'd be telling her she was imagining things, yet something terrible had happened to him. There was a connection between it and his work, she knew, something the police had missed.

She lay there with her eyes open. The wind blew against the windows. She imagined it blowing round the house and over the roof. She imagined it blowing through the open dormer window and down to her room. There were some things you couldn't explain. No one could explain the hole in the roof. She looked at Luca's book on the shelf. Was he trying to cheer her up or tell her something?

She closed her eyes. The shadows played on the window and the wind blew away northward over the heath. The bars on the spectrum analyser didn't move. They flickered a few hours later but she was fast asleep.

21

Just after eight, Jodie was woken by a vibration. It spread up her arm to the left side of her face. At first, she thought she was dreaming, but the throbbing continued. She felt beneath her pillow and touched cold metal. It wasn't the spectrum analyser. It was her phone. She looked at the display. It was Luca.

'Are you awake?'

'Just. What is it?'

'I went over to Kamran's last night. We got that video working.'

She sat up quickly. 'You did?'

'Yeah, you need to come over.'

'Why?'

'I think it's best you see for yourself.'

She jumped out of bed, her heart racing.

*

181

Kamran lived on the other side of the road from the school, in a small semi-detached house. Whenever they went round, the smell of curry wafted halfway down the street, but today there was a smell of burning like someone had lit a bonfire. It stung her eyes.

His mum opened the door. She wore a bright pink Asian suit that made her look like a giant flower. She gave Jodie a big smile and showed her up the stairs.

Luca was at the top, holding a screwdriver. He looked tired and unkempt.

'You slept over?'

He nodded and led her into Kamran's room. It was dark inside. On the wall was a plasma screen TV and, underneath it, a silver VCR machine. Kamran was crouched down beside it.

Luca picked up the old video tape. It was broken into pieces. 'The thread went on the screws. I had to smash it up.'

She stared despairingly at him. 'What about the tape? I thought you had it working?'

'We managed to transfer it.'

Before he could say anything more, there was a knock at the door. Kamran's mum came in with a tray of mango juice and Asian bread.

She smiled at them. 'Breakfast.'

There was an uncomfortable silence as they waited for her to go. When the door closed, Luca went to the VCR and pressed play. The machine started to whirr and grind.

Jodie sat on a pouffe at the foot of Kamran's bed. Luca sat next to her.

The screen went dark, then crackled into life. Flashes of light zigzagged across it. Then the picture cleared. There was a man lying down on a table with what looked like electrodes strapped to his head. The picture was grainy and in black and white, but she could make out he was in some kind of cell. The camera panned slowly across the room to another man, this one wearing a white coat. He was talking soundlessly to camera and pointing to a strange machine with large dials and levers on it. It made her think of her father's machine in the attic.

'How come we can't hear anything?' she asked.

Luca put a finger to his lips. 'Wait.'

Crackles of dialogue suddenly burst out. It was hard to pick out what the man was saying; it sounded like a foreign language. They watched as he put headphones on and turned the dials on the machine, then walked over to the man on the table. At first, nothing happened, then the man on the table started to shake like he'd caught a fever. The shaking became more violent till it seemed his organs were trying to escape from his body. He struggled against the straps. Then the screen went dark and the tape flickered. There was a circle of light ahead like the eye of a telescope or the top of a well. It got bigger and bigger till it filled the whole screen. The man in the white coat was there again. He was in another room. There were lines of machinery against the walls and a lot of men sitting in the centre. Some looked like soldiers with short-back-and-sides haircuts; others were older and looked like college professors.

The picture froze, jumped, then started again. There were more glimpses of the men, then close-ups of the machinery and the man in the white coat addressing them. Suddenly, the picture jolted like someone had dropped the camera. The men were no longer sitting down but running about. They were running away, bumping into each other, scrambling over chairs. Some were fighting.

Jodie sat up. The camera started to move from side to side. There were shots of a subterranean floor and a high ceiling and men running in all directions. The sound was intermittent, but every now and then something cut through like someone was screaming into a microphone.

Jodie felt her heart thudding in her chest. The man in the white coat reappeared. He spoke very closely to camera, his face sweating and terrified.

He looked behind him. '*Is it uncommon,*' he said.

'What?' she said.

Luca shrugged. 'I dunno.'

The man ran down a corridor, his footsteps heavy on the ground. The screams had gone but the camera was unsteady. There was someone ahead, sitting slumped against a wall. The camera edged slowly towards him. It was the man who'd been on the table. He stirred for a moment, seemed relieved, then his mouth opened and he screamed. The sound on the VCR distorted horribly. Then the picture cut to black.

Jodie stared at it, immobile, then at Luca.

'It's not finished,' he said.

The screen flickered again. There was some coughing and the sound of footsteps. A torch was flashing down a long red-brick tunnel.

'It's dark down here. Oppressively so.'

Jodie caught her breath. The voice was clear now, and speaking in English.

'We're nearly there. I can understand why people talk about this place. In all the tunnels I've been down, I've never felt anything like it. It really is eerie.'

There was more shuffling.

'There's a wind blowing. It's come up from nowhere.'

She could hear a dull roar on the tape like a passing train.

'I'm going to stop. The temperature has dropped and the readings are jumping. I can't pinpoint where they're coming from.'

Readings? The word shot through her. The voice.

The screen went dark again. There were flashes of tunnels and rail lines disappearing into the gloom, then footage of people walking down them. A light cut across the tracks, rats scurried in narrow culverts, and water dripped down moss-filled walls. Suddenly, numbers flashed across the screen like they did on old movie reels. There was a few seconds of dead tape, then a deeper, impenetrable black. The sound of footsteps on the concrete floor grew louder.

Jodie's heart was on standby.

'I've got the answer.'

A light came on, throwing a narrow beam against a tunnel wall. A middle-aged man came into view. He wore silver rimmed glasses and a blue anorak.

He looked quickly to his left and right.

'I've just got to get out of here.'

Lights out.

Jodie stared at the screen.

Kamran and Luca were quiet. The only sound was the whirring of the VCR.

'Was it your dad?' Luca asked.

She nodded.

'What did he mean, he had the answer?'

'I don't know.'

There was a noise from the video machine just before it cut out, and the sound of spools winding round nothing.

'Oh, crap,' said Luca, reaching for it.

'What is it?' she said, the spell broken.

'It's eating the tape.' He pressed stop, then eject, but the whirring continued. He tried to open the top. 'It's jammed.'

'It's really old,' said Kamran. 'I'm surprised it worked in the first place.'

Luca peered in. 'Thanks for telling us now.'

Jodie got off the pouffe and knelt beside him. 'Can you get it back?'

Luca opened the back with the screwdriver. With a few heaves and pulls, the metal came away. There was tape coiled across the heads and knotted in the rollers. He tried lifting it out but it didn't give.

'You won't get this out without splicing it. It's ruined.'

Jodie looked at Kamran. 'Thanks a lot.'

He looked hurt. 'What did I do?'

'You just shredded my dad.'

22

The Roundhouse coffee bar was deserted. They took the table in the corner and sat down. Luca and Kamran looked as though they were about to fall asleep.

'Well?' Jodie said.

'Well what?' said Luca.

She set the spectrum analyser down on the table and switched it on. 'You must believe me now?'

'I never said I didn't.'

'You didn't need to. What happened to my dad was because of what he was doing. You saw the tape, those people running round. It's all to do with infrasound. The psychic said there was a price to pay for it. He warned my dad away.'

Luca put a hand on his head. 'So what do you want us to do?'

Jodie took her father's paper out of the bag and put it in

187

front of him. 'Read it.'

She followed his eyes to the bottom of the page, making sure he read every word.

When he finished, he raised his eyebrows. '18.98 hertz?'

'The level you see it all, Luca. I want to test it. If we can show that places where ghosts and spirits have been seen are high in infrasound, we'll know my dad was right.'

'Well, how are we going to do that?'

She scrambled in her bag and brought out his book. '*Haunted London*,' she said. 'It has a list of all the haunted places in the city.'

'Jodie, this isn't *Scooby Doo*.'

She stared at him and tried to find the understanding she'd seen yesterday. He seemed like a kid again. 'You haven't listened to a thing I've said, have you?'

'Yes. And I saw the tape. Which is why I'm worried. Not about me or ghosts or spirits. I'm worried about you. I want you to be okay, and I don't see how this helps.'

She went quiet. 'My nightmares are connected to all this, Luca. You don't know the things I've seen. They're not just in my head. Aunt Gene thought I had the answers, and I'm beginning to agree with her.'

'But, Jodie, it's not real,' he said. 'Spirits aren't real.'

Kamran shuffled in his seat. 'I believe in them.'

She shot a look at him. 'Well, who asked you?'

'We call them jinn. Most of the time you can't see them, but you can be possessed by one.'

Possessed. The word lodged itself in her head. Was she possessed by the demon? Was that why it was following her? She had a flashback of the bird woman and the shadow on the ceiling.

'A bad jinn can make you do things. They have to be cast

188

out.' Kamran stirred his cup slowly. 'Like an exorcism. If you're a woman, it's worse. You can be possessed by a zar. You have fainting fits and hysteria. You have to do a special dance to get rid of it, put the victim into a trance.'

Jodie watched the chocolate iceberg dissolve in his cup. Kaleidoscope rings circled around it. 'How do you know all that?'

'My dad's a Sufi Muslim. He believes in spirits and reincarnation. I've grown up with it.'

Jodie turned to Luca. 'You see?'

Luca shrugged his shoulders. 'What do you want me to say?'

'I want you to help.'

She put the book down in front of him. His face went suddenly older and more serious.

'Okay, Jodie,' he said. 'It's your call.'

Haunted London had comic illustrations and naff titles beside each story: the Golders Green Ghost, the Highgate Vampire, the Witches of Winchmore Hill. They didn't sound particularly scary, but beneath the humour were stories and sightings dating back to the Middle Ages.

'How about St. John's Church on Church Row? Bram Stoker was meant to have written part of Dracula there.'

'No way,' said Kamran. 'Too spooky.'

She gave him a withering look. 'Who said you're coming?'

He looked hurt, like a puppy waiting for a bone it knew would never come, and she felt bad.

'I thought you might want the company.'

'You may as well let him,' said Luca. 'The more the better. Makes it more scientific.' He turned back to the book. 'How about the William the Fourth pub? A doctor murdered his wife and buried her body there. Or the Spaniards Inn on

Spaniards Road? It was meant to be a haunt of Dick Turpin. You can hear him ride across the car park in the dead of night.'

She didn't know whether it was because Kamran was there and he was trying to act blasé, but she got the feeling Luca still wasn't taking it seriously.

As she was about to reply, the phone in her coat pocket rang. She thought it must be Aunt Gene checking on her again.

She took it out and looked at the screen. The number was withheld.

Her finger hovered over the reject button but something told her not to. She put the phone to her ear. 'Hello?'

There was a small pause, then a click on the other end. 'Jodie?'

The voice seemed eerily familiar. It rolled down the heath towards her.

'Who is it?'

'It's me, Jodie.'

'John?' she whispered.

At the mention of the name, Luca stirred. She thought of Laura and wondered whether he was feeling the same jealousy as her. For a second, the briefest second, she felt a small, incalculable triumph.

'I need to see you.'

'What is it?'

'I have something important to tell you.'

She tried to keep calm. 'Can't you tell me now?'

'It's too dangerous.' She could hear the anxiety in his voice, imagined him in the waiting area or in the library, on his own. 'Can you meet me tonight? On the heath?'

'I'm not sure.'

'I'll be on Boudicca's Mound. At ten.'

Before she could reply, there was another click and he was gone.

She turned to Luca. 'The Spaniard's Inn is on the heath, isn't it?'

He nodded.

'I think we should try there.'

'Any particular reason?'

'We have to meet someone.'

Luca exchanged a quick look with Kamran. 'Someone we know?'

'You will do. Will we pick up readings there?'

'Yes,' he said. 'The radio mast isn't too far away. You can see it through the trees. If we can find those signals, at least we know what we're doing.'

'So you'll come?'

He nodded slowly.

'Now?'

'I need some sleep first.'

'Tonight, then?'

'We have a Psychology exam in the morning.'

'I don't care.'

'My mum and dad will.'

'Luca . . . '

Kamran finished off his hot chocolate. 'I'll come if he won't.'

She stared at him and knew he would. He'd follow her anywhere.

Luca got up from the table. 'One day you're going to get us in big trouble, you know that? What time?'

'Eight.'

'You better tell your aunt you're not going to be in. I don't want her ringing my mum again.'

'I'll tell her we're studying at Kamran's.'

'What if she rings and finds we're not there?'

She shrugged.

The spots on Kamran's forehead took on a benign, browner pallor. He smiled. 'I'll make sure my mum answers. She doesn't speak English.'

Luca rolled his eyes. 'Nice.'

*

Jodie didn't think Aunt Gene would be in when she got back. There was usually a window of free time before she returned from the hospice. But today was different. The builder's van was still parked outside. Most of the dust and dirt had been cleared from the hall, but there was a strange coldness about the house, like the sun had withdrawn from it.

She was about to go up to the attic when she heard a scrape across the kitchen floor and the clink of a bottle. The sound surprised her. She thought maybe the builder had helped himself to a cup of tea. She pushed the kitchen door open slowly. There was no builder, just Aunt Gene. She was sitting at the table, holding a glass. She turned her head and looked right through her. There were tear lines on her cheeks. Beside her were a bottle and a white handkerchief.

Jodie pulled up a chair. 'What's wrong?'

Aunt Gene's eyes settled on her. There was a film of water over them, like a dam about to break. Jodie picked up the bottle. It was nearly empty.

'Don't worry. I haven't drunk it all today.'

'What's the matter? Why are you like this?' Aunt Gene had always warned her against the perils of drinking.

'Did you sleep okay?'

Aunt Gene's voice was slurred.

Jodie nodded.

'No nightmares?'

'No.'

'Maybe cleaning the attic did the trick?'

Jodie stared at her glass. 'Aunt Gene, what are you doing?'

Aunt Gene blinked the film of water away. 'I'm thinking.'

'About what?'

'William wants to see you again.'

Jodie watched her drain the rest of her glass and put it down on the table. It rang dully.

'He'll help you find out about your father.'

The words knifed into her. 'How?'

'He wants to conduct an experiment. I'm afraid we argued about it. It's up to you now. If he's right about what happened to Kate and Malcolm, the experiment will put you both at great risk.'

'What does he think happened?'

Aunt Gene's eyes re-focused. It was hard to know whether she was looking at her or through her. She picked up the glass and looked at the bottle. 'Is there any left?'

Jodie took the glass out of her hand and put it on the side. 'I think you've had enough.'

'Are *you* looking after *me* now, Jodie?'

She watched her aunt fall asleep where she sat. There was something horrible about it. One moment she was there, the next she was gone. It made her think how fragile things were. Without Aunt Gene, she'd be on her own in the world.

She looked at the kitchen clock. She'd only been back fifteen minutes but it felt longer. She didn't know how long it took people to sober up but there was no way she could leave her like this.

193

As she got up, there was a knock on the kitchen door. She hadn't heard anyone come down.

'Hello?'

It was the builder. 'Just finished, luv.'

He looked at Aunt Gene with her head on the table. Jodie thought how embarrassed she'd be if she knew.

'Is she okay?'

'She has a headache.'

He nodded. She guessed he must have seen a lot worse in other people's houses.

'Has she paid you?'

'Don't worry, luv. I'll sort it out when she's better.'

He smiled at her. Jodie saw him to the door. She watched him load his ladders and buckets into the back of his van.

'The roof's fixed, then?'

He winked at her. 'Nothing will get in now. Or out.'

She watched him drive off, then went back inside. The house was deathly quiet. She went up to the attic. Something seemed to beckon her. The builder had cleared it. There was no more plastic sheeting, no more bags of rubble. It looked a little like the room she'd slept in, but something had changed: something fundamental. It was bigger, cleaner, newer. There were no cupboard doors and boxes and cobwebs. And no strange vibrations. The open window seemed to offer not just fresh air, but a fresh start. In the sunlight, it was hard to believe the place had been so full of shadows and nightmares. Even if she tried to conjure anything up now, she doubted she'd be able to.

Her father's stuff had been left on one side of the room. In reality, there weren't as many boxes as she'd first thought. She started to open them. They were full of books and papers. Some of the books wouldn't have looked out of place on Habborlain's shelves. She wondered if her father had borrowed them, too.

When she'd taken everything out, it seemed a whole lot less, especially for a man's life. She looked through the papers closely. Most of them were technical and typed out but there was handwritten stuff, too. She put them on her knee. There were newspaper and magazine articles and some official-looking documents from London Underground.

The headlines read like episodes of *The X-Files*: *Ghosts on the Underground, Dead Body Train, Bakerloo Line Haunting*. At the bottom of the pile was a map of the network with little green and red pen marks on it. There was a concentration of them in several areas: South Island Place, Covent Garden, Kennington Loop. But around a place called Pages Walk, there were more pins than anywhere.

She stared at it, wide-eyed, then looked down. Underneath was a battered red notebook. She flicked through it and saw maps of tunnels and shafts. There were scribbles on each page, and numbers. She recognised the terminology now: 12Hz, 20db; 12.4Hz, 22db. He'd taken readings. It was a log of some kind. Names of Tube stations and lines leapt out at her. He must have been working on it before the end. The image of her father in silver-rimmed glasses and a blue anorak came into her head.

She turned to the back of the book and found it blank. An immense sadness welled up inside her. She tried to hold it back but it was impossible. It was like a huge wave had come along and swept her overboard. Tears came rushing down her cheeks and her soul emptied.

She shook, not with fear this time, but with grief. The full realisation of being alone in the world finally hit her.

23

'Well, what do you think?' Luca said, holding the phone up. 'Not bad, eh?'

'It looks like the spectrum analyser.'

'Twenty quid. Kamran's brother does them up. Customises them.'

'Did you tell your dad about the last one?'

He looked at her guiltily. 'I told him I exchanged it.' He pressed a button and caught her in the camera lens. 'Eight million megapixels. If we see anything tonight, this'll capture it.'

She stared at him. 'I'm half hoping we won't.'

She cleaned the kitchen table of notepaper and psychology books.

'You're taking all of them?' he asked.

'I have to make it look convincing.'

'Where's your aunt?'

'Upstairs. She's not feeling well.'

'Won't the books weigh you down?'

'I can always throw them later. You ready?'

He nodded.

She scribbled a note for Aunt Gene and left it on the kitchen table. She felt bad writing it. *I've gone to revise with Luca and Kamran. Jodie x.*

She underlined the word *revise* twice.

She stopped at the front door and had a sudden urge to check on her again. She ran upstairs and peered into the grey twilight of her bedroom. She'd drawn the lace curtains after she'd helped her up there. The glass of water was untouched beside the bed. She closed the door and felt a shiver down her back. The dormer window was open but the smell of plaster still hung heavy in the air. Her heart was uneasy.

They slipped out of the shadows on the porch into the midsummer evening. There was a warm, balmy feel to it. She felt a sense of adventure as well as trepidation. Luca was right about the books. They were heavy already. She clutched the bag to her side and felt the metallic cover of the spectrum analyser through it.

*

They met Kamran on the corner of Haverstock Hill. He was kicking a greasy kebab wrapper down the road. Luca tackled him and sent it spinning into one of the ditches. She didn't think it had quite sunk in with them yet. But it would.

They caught a 168 to Hampstead and got off by the pond on North End Way. She could just make out the old houses of the Vale of Health on the other side of the road. They crossed over, turned on to Spaniards Road, and passed the entrance to the heath. The grass swept away south and eastwards like the fairway on a golf course. She caught glimpses of the city through the foliage and the flash of birds flitting from branch to branch. They reminded her of the rook on her window ledge.

After five minutes, she saw the radio mast breaking through the trees. It was impossible to get to it from the road unless you vaulted over fences and gardens, but you could get near if you went down the old horse paths.

Luca stopped and got out the book. 'Find the pathway by the radio mast and follow it downhill. A dark figure on horseback is meant to come riding along it.'

'Fine, but we're going to the Spaniards Inn, aren't we?' she said.

She looked into the woods. The evening sun had painted it red. Car headlights now flickered through the trees and red taillights gleamed like eyes.

Eventually, they came to a cream coloured pub on a bend in the road. It was set on three floors with a mock Victorian gas lamp over the porch and black windows from which came a warm orange glow. On one side was a sign. It was hung haphazardly with two crossed swords above it. *Spaniards Inn 1585 AD*.

'Why did they call it the Spaniards Inn?' she asked.

'It used to be the home of a Spanish ambassador,' Luca said. 'It was turned into a pub in the eighteenth century by two brothers, also Spanish, who fought a duel over a woman.'

He tapped the book.

'Well, don't you two get any stupid ideas,' Jodie said.

Kamran looked at her strangely, then stared at the evening sky. 'What are we looking out for, then?'

'We're not looking for anything,' she said. 'We're testing something.'

She took the spectrum analyser out of her bag.

'*Not to be taken out of the department,*' he read. 'Nice.'

'We were lent it.'

Luca pointed across the road. 'The car park is over there. Most sightings have been on the West Heath.'

Jodie turned the machine on. The light glowed in the dark. She set the frequency to between fifteen and twenty hertz.

Luca looked over her shoulder. 'Well?'

The green bars were flat.

'Try widening the frequency level.'

As soon as she did, the bars began flickering.

'Look, that's us talking.'

The bars peaked and fell.

'Go higher.'

She extended it some more.

'All that high frequency stuff will be the radio mast, I'm pretty sure. It's picking up loads.'

She reset the levels to below twenty hertz.

They crossed the road and skirted the pub until they came to an old stone wall. It was all that divided the car park from the heath. The shadows lengthened and the sun sank behind the trees. Thickets grew darker and the under-growth became indistinguishable from the ground. Jodie had her eyes fixed on the green bars.

'Anything?' Luca asked.

She shook her head.

'Shall we try further along the path?'

She didn't know why it felt such a let down. She had no right to expect anything. They walked down the paths and all the time the darkness seemed to creep up on them.

Luca stopped. 'Still nothing?'

She shook her head again.

'Here, try adjusting the amplitude. There will be infra-sound, I'm sure. It'll just be really low.'

He changed the settings and the green bars flickered again. 'There, did you see that?'

It peaked at five decibels, then flattened.

'Yes, but it's not the right frequency. That was ten hertz.'

'Maybe we have to wait for the ghost?' Kamran said.

She pulled a face at him.

They looked back along the path. It was hard to see anything in the twilight.

'So what do we do?' asked Luca.

'We wait,' said Jodie.

She pointed into the woods. The path disappeared into the gloom and the land rolled away on either side. They passed mounds and hollows filled with bracken and gorse. Small ponds glinted like mirrors in the delves. There was a *rap-tap-tapping* in the darkness and the rustling of the purple curtains of twilight. Behind them seemed to walk a monstrous terror. The sound of cars passing grew fainter.

Kamran became more agitated. 'This place is creepy.'

She stared at the spectrum analyser. There were no further jumps. She sat on a log beside the path and put her bag down. It was making her shoulder hurt.

Luca looked round. 'Dick Turpin knew what he was doing. This is a great place for a hold-up.'

'Yeah, but who's going to come down here?' asked Kamran.

Jodie thought about John. He went walking the heath at night.

'Nutters,' she said.

Kamran shuffled his feet. The sound magnified along the path. As if in response, there was another shuffle in the thickets opposite them.

'What was that?' he asked.

The thicket continued to shake, then something broke cover and scampered across the woodland floor.

'Whoa, what is it?'

Luca peered into the gloom. 'It's not Dick Turpin.'

Jodie ignored him. Her eyes were fixed on the green bars. She was surprised how calm she felt. The heath wasn't like her room or the tunnel. It was open and free.

'Maybe we should try the other side?' Luca asked.

'I thought you said the sightings were here?'

'Well, it doesn't look like anyone's coming.'

'You go. I'll wait here.'

'All night?'

She shrugged.

'Come on, Jodie. We can't leave you. It's not safe. We'll take one of the horse paths by the radio mast and go back that way.'

Disappointment and embarrassment crushed her. She couldn't blame them for wanting to go. It *was* like *Scooby Doo*. Did she really expect to hear horse's hooves come down the footpaths and a highwayman emerge from the thickets?

*

The last ounce of daylight was squeezed from the woods and an oily blackness spilt across the sky. They crossed Spaniards Road and disappeared down one of the bridle-ways on the other side. The trees were bigger there. They were taller and older than those on the West Heath and towered above them like giant tripods. Through them, they could see the radio mast rising up. The paths narrowed and forked and soon they were totally lost in shadow. They tried to keep the mast in sight but, as the path meandered away to the left, they soon found themselves going down and away from it.

'So, who's this guy we're seeing?' said Kamran.

'The psychic's son.'

'Bit weird he wants to meet us here, isn't it?'

'Not for him. He spends a lot of time here.'

'Doing what?'

She looked into the trees. 'Thinking.'

Luca pulled up beside her. 'You feel it, too?'

'Yeah. Since we crossed the road. Like something's following us.'

'Maybe it's your friend?' Kamran said.

No one replied. It was easy to laugh off getting lost during the day but not now. They weren't walking along the road, or on the top of Parliament Hill watching the kites. Joggers and cyclists stuck to the open spaces, not these dirt tracks.

They looked around and waited for whatever it was to break cover, but the trees closed ranks and the spaces between them got narrower and darker. Nothing stirred.

'I think we should get back,' Luca said.

'I said I'd meet him on Boudicca's Mound. We can't go back.'

'We're gonna get lost.'

She searched the woods for a recognisable landmark, found none. The trees grew thinner but the sense of being watched didn't leave her. If anything, it grew with every step. Yet the bars on the spectrum analyser hadn't moved.

After ten minutes, they came to a black-and-white building set back from the path. On one side was a sign saying *Ladies*: the other, *Gentlemen*. She'd passed the toilets during the day but never dared use them.

'I think we need to go that way,' she said, pointing down the path.

'You sure?' Luca said. 'You said it was between the radio mast and Parliament Hill.'

Jodie looked into the dark selvedge of the trees and remembered nothing. She imagined a pair of eyes looking at her from within.

She turned to Kamran. The look on his face said it all: *Just get us out of here.*

After ten minutes of scrambling through thickets and being forced downhill, they came to one of the large ponds at the bottom of the heath, crossed by a large stone bridge. They heard voices coming through the trees ahead of them. It was a pair of joggers, heading up the hill. But, before they could call out to them, they'd gone.

The moon came out, glimmering on the algae-filled water. A cool breeze blew across it.

Jodie noticed someone standing there. At first, she thought it was one of the statues, but then it bent down to pick something up and her heart raced. She waved her arms to get their attention.

'Hey!'

Luca turned. 'Who are you waving at?'

The figure looked up at them and quickly disappeared into the trees. It was John. Jodie ran round the pond to catch him.

He slipped through the undergrowth. She could see him ahead of her. Then he vanished in the moonlight as mysteriously as he'd appeared.

Luca and Kamran came lumbering up behind. 'Who was it?'

'John,' she said. 'The psychic's son.'

Kamran had his hands on his knees and was breathing like an old steam engine. 'Can we stop, please? I think I'm having a heart attack.'

Jodie checked the treeline, hoping for another sight of him, but there was none.

'Are you sure?' Luca asked. 'You're meant to be meeting him on Boudicca's Mound. What would he be doing here?'

Then a voice came out of the darkness behind them. 'Making sure she doesn't get lost.'

They all turned.

John was standing in the moonlight. He had a long coat on and his face looked like marble. 'The heath's a dangerous place to get lost.'

Luca turned to Jodie. 'Are you checking your readings?'

Jodie looked at the spectrum analyser. There was a flicker of life at the ten-hertz level, but nothing more.

'Your machine won't work here,' he said. 'I'm not a ghost.'

'You know about it?' asked Jodie.

'I've been following you for a while. You make a lot of noise.' He marched over the bridge. 'Try to keep up.'

She ran after him.

He led them through the trees and up the hill on the other side. In the distance, she could see the lights of London twinkling away. She recognised Parliament Hill to the east, its barren top like a bald crown.

At the top of the hill, he stopped.

'Why were you following us?' Jodie said.

'Following isn't the right word. I was checking you got

here on time.'

'Why?'

'Because we haven't much time. I need to show you something.'

'What is it?'

'It's to do with the day you came. I know what happened. I know why Mrs Carstairs was attacked.'

The running and the night air made her head spin. She was back in the room with the shadow on the ceiling. 'What?'

She felt herself going fainter.

'Best you come to the house and I'll explain. My father won't be in.'

*

Jodie stared at the top of the hill and felt the cool air on her face.

Luca was fidgeting beside her. 'How long's he gonna be?'

She looked at John, etched against the moonlight. 'I think he's nearly done.'

'What's he doing?'

'Trying to find a ley line.'

Luca tapped his head. 'I don't think he's all there.'

'Maybe. But you heard what he said?'

'Yeah,' Luca said. There was more than a touch of dismissiveness in his tone. 'He's mad.'

'So you're not coming?' she asked.

'To his house? It's nearly eleven.'

'We'll be back by midnight.'

'Yeah, and we have an exam tomorrow.'

'I can't wait, Luca.'

John was waving at them to follow. She ran up the hill towards him.

Luca looked at Kamran.

'That's why I don't have a girlfriend,' Kamran said.

'Yeah, of course,' Luca said.

He looked into the oily blackness.

24

John led them quickly over the heath, navigating the dark paths with an unerring and unfaltering ease. The woods clearly weren't a place of terror for him. He brushed through them like the wind.

'Do you come here every night?' she asked.

'It's my refuge. People used to come to the heath to escape the plague. I come here to escape life.'

Luca rolled his eyes at her.

They passed the Highgate ponds where she'd first met him — she recognised the pier sticking into the water like a needle – and eventually came to more broken woodland. The ground broke and snapped beneath their feet. Once or twice, Luca's hand touched hers, but she felt disconnected from him, and distracted. She kept seeing the bird woman and the shadow on the ceiling.

After a final copse, they came to a road. It wound round in

the darkness, past still and silent houses. Up ahead, she could see the glint of long, iron railings, and through them the sombre lines of gravestones.

'We're near now. We have to cut through the cemetery. Be careful.'

'What of?' Luca asked.

The headstones gleamed in the moonlight, white and ebony.

'Well, the Highgate Vampire, for one. If you see a grey figure or a tall man in a hat, or a woman in white, let me know.' He turned to Jodie. 'People rip up the old graves and knock over tombstones and claim the undead are after them. They forget real people are buried there.'

He vaulted the railings and disappeared into the shadows.

Luca gave her another look.

'It'll be okay,' she said, and clambered over.

John picked his way through the stones, pointing out the graves of famous people. Once or twice, he stopped as if he'd heard something, and she imagined the ground about to open up beneath them.

He stopped to pick up some flowers and gave them to her. 'My nanny used to say you were giving them away to folks that didn't need them.'

'How did she figure that out?'

'She said heaven was full of flowers that never died.'

Jodie looked at the faded blooms and read the inscription on the headstone: *Trust in the Everlasting Mercy of Our Lord*.

'That's a nice thought,' she said.

'Very,' said Luca.

John got on his knees and swept the leaves away.

'We used to play together when we were young.'

She looked at him. 'We did?'

'My dad told me. I never had any other childhood friends.'

'What about at school?'

'I was taught at home. Do you want me to show you something?'

The wind blew up and she felt spots of rain on her face.

'I'm not sure.'

'It won't take a minute.'

Before she could say no, he'd leapt between the stones. She saw glimpses of his coat flickering behind him. He cut this way and that until he came to a plain and unadorned grave.

'What are you doing?'

He shifted the headstone to the right. 'She's already gone to heaven.'

He reached into a hole in the ground and brought out a small metal box. He swept the dust from it and handed it to her.

'What is it?'

'Open it,' he said.

Her nails caught on the edge. 'It's not bones or something freaky?'

He shook his head.

She prised the lid off and looked down. Inside were the broken pieces of a green plastic dinosaur. 'I don't understand.'

'Have you ever wondered what it must be like to save someone's soul?'

'No.'

'I have. I look at all these people and wonder how many went to heaven and how many were damned.'

The wind whipped up and she thought of her mother and

father lying in the cold earth.

'I didn't think you believed in stuff like that.'

'The Victorians called it honest doubt.' His eyes sparkled within the cowl of his hood. 'How grateful would they be if you saved them, do you think? Would they be bound to you for what you'd done?'

She looked at the tombs and headstones and angels' wings. 'I would think so.'

He stared at her fathomlessly. 'That's what I hoped.' He took the metal box from her and laid it in the ground. 'You don't understand now, but you will.'

Luca looked at her. 'What the hell's going on?'

John gave no sign he heard. He led them back through the graves.

Eventually, they came to another long, tree-lined road. She didn't recognise it in the dark, but when they came to the end and she saw the stone owls on the gateposts, she knew where they were.

Luca whistled. 'Nice house.'

John led them up the gravel drive. He looked about him. His garrulousness on the heath was now replaced with a growing unease.

'You okay?' she asked.

'Yes. It's just a risk bringing you here.'

'You're telling us now?' Luca said.

John said nothing and led them inside. There was an eerie quiet in the waiting area. The pictures on the wall looked more sinister and ethereal. It was hard to know where they ended and the room began. The trees seemed to crawl out of their frames and shadows played on them like fingers.

'My father doesn't like visitors. I'm never allowed to bring people round. But we should be okay for a few hours.'

'Where is he?' she asked.

John stared at her. 'Probably off trying to summon the devil.'

He opened the dark, oak doors into the library. The first thing Jodie noticed was the cold, like someone had breathed frost into the room. It was so different from the last time she was there. She looked at the leather seats and imagined the old man with the walking stick and Mr and Mrs Carstairs. The room was holding its breath.

John closed the doors, turned the wall lights on, and went to the table in the middle. Jodie could see the outline of the black magic mirror under the purple cloth.

'Don't worry,' he said. 'It's quite safe.'

Luca and Kamran joined them, as bewildered as she was the first time.

'Your dad's a medium?' Luca said.

'That's how he describes himself.'

Jodie noticed a shadow under his eye.

'I wasn't going to tell you about what he was doing. I wasn't going to say anything.'

'So why change your mind?'

He looked at her strangely. 'I'm not invited to séances normally. My father doesn't like me with him.'

'Why not?'

'He thinks I'll give him away.'

The words took a moment to sink in.

'Give what away?'

'This,' he said, indicating the room. 'What he does here.'

'I don't understand.'

John paused. 'My dad's desperate to be able to communicate with the dead. He believes in the afterlife, but he's no psychic. He's just a conman who makes his living preying on rich old ladies. They listen to him because he's good at what he does. He makes them believe.'

'You mean Aunt Gene?'

'Yes. He's strung her along for years. Telling her the answer will come. But nothing does. That's why he was so interested in you. He thinks you're the best chance he has. He was delighted when your Aunt told him you'd started having dreams again. He knew you when you were little, you see?'

Jodie was furious with him, and embarrassed. 'Why are you telling me all this?'

He put his hands on the table. 'Because you're in danger from him. He thinks you'll provide him with access to the spirit world. I've heard him talk about you. When I met you on the heath I had no idea it was you, but when I saw you at the door, I understood. I knew something was up. He'll never leave you alone until he's made contact with it.'

She felt a terrible rage growing inside her. Aunt Gene, Habborlain – were they part of some terrible conspiracy? For a few seconds, she said nothing. The import of what he'd said was lost in the fug of confusion.

'But that's impossible . . . ' She stopped.

'Is it?' asked John. 'My father knew your father. He knew what he was up to. He's had his books out in his study for the last three days. He thinks you have an ability, that you can make spirits appear for the rest of us.'

Jodie looked at Luca and Kamran's disbelieving faces. Anger pinned her tongue down. Who'd believe a thing like that?

John left the table and went to the bookshelves. His movements were quick like he'd rehearsed it. He brought a book down and Jodie knew what it was immediately.

'Page sixty-eight?'

She nodded.

He opened the book and put it in front of her. The horned demon stared back at her. Luca and Kamran were still.

'How did you know?'

'I overheard everything. After you left, dad took the book out and stared at it for hours. Something you said disturbed him greatly. This is a demon from hell. He thinks you've allowed it into this world. '

There was a grim silence.

John shuffled next to her. 'My father's spent his entire life searching for the spirit realm. I think he'd do anything to open the door, to see what's on the other side, to convince us our nightmares exist.'

Luca looked at the picture closely. 'This is the thing that's been chasing you?'

She nodded. There was a low chime from a distant clock, then eleven more.

Kamran shuffled uneasily. 'We need to get back, yeah?'

Luca nodded. 'Jodie?'

But she couldn't draw herself away. 'I need to check something first.'

She took the spectrum analyser out of her bag and turned it on. The green bars were flat. As the twelfth chime died, it was answered by another, this time from outside. It was harder and heavier.

John's face turned instantly.

'What is it?' asked Luca.

John ran to the doors. '*My* worst nightmare.' He opened them a fraction. 'We're too late.' He ushered them back into the room. 'Let me do the talking, please. If you say anything, it'll only make things worse.'

'Why?' asked Luca.

'Just do as I say.'

The library doors were thrown open. A tall man with a long coat and cane stood in the doorway. His silver hair glinted in the light and his grey eyes bore out the darkness like a wolf's. He stood there a moment as if he was about to cast a spell on them. It was William Habborlain.

Kamran murmured a prayer under his breath. Fear gripped them all. Habborlain shut the doors and stared at each of them in turn. When his eyes got to Jodie, they seemed to look into her mind. She thought of what John had said: *he's good at what he does.*

'Well, John. This is how you repay my trust? You open my library to strangers when I'm out?'

'No, father.'

'Then you caught them breaking and entering? In which case, we must ring the police.'

'No, father. They weren't.'

'Then do you want to tell me why they're here?'

His voice had dropped to a whisper.

John didn't move.

Habborlain's cane beat the floor as he approached. His arm flashed out and struck John full in the face, knocking him over.

The violence made Jodie reel. She stared at John and thought of the shadow on his cheek.

'He's okay, Jodie. John's quite the actor when he wants to be. He says all sorts of things to get attention.' He glanced down and saw the book on the table. 'Just like you. Have you missed your old friend? Is he still bothering you?'

She looked at Luca for help.

'Why don't you leave her alone?' Luca said.

Habborlain turned. 'Why don't you stay out of it, boy? You're in my house. Do you know what you get for breaking and entering?'

'We didn't mean any harm. John invited us.'

'Not very likely. John has no friends.'

'He wanted to tell us something.'

Habborlain picked up the book. 'Tell you, or her? It must have been very important.' He stood next to Jodie. She could smell his coat. 'Why have you come back, Jodie?'

She had to bite her tongue to keep herself from saying what John had said.

'You know who killed my father.'

The words came tumbling out. Habborlain's eyes flickered.

'So that's why you came?' he whispered. 'To find out?'

She couldn't move.

'I warned your father before he died that he was meddling with things he didn't understand. I told him to his face. But he was dead set on proving me wrong. I was one of the few who suspected.'

'Suspected what?'

'That things weren't all they seemed.'

Her thoughts ran madly ahead of her. 'What do you mean?'

'They never found anybody, did they? The poor police.'

'You didn't believe them?'

He laughed dismissively. 'Of course not.'

'Then what?'

Habborlain drummed his fingers on the table. 'I think something came after him, Jodie. Like it's coming after you.'

She thought of what he'd said to Aunt Gene, that there was a monster on the Underground. 'It's not possible,' she said.

Habborlain's grey eyes went through her. 'Everything is possible, Jodie. Everything in heaven and earth. You see, I believe you now. I believe that if I sit you down, the same thing will happen. You'll see a demon come from the roof and pluck your heart out. You need my help. I can help you control it. You connect so strongly to the spirit world, but you don't understand its power. You have to let me help you. I felt something that night, something otherworldly and dangerous. I felt fear in the room. A fear so strong your mother and father wouldn't even come in. Their spirits refused to enter. There was something in here.'

He lit the candles round the table and pulled the chairs out. 'If you really want to know what came after him, maybe we should see what's coming after you?'

He looked into her eyes. She watched as the wall lights dimmed and he pressed the switch. The blinds were drawn and the fans began to rotate.

'Jodie, we can't stay,' said Luca, pulling her arm.

But she couldn't take her eyes off Habborlain.

'Why don't you leave her, boy? She needs to know. How else will she sleep at night?'

'Come on, Jodie.'

Luca sounded like he was coming through a tunnel.

Habborlain sat down in front of her. She stared at the ceiling.

Luca tugged at her but she couldn't move.

'What have you done to her?'

'She's here of her own volition. Why don't you and your friend join us?'

Kamran clutched one of the candle stands for support.

'Don't break the circle, if you value your life,' Habborlain warned.

Jodie watched the blades turn, beating cool air on her face. She knew Luca and Kamran were beside her but she could no longer see them. The room was spinning, bringing with it the sickness she'd felt before.

The spectrum analyser dropped from her hands.

'Get me out of here, Luca.'

He bent to pick it up and called out to Kamran. But Kamran wasn't listening. He was staring at the ceiling and ducking.

'There's something here,' he said.

Habborlain's face was incandescent, following his gaze.

'Can't you feel it, Jodie? It's up there.'

The blades spun faster and faster. She couldn't see anything now. The whole room was grey. A rain fell in the corners of her eyes, growing like a cloud. Shapes shifted and flickered like matchstick men dancing on a page. She turned her head to catch them but they vanished into the mist. Luca had his arms round her waist, pulling her. She could see green lines playing in his hand, vaulting up and down.

'Luca, look.'

'What do you see, Jodie? Is it there?' Habborlain was on his feet. 'Where are you? Show yourself.'

The green lines grew out of Luca's hand like a blaze of ectoplasm. They cut through the grey lines of matchstick men and electrified her eyes. Her stomach churned. She was aware of voices, panic-filled and strident, but they were lost in the cloud. She felt herself losing consciousness. The floor opened like a black pit in front of her.

As she was about to disappear inside, she felt something blow against her face. She'd felt it before, in the Underground tunnel, in the science lab, at the zoo. It wasn't the

217

fans. It was too fast. It was the wind rushing, unstoppable and unseen. Something was flying through the darkness, beating its wings towards her. She opened her mouth and emptied what was left in her lungs. The scream shook her body and brought vomit to the back of her throat.

Habborlain covered his ears. 'Don't break the circle!'

It was too late. Kamran knocked over a candle stand and shouted. Luca gave a last heave and finally managed to pull her away. She felt herself being dragged along, trying to keep up with them. She could feel liquid spilling from her insides. The smell of it made her gag. They ran through the waiting area and the pictures on the wall flickered like grainy images in an old black-and-white film. Behind them, she heard the wind, and then the dark oak doors slamming shut.

She looked back and saw Habborlain with his back pressed against them, as if he were holding back the very gates of hell. There was anger in his face, and fear. He knew what was in there.

Luca tried to drag her to the front door, but she couldn't leave. Not yet.

'What the hell was it?' she cried.

Habborlain stared at her, ashen-faced. 'It was your demon, Jodie. Someone has summoned it again. Maybe that's what your father found. The way to call it. A projection of the unconsciousness, perhaps? Concretisation, Jung called it. The ability to project things into reality. A realm between mind and matter where bodies could manifest themselves in mental as well as material form. What if your poor father had found that?'

'How do I stop it?' she said.

Habborlain shook his head. 'You can't, Jodie. Even if they

218

rewired your brain. It's coming for you.'

Luca pulled her again. 'C'mon, Jodie. He's mad.'

Habborlain's eyes flashed angrily at him. 'Mad, boy? And what would you propose to do? Do you think the drugs you use in your playground are going to do her any good? There are far darker forces at work here. We're talking about her soul.'

The word froze her. Her *soul*?

'There must be an answer,' she begged.

The wind relented and a slow, sadistic smile appeared on Habborlain's face. 'If there is, there's only one place you'll find it.'

Her heart stopped. Of course there was. She'd known it the day the slate came off the roof and she looked in the attic.

'The Underground?' she whispered.

'Yes, Jodie. You must follow in your father's footsteps and confront your fears. Maybe you'll find all your answers down there?' He turned to the paintings on the wall, the pictures of the heath and cemetery. 'But you better beware. If your nightmare knows you want to wake from it, it may come after you first.'

She felt Luca's grip on her hand tighten. Before she had time to reply, he'd dragged her away. He pulled her through the front door and pushed her out into the night.

They ran down the gravel drive through the gates with the owls on and didn't stop until they'd got to the road by the cemetery. Kamran doubled up, holding his face. His whole body shook. It took a few moments to register that he was crying.

'Shit, what the hell was in there?' he sobbed.

The midnight air blew the grey cloud from her eyes. It

was unnerving seeing him so distraught. It made her think how real things were, and how dangerous.

Luca put his arm round him. 'There was nothing there, Kam. It was a trick.'

'A trick? Something was taking swipes at me. It was flying around.'

'You saw it?' Jodie asked.

'I saw something.'

'What was it?'

'I don't know. It was like smoke.'

Jodie's heart throbbed in her chest. She turned to Luca. 'So I'm not the only one.'

'Jodie, it was a trick. The guy plays it every chance he gets. You heard what the weird kid said. He's a conman.'

'I don't think so.'

Luca waved his arms in resignation.

'You didn't see anything?' she said.

'I saw a psycho go off his nut and punch his son in the face, then you two acting like you were drunk.'

'What about the spectrum analyser?'

'What about it?'

'You picked it up.'

'So?'

'So it was going crazy. You saw it.'

'I didn't see anything.'

'We set if for between zero and twenty hertz.'

Luca ran his hands through his hair.

'Just tell me what it showed, Luca. For God's sake.'

He paused. 'Nineteen, maybe. Nineteen hertz.'

He banged the cemetery gates.

'Tell me we're not going back there. You've got what you came for,' Kamran begged. 'My mum's going to kill me.'

Jodie thought of Aunt Gene sleeping in her room. What would *she* say?

Luca stared at the graves.

'Are you mad with me?' she said.

'I'm mad at myself for letting you come.'

'I had to.'

She put her hands on his. 'I'm sorry, Luca.'

25

Aunt Gene looked through the gap in the curtains at the streetlight outside. It shone directly into her room with a pale, unearthly glow. For a moment, how she got there was just as mysterious. She didn't remember going to bed. She tried to move her head but it was weighed down like a sandbag. She managed to roll it to the side, and when she saw the glass of water, bits and pieces of the day assembled themselves like a jigsaw: the builder, the roof, the bottle of gin.

'Jodie?'

There was no reply. She strained to look at the bedside clock, but the hands merged into one. Eleven, twelve, she couldn't tell. She struggled on to her side. Her head throbbed. Every time she moved, it sent shockwaves into her skull. Something else was there, too: a ringing sound. She tried to shake it away but it cut through the air insistently. She thought it may be an alarm but it kept stopping and starting. This time it seemed louder. It stripped away the torpor and filled her with dread. It was her phone. A blue light was flashing now like an ambulance's. She reached her hand out and grabbed it.

'Genevieve?'

It was *him*. His voice was not the soothing balm it normally was, but irritated and aggressive.

'I've been trying for ages. Where have you been?'

It was difficult to think in the fog.

'I was asleep.'

'Asleep? Do you know who came to my house tonight?'

The dread rose up from her stomach.

'I came home to find her in my library along with her friends.'

'Jodie?' she whispered.

'Yes. Jodie. John found her wandering around the heath with an infrasound sensor, trying to prove her father's theories. She's a danger to herself, Gene. She needs to let *me* help her.'

'Yes, William.'

The pain in Aunt Gene's head was replaced with anxiety. 'Where is she now?'

'She ran off with her friends.'

'What do you want me to do?'

'I want you to find her. If you want to know what happened to Kate and Malcolm you'd better get her back here quickly, before she harms everyone round her.'

'What?'

'You heard.' His words were measured now, and sober. 'She might be dead before we find out the answers.'

The phone whirred. He'd put it down.

She struggled up, went on to the landing. A light breeze blew down from the attic. She looked in Jodie's room opposite. Her bed was empty. She rang her number but there was no reply.

She went down to the kitchen. Everything was cleared away. There were no glasses and no gin bottle, just a note. She picked it up and read it slowly.

I've gone to revise with Luca and Kamran. Jodie x

The lie didn't hurt as much as other lies she'd told – if there was a reason she couldn't tell her things, that was her fault. She looked at Jodie's name and the x beside it. It would have been worse without it. She folded up the paper, sat on the chair then picked up the phone. She steeled herself against the long night and what would happen when they found Jodie. *If* they found her.

*

At half past one, she went to her bedroom and lay on the bed like a corpse. She heard the front door open and Jodie's tentative footsteps in the hall. She heard her climb the stairs and pause on the landing. She watched the handle of her door turn slowly, then Jodie put her head round and made a couple of steps into the room. It was like she was a little girl again, coming in to see her when she was frightened, wanting to sit on her bed and feel the reassurance of an adult.

'Jodie, thank God.'

'I thought you were asleep.'

'I was.'

'I'm sorry I'm late.'

'William is beside himself with worry, Jodie. He told me what happened.'

Jodie's eyes burned in the half-light.

'You have to speak to him, Jodie. He's the only one who

can help you.'

'I can't talk about this, Aunt Gene. Not now. I'm sorry.'

Aunt Gene could tell she no longer trusted her. She watched her creep back to the door. 'I love you, darling.' She used to say it to her every night. Now, she meant it more than ever.

'I know, Aunt Gene.'

The door closed softly. She rolled on to her side and stared at the streetlight. She watched a wave of insects flitting by, a wingspan away from the webs and burning fire, and knew she had to watch over her more carefully than ever.

26

Jodie had left home early to avoid Aunt Gene's little 'talk'. She sat in the common room studying her father's papers, trying to make sense of everything. There was no way she was letting William Habborlain experiment on her, whatever her aunt said. She had to find out the answers for herself.

Luca had his head on the table next to her. 'I don't think I've ever been so tired.'

'I'm sorry, Luca.'

'It's my fault. What do they always say? "Don't leave your revision to the last minute."?'

'Maybe you did better than you thought?'

'I don't think so.'

She laid the black folder on the table. 'I can't stop thinking about last night.'

'I was trying to forget it.'

'Habborlain and Aunt Gene are right, you know. I have to face this. Just not in the way they want. I have to go back to where this all started for Dad.'

'The Underground? I don't think that's a good idea, do you?'

'All the answers are down there.'

'Yeah, and a whole lot else, probably.'

'I didn't think you believed in the supernatural.'

'I don't know what to believe.' His tone was resigned and sad.

She took another folder out of her bag and laid some pictures on the table. Luca raised his head and scrutinised them. There were charcoal prints and computer generated screens and a few sketched self-portraits. Her expression was the same in each one.

'Have you ever drawn something that wasn't completely depressing?'

As he reached the bottom of the pile, one suddenly caught his attention. It was a picture of a ceiling with a dome in the centre and two giant fans. From the fans were suspended the green, reptilian limbs of the demon. Its wings spread behind it and its red eyes searched the floor. It was looking for something. Where the oak doors should have been, there was a tunnel, black and impenetrable.

'Did you see it last night?'

'Yes, it was coming for me.'

The room went quiet.

'If your father was right about infrasound, Jodie, how come only you could see something? I was there and didn't see anything.'

'What about Kamran? He did.'

'Kamran would say anything you asked him.'

227

'What does that mean?'

He shrugged. 'Nothing.'

'He was scared out of his wits, Luca. And so were you.'

'How could I be scared of something I couldn't see?'

'Isn't that the point? You don't. You feel it. Maybe some people are more susceptible?'

He picked up the picture and pondered. 'Or the levels of infrasound have to be higher, maybe?'

She had a sudden flashback of people running round in a grainy black-and-white film and a man with electrodes strapped to his head. 'That's it,' she said. 'The experiment on my dad's tape. Do you remember what Mr Cronin said? That the Germans were working on something?'

He nodded vaguely.

'Maybe that's what he found?'

'I don't understand.'

She looked at him. 'They reacted the way we reacted. No bombs, no explosions. Just silence.'

She stared at the words above the doors: Common Room. *'Is it uncommon,'* she whispered, then leapt to her feet. She ran out of the room as if the demon was still after her. 'Come on.'

*

The computer room was deserted. Jodie sat in front of one of the terminals and typed as fast as she could.

'Do you want to tell me what this is all about?' Luca said.

'I want to know what that man said.'

'Which man?'

'The one in the white coat. In the video. He said something to camera when everyone was going crazy. I asked you at the time. No wonder I couldn't work it out. He was speaking German.'

She brought up an online translator, clicked on English to German, and typed in the words *is it uncommon*. The reply came back instantly: *ist es ungewöhnlich*. She tried *uncommon* on the German side and got the same word back.

'If it's German, the last word will probably be a verb,' Luca said.

'How do you know that?'

'Trust me, I'm smart.'

She went on Google, clicked on a list, and read down the words, looking for anything that sounded like *common*.

Luca pointed at the screen. 'What about that?'

She looked above his finger. *Kommen v. to come.*

'Is it coming?' she whispered.

'Click on "conjugations",' he said.

'What?'

He took the mouse from her, brought up another list of words, and read down them. '*Ich kam, es kam, er ist gekommen, es ist gekommen.* Is it, *es ist*, is it, *es ist*. You say them.'

She ran them through her head, trying to remember how the man in the white coat had said it. '*Es ist gekommen,*' she repeated. 'It's not right, even in a German accent. I'm sure it was "uncommon".'

'Then we need to find all the German words with *kommen* in them.'

He clicked again and brought up a longer list of verbs. She put *es ist* in front of each one, imagined herself stuck in a tunnel, looking behind her. Every time she came to a word with *kommen* at the end, she stopped and a strange paralysis would take hold.

She felt Luca's breath on her arm. His hand reached out the same time hers did.

Entkommen. Uncommon. It was almost the same.

She looked along the line. *v. escape, run away, get away, flee, take flight.*

She grabbed the keyboard, typed *es ist entkommen* into the translator, and waited for the answer.

It came back in an instant.

It has escaped.

The paralysis grew up her arms and down her legs, welding her to the chair.

'Those guys meant business, didn't they?' he said. 'What the hell was down there with them?'

She nodded, remembering her father's words: *I've just got to get out of here.* 'He died before he could tell anyone.'

Luca looked at her. 'You think he knew what was coming after him?'

She nodded. 'There was definitely something in the tunnels with him.'

Luca paused. 'But he didn't die in the tunnels. He died at home.'

She turned to the screen. The words leapt off it, into the mouth of the German, through the dark, subterranean tunnels, to a man in a blue anorak and silver-rimmed glasses.

Es ist entkommen.

'So he brought it back with him.'

The words sank in slowly and took her down, down into the bowels of the earth. She thought of the map and his notebook.

'I found a diary of his yesterday when I was unpacking. It was a journal he kept of the Underground. There were readings from every Tube station.'

'So?'

'So, if we go there, we can find out.'

'Find out what?'

'What it was.'

He looked at the screen and swallowed. 'Now, you are joking.'

'Please, Luca.'

He ran his hand through his hair. 'What makes you think we can just go down there and take the readings, anyway?'

'Because my father did.'

'He was a lecturer at Imperial College.'

'Yeah, and we're not kids any more.'

He fingered the ring on his finger. 'If we go, I want you to promise me something.'

She guessed what it was: if it didn't work, would she drop it? It was impossible. No matter what he said, she knew she was near to finding the answer. She wouldn't give that up for anything.

'What is it?'

'I want you to promise you'll listen to me when I need you to. You won't run away, you won't get cross, you'll hear me out.'

It caught her unawares. 'Why do you think I wouldn't?'

'I just want to know you would.'

She nodded slowly.

They made their way back to the common room and picked up her folder.

He looked again at the picture of the demon on the ceiling. 'If this is part of your art coursework, I'd leave it out.'

'Why?'

'You wouldn't want to give others nightmares, would you?'

The noise of the common room came rushing back. She chose three others from the pile. She looked round the room and imagined everyone's picture on the wall for next year's School Leavers' Ball. They were all there except hers. She had the feeling she'd be back next year with the word FAIL written across her forehead. Everyone would be moving on without her.

As she got up, she saw him glance behind her and his expression change fleetingly.

He didn't give her time to find out what it was. He put his arm round her waist in a protective ring and led her away. It seemed kind of naff and cheesy when other couples did that, like they didn't know what they were doing, but this time it felt different. It was his hand and her waist and she left it there for all to see.

As they left the common room, she gave a last look back. Part of her wanted to capture the moment, to remember what it was like to be there, at that time, with those people. She wanted to take it all in. She saw familiar figures that would soon become ghosts: Mr Green, with a smile on his face; Kamran, with his hair freshly combed to the side; Trent, looking gloomy and serious and all the things you'd expect from the graveyard; then, to her shock, Laura.

She was by the drinks machine where they'd been sitting. She wasn't talking to anyone; she was looking over at them. Her hair was down and Jodie thought she'd never seen her look so beautiful or so cold. She thought about Luca putting his arm round her.

He'd protected her. It's what any boyfriend would do.

She's jealous of you.

Jealous? Maybe it wasn't so hard to believe.

*

Jodie lay on her stomach in the long grass. A strong head-wind rattled the kites on Parliament Hill. They pulled and strained at their umbilical cords, eager to sever their ties with Mother Earth. Some succeeded and rode the unseen aerial waves for a while before crashing back down.

'Well, what do you think?'

Luca turned the last few pages of her father's red notebook. He had grass in his hair from lying down. 'I'm sorry for not believing you, Jodie.'

She rolled on to her back and looked up at the sky. 'I wonder if he's looking down at me.'

He picked up the notebook and flicked through it again. 'He keeps mentioning a place called Pages Walk. *The Walkers have seen something. Go and see George. The levels are unbelievable.* What are Walkers?'

'I don't know.'

'The levels are very high. And all between eighteen and nineteen hertz.'

'Shame we don't know George.'

'Yeah, but we know where he lives.'

Her eyes shot open. How come she hadn't seen that? She sat up, snatched the book, and looked to where he was pointing. There were some names and addresses scribbled at the bottom of the last page. One or two were circled. The last was George Jones. He lived in a flat in Southwark.

She kissed him hard on the mouth. 'You're a genius.'

She didn't give him a chance to reply. She was already running down the hill. He dusted down his jeans and jacket and looked after her. 'I know.'

27

The train pulled in to Belsize Park Tube station, bringing with it a suffocating heat.

Luca held her arm. 'It's right across town, Jodie. We couldn't have taken the bus.'

She took a deep breath as the doors slid open. There was no going back. She looked at the billboards through the windows and felt relieved. Her eyes were still okay. Then the doors snapped shut.

The train jerked, accelerated into the tunnel, rattling along the tracks. The moment it did, she started to feel unwell and the billboards blurred. They passed through Chalk Farm and Camden and all the while she waited and wondered how long they had left and whether a wind would come rushing down the tunnels. A few minutes after leaving Euston, there was a screech of brakes and the train ground to a halt. Jodie felt her heart pick up speed. The passengers continued reading their newspapers, listening to their iPods, but fear clutched at her.

A voice cut through on the Tannoy: 'I'm sorry, ladies and gentlemen. There's a red signal ahead. We have to wait here till the train in front moves on.'

Jodie thought of her father in the tunnel and things on the line. She thought of the man on the table and the screams in the dark. If anything should happen now? *Es ist entkommen.* She took some deep breaths and reached out for Luca's hand. The train seemed to sway, the darkness outside to peer in and grab her. There was a jolt above their heads and this time people looked up.

Her breathing came quicker. There was a noise on the roof like something scrambling about.

'Can you hear that?' she said.

'Hear what?' Luca replied.

'On the roof?'

'Maybe something's snagged?'

The train shuddered again and the carriage rolled to its side. Now, everyone was looking around. Everyone but a little girl in a red coat who stood staring at her.

Jodie's eyes rolled. She felt cold and her ears popped. Sounds fought their way through.

There was a loud scraping on the roof like metal being peeled back. The train inched forward. There was a crackle of static and the voice on the Tannoy cut in again.

'I'm sorry, ladies and gentlemen. I've just been informed that something's blocking the track. Maintenance engineers are on their way down to sort the problem out.'

Blocking the track? Jodie imagined the engineers running down the lines, their torches flickering in the dark.

Luca held her. 'You okay? We'll be out in a bit.'

She pressed against him, hoping the noise in her ears would go away. But it didn't.

There was more scraping, no longer random, but confined to the ceiling above her. It grew in intensity. She moved down the carriage to get away. As soon as she did, the scraping stopped. She thought of the attic and a terrible fear caught hold of her. It was following her. People got up, screaming. The little girl and her mum ran towards her.

'What the hell is that?' someone shouted.

'Get out the way!'

Jodie felt a familiar dizziness disorientate her. The train shuddered and the carriages were plunged into darkness. She lost hold of Luca.

'Help!'

Her cries were lost in the panic. She looked up at the roof and imagined the cold tunnel above it. Something was crawling along it, looking for her. The carriage swayed in the darkness.

Jodie?

It was calling her.

'This side. Get to this side.'

The words didn't mean anything. There was a wind coming down the tracks, blowing into the carriage. The metal shell was not enough to protect her.

Jodie!

She felt her arm being tugged, then a mist descended over her eyes.

A deeper black swallowed her up.

*

The next thing she knew, the lights in the carriage were on. Luca was beside her with a middle-aged lady.

'She okay?'

'Yeah, she bumped her head.'

'You should sue them for that. It's a bloody disgrace.'

The doors opened and the lady dusted herself down and targeted a London Underground worker.

Luca led Jodie off the train. They were at Goodge Street. There was station staff everywhere and police in yellow fluorescent jackets. Everyone was talking. She caught the gist from their conversations. A beam had fallen on to the tracks. The tunnel roof had been damaged.

She looked up at the carriage roof. It looked like someone had taken a giant can opener to it. She pulled at Luca's hand.

'Bloody hell,' he said. 'It's just ours. We were really lucky.'

Jodie got as close as she could. Some police warded her away.

'What's a beam made out of?'

'Metal, I guess.'

She looked at the knife-like incisions. They could have been cut by a surgeon's scalpel. The thick wedge of a beam couldn't have done it.

Something else had.

*

They left the station and caught a bus on Tottenham Court Road. The West End crowds, five and six deep along the pavements, were as squashed as those on the Underground. They swarmed like angry ants. From the top of Parliament Hill, you could feel the city's proximity, but not its excitement or its rush. Here, everything was done at a faster pace. Even Camden market seemed quiet in comparison. The closer they got to the Thames, the faster things got. Everything, that is, except the traffic.

They sat on the top deck. Luca was puffing his cheeks out, trying to cool down. 'It must have been a beam. There's nothing else.'

She stared at him. 'You know that's not true, Luca. It's getting nearer.'

The approach to Waterloo Bridge was gridlocked. She looked to her right and saw Cleopatra's Needle on the embankment and the white spokes of the London Eye on the other side. Riverboats cruised down the grey waters. Compared to the slow crawl of the bus, they seemed to be flying.

'How far is Southwark?'

'About a mile. We can walk if you want?'

She shook her head. 'We've come this far. Another half an hour's not gonna kill us.'

She took out the red notebook and read the last few pages again. The word *Walkers* leapt out. She knew they must hold the answer. It was the last thing he'd written.

The bus shuffled along the bridge, coughing and spluttering till they reached the South Bank. They passed the National Theatre where her sixth form English group used to go to see plays. That part of her life already seemed a long time ago.

They got off at Waterloo and headed into the back streets. This part of town lacked the polish of Belsize Park. The buildings were large and squat with flat roofs. There was uncollected refuse on the streets and graffiti on the walls. They were only a stone's throw from the Thames but they already seemed a long way from pleasure boats and open top buses. There were things the London Eye couldn't see and which even the summer sun failed to inspire.

Luca seemed to know where he was going. Either he'd memorised the *London A to Z* or he had a sixth sense. He cut down streets that didn't appear to exist and seemed to lead nowhere. He led her down a couple of back alleys until they came to a long, gentrified road. It had tall trees on it and bikes chained to railings. The houses were terraced and on three floors. Some looked really well maintained, with stone steps leading up to newly painted doors and long, beige curtains hanging in the living rooms. Others looked like they'd been condemned and were occupied by crack addicts.

Luca stopped outside one in the middle and squinted his eyes at the number. 'What's the chance he still lives here, do you think?'

'Not much, I guess,' she said.

He looked over the railings down to the basement. The windows were open.

'Do you know what you're going to say?' he asked.

She didn't. She hadn't thought about anything other than the name in the notebook.

The steps down were barred by a metal gate. Inside, her stomach churned. She thought of her father coming here twelve years ago. She opened the gate and it creaked loudly. She took the steps down into the concrete yard. There was an old, steel dustbin with a lid perched precariously on top. Knotted Tesco bags and bottles propped it open. The yard smelled of disinfectant. There was some graffiti on the wall that had been half rubbed off. She stared at the doorknocker and then at Luca. Before she had time to rap it, the lid came crashing off the dustbin and set a steel-band accompaniment of pots and pans. A loud Cockney voice came bawling through the window.

'I thought I told you lot to clear off!'

There was a sound like a rhino charging behind the door. Jodie measured the distance to the steps but it was too late.

A bald man in his sixties, with arms like tractors and a stomach like a bale of hay, had thrown it open. He was sweating from every pore, carrying a large kitchen knife.

'Well?'

Luca was halfway to the steps, but Jodie stood there, spellbound. She stared at the knife in his hand and a shadow crossed her heart. She had a sickening feeling of déjà vu. She'd been down these steps before.

'George Jones?'

He stared at her suspiciously. 'Who wants to know? How do you know my name? You been pinching my mail?'

She shook her head and looked at the knife point. 'My dad knew you, Mr Jones. I came because of him.'

He held the knife out, its blade like a fang. She blinked and saw blood on a wall.

'Is this a game?'

She shook her head. 'His name was Malcolm Lawrence.'

She took out her father's red notebook, found the page with his name on, and handed it to him.

He took it in his knife hand. The change in him was so sudden, it was like he'd been drained of blood. He put a hand on his head and stared at her as if she were a ghost. 'Christ, you're his little girl?'

She nodded.

'The girl in the papers.'

'I need to talk to you,' she said.

*

The smell of fried food permeated the whole flat. The carpets were threadbare and woodchip wallpaper hung from the walls and ceiling like old, frayed plasters. The whole place looked like it hadn't been touched for years and was in desperate need of renovation.

George led them into the living room. There were a few photos of railways on the walls, and a black-and-white picture of a sailor on the mantelpiece, but nothing that could really be called decoration: just an old sofa and a dining table with some dead-looking flowers in a vase. He opened the window wider and looked through the netted curtains.

'I thought you were kids when you came. Little sods. They tried to set fire to my bin last week.' He put the knife on the table. 'I'll kill them next time.' He sat on the sofa and wiped his bald head with the back of his arm. 'Can I get you a drink?'

They shook their heads. He indicated they should take the chairs at the dining table.

'I'm sorry for calling at a bad time,' Jodie said. 'My father never left your number.'

'There's *only* bad times when you reach my age,' he said. He stared at her as if trying to remember something. 'I never thought I'd see you. Bloody terrible what happened. Sure you don't want a drink?'

'No. Really.'

'Haven't spoken about it for ages. There were police and reporters at the time. Loads of 'em.'

He paused a second. 'You're not reporters, are you?'

'No.'

'They got the wrong end of the stick, as usual. Thought I had something to do with it.'

'We know you didn't.'

'So long as you know. I did my best.'

'We didn't really come about the case, Mr Jones.'

'No?'

She shook her head.

'What, then?'

'My father mentioned you in his notes. He said you'd seen something. You and the Walkers. You knew about infrasound.'

George went quiet. The sun went in and a shadow crossed the room. 'Infrasound? Yeah, that's what he said it was.'

He looked into the distance as if he was staring down a tunnel. 'He said it was making people hallucinate. But I knew it wasn't. I saw other stuff, you see. I tried to tell the reporters but they didn't want to know, either.'

The shadow grew darker and her heartbeat quickened. 'What other stuff?'

'Things infrasound couldn't explain. I mean, hallucinations can't strangle you, can they?'

She glanced at Luca to see his reaction, but his eyes were fixed on George.

George got up and removed his shirt. His stomach sank over his trousers. He was wearing a large white vest. He turned round and lifted it. There was a long pink scar running round his neck and down his back.

'I couldn't talk properly afterwards. I felt my windpipe had been crushed.'

She felt sick. 'What was it?'

He stared at the picture on the mantelpiece. 'A devil, luv. Tentacles thicker than a man's waist. I told my bosses. They said I'd just fallen, caught myself in the wires. They said I'd been drinking. I couldn't go back after that. Your father wanted to go public but they told me to keep quiet or I'd lose my pension. I regret that. I told him to stop, too, but it was too late.'

'Too late for what?'

'He'd already gone.'

'Where?'

He stopped.

'Pages Walk.'

The diary and the map with flags on it flashed in front of her, then some faded red letters on a video. '. . . *ages*,' she whispered.

Luca looked at her.

'The letters on the video tape,' she said. '. . . *ages*. Pages Walk.' She turned to George. 'What is it?'

'It's a disused tunnel that used to connect the Bakerloo Line to the District. It gave me the bloody creeps. I wasn't the only one, either. Others saw things down there, though they soon shut up when the bosses asked. I showed your father where to look. We had a job near the old substation. He wanted to take readings. Some of the Walkers had seen something. The Underground started closing some of the tunnels. I couldn't go in after what happened but I waited for him. When he came back, he was breathing heavily. He was excited but frightened, too.'

'Why?' Jodie's heart was racing down the tunnels with them.

'He said he saw something that proved it.'

'Did you tell the police?'

'Of course, but they weren't interested. They were more concerned with where I was the night he died.'

'You never saw him again?'

'Not till I saw his picture in the papers. I felt sick when I saw it.'

George put his shirt back on. She stared at the empty leaves in the back of the red notebook and fought back the tears. He picked up the picture of the sailor from the mantelpiece. 'I know what it's like to lose a father, luv. It broke my heart.'

She steeled herself against the pain. 'What do the Walkers do?'

He fixed her with a steady eye. 'They're trackwalkers. They check the tunnels when the network's closed down. It's the loneliest job in the world. And the creepiest. Not a job anyone would want.'

Jodie thought of the tunnel at Chalk Farm and the train at Goodge Street. She knew where she was heading. Even the mirrors on her dressing table had shown her. She had to find out.

'I need you to show me, Mr Jones. I need you to take me where you took my father.'

'I won't go down there again, luv. Not for anything.'

'You have to.'

He looked at the picture again.

'Please.'

He waited a moment, unsure of himself, then put the picture back on the mantelpiece. 'You know Embankment station?'

She looked quickly at Luca.

'It's by Hungerford Bridge. I'll meet you there tonight. Eleven o'clock.'

'Thank you, Mr Jones.'

He turned to her. 'Tell me that when you're out.' He paused. 'You are who you say you are, aren't you? I wouldn't go back for anyone else.'

'I am.'

Jodie looked at Luca. His face had lost its glow.

George showed them to the door. The smell of fried food seemed less overpowering than when they'd come in. Maybe she'd just got used to it. When they got to the yard, they helped him pick up the bags that had fallen out of the bin.

'I need a new one,' he said. 'I can't keep lugging it up those steps.'

They climbed up. At the top, she turned and looked back. George was staring up after them.

'There was someone else asking after infrasound round the same time, you know?'

Her heart stopped. 'Who?'

'He was a weird fella. Straight out of Sherlock Holmes. Carried a cane. I remember thinking not many people carried those any more.'

Jodie gripped the iron railings. A name came whispering through the darkness. She saw a library and two dark, oak doors. They were thrown back, and a man with silver hair came in from the shadows.

William Habborlain.

28

'How can you be sure?'

'I know it was.'

They sat on the canal towpath, dangling their legs over the side. The late afternoon sun glinted on the brackish water. Bluebottles swarmed round their samosas, dive-bombing into the chilli sauce. Kamran had given them extra of everything.

Luca shooed them away. 'Even if he had gone to see George, it doesn't mean anything. They were having an argument. Science versus superstition. Maybe he was just curious?' He took a bite out of a samosa. 'Whoa, that's hot.'

Jodie held a long blade of grass out like an imaginary fishing line. 'You promised to go.'

'That's before I saw the marks on his neck.'

'You can't go back on a promise.'

'Why not?'

'It's unchristian.'

'So is consorting with the devil.' He finished chewing. 'Jodie, we can't go. It's too dangerous.'

She brushed the grass from her jeans irritably. 'If you have another football practice, why don't you just say?'

Kamran came over to sit with them. 'What do you think? I cooked them myself.'

'The flies like them,' said Luca.

'Too much chilli?'

Jodie shook her head. 'They're delicious.'

'What are you both doing later? Want to come over?'

She looked at Luca. 'Luca will. He's got no plans.'

She got up and threw the samosa away. It dropped into the canal with a plop.

'Where are you going?' Luca said.

'Home. I need to get the spectrum analyser.'

'Jodie, you're being ridiculous.'

'You're asking me to stop before I get to the end. I can't do that, Luca.'

'I'm asking you to stop before something bad happens.'

She walked on. 'It already has.'

She headed towards the market. He shouted out, but she wasn't listening. Not any more.

*

Aunt Gene was home when she got back to the house. She could smell the warm pastry from the kitchen.

'I thought we could talk tonight over dinner. We could have a little celebration for you finishing your exams?'

'Vegetable pie?'

'Yes, I made two. Why don't you invite some of your friends round?'

'I'm going out.'

'But, Jodie, you promised to talk to me.'

'There's a leaving do at school. Everyone's going.'

'You never mentioned it before.'

'I just found out.'

Aunt Gene looked at the pies. 'Well, we'd better talk now then, hadn't we? Sit down.'

'Aunt Gene, I can't do this. I can't do what you and Habborlain want.'

'All that I ask is that you speak to him. He's arriving shortly. It's for your own good, Jodie.'

Jodie grabbed her bag and went upstairs. Something had happened to Aunt Gene. It was as if Habborlain had a hold over her. The change was scary.

She went up to the attic and picked out a purple t-shirt and some battered Jane Norman jeans, sat down at the dressing table, and turned the side panels of the mirror towards herself. She got out the makeup bag and applied some mascara and eyeliner, then worried she'd put too much on and wiped it away.

Finally, she threw on her three-quarter-length coat – her theatre one – grabbed the spectrum analyser, and ran back down the stairs straight out of the front door. William Habborlain was nowhere to be seen.

*

The atmosphere round Camden Lock changed in the evening. Stalls closed and bars opened. The shouts of children were replaced by the aggressive shouts of men. There was an intimidating swagger in their voices that put Jodie on edge. She held her phone tightly and hoped Luca would turn up soon. He'd texted to say he'd meet her. She knew he wouldn't let her go on her own.

Some guys in short-sleeved shirts passed by. One leered

at her. He must have said something because the others turned round and laughed before disappearing into Jongleurs comedy club.

She walked towards the market and waited outside another bar. Her hand vibrated. Another text had come. It was hard to read.

Hey guess wat. Ive found my old sim.

It was from Luca's old number.

Where are you? she texted back.

She looked round but couldn't see him.

Her hand vibrated again.

Right behind you.

She turned and looked towards the canal. There was no one there. She looked into the bar. He wasn't there, either.

Then it rang.

'Why are you being stupid?' she said.

There was no reply.

'Luca, would you stop it. Where are you?'

'Why don't you look behind you, Bella?'

She nearly dropped the phone. The shock of hearing the voice sent her heart racing. Laura's hair was down and cut into a Cleopatra fringe. She wore a tight bodice and a long black coat. Trent was beside her. His eyes were like a cat's, cut into slits by his guyliner.

'What do *you* want?'

'To talk to you.'

'About what?'

'Luca.'

'What about him?'

She was up close now. 'I know he won't have told you.'

'Told me what?'

Laura smiled and her eyes glinted in the failing evening

249

light. Other shadows appeared in the corner of Jodie's vision: Bethany, Cheryl, all the ghouls from school.

'What a bad boy he's been.'

'You're just jealous.'

Laura's smile withered. 'Shouldn't that be the other way round, Jodie?' She grabbed her bag.

'Leave it alone.'

But she hadn't the strength. Laura's fingers prised it from her, little by little.

'Do you know what's happened to me since your master class at the station? Do you know what it's like being accused of things you haven't done? Or have someone set you on fire?'

'I didn't.'

'Yes, you did. And you never paid for it.' She took the spectrum analyser out of the bag. 'What's this?'

'*It's not yours.*'

The voice came from behind her.

Jodie looked round.

Luca was there with Kamran and the men from the Asian takeout. He'd come just in time: her knight in shining armour.

Laura stared at him defiantly.

He walked through the ghouls towards her, bent her fingers back, and loosened the spectrum analyser from her grasp. It slipped through Laura's fingers and fell to the ground. Jodie rushed to pick it up but Laura placed her black boot on top of it.

'If you touch it, I'll break your fingers.'

Jodie tried to get it free but the boot sunk lower.

'Why don't you let Luca try?'

Tears of frustration leapt to Jodie's eyes. 'Just leave it,

will you?'

'Tell me what it does, first.'

Luca knelt beside her and moved her hand away. 'Let it go, Jodie.'

Laura removed her boot.

He dusted it down and switched it on. The machine powered up. 'It measures supernatural activity. Lets you know when ghosts are around.'

Laura smiled at him, sarcastically. 'Really? And what does it say now?'

He set the frequency level and played with the buttons. The green bars were flat. 'It says, despite all the evidence to the contrary, that there aren't.'

There were smiles from the ghouls' gallery.

Jodie took it back. 'If you don't believe him, why don't you come along and test it?'

Laura threw her a disparaging look. 'I don't tag along with anyone, Bella.'

'I thought you liked playing games on the Underground? You can bring Trent if you like, hold his hand when you get scared.'

The words resonated in Laura.

'Jodie?' Luca said.

Laura stared at her and then back at Trent. 'Okay, Jodie. On one condition.'

'What?'

'If your ghost doesn't turn up, you give me the machine.'

Jodie saw a long tunnel ahead and Tube lines that disappeared into blackness. The green bars flickered.

*

They walked along the towpath towards Camden High Street. Jodie felt Luca's hand and the cold metal of his

251

ring brushing against her fingers. She felt moored to his side like a boat against the bank. The men from the takeout had gone, but Kamran was still with them, acting as sentry.

The air by the canal was stifling and warm. The smell of weed hung over the towpath, sending strange signals into her brain. She could hear the clink of glasses and, behind her, Laura and Trent's footsteps, like distant echoes.

'Thank you,' she said.

'Well, I wasn't going to leave you, was I?' he said.

She went quiet. 'What made you change your mind?'

'Henri, Bergkamp and Van Persie.'

'They rang you?'

'In a way.'

'So you missed practice?'

'It was a trial, actually.'

The words hung heavily on her. 'I'm sorry, Luca.'

He held his cross like he was praying for strength and guidance, the way she'd seen footballers like Ronaldo and Messi do. 'Everyone has dreams and not everyone gets them,' he said. 'My dad told me that when I first got over-looked. Others move on, with more speed, more skill, maybe more determination. In my head, I could have succeeded. But not today.'

'Because of me?'

He shook his head. 'No. Because of me.'

The footsteps behind them got closer. She looked back and saw Laura's eyes fixed on her. Over the canal, a sickly orange haze spread over the city. It looked like a demon had set fire to it.

They turned on to Camden High Street.

'Those marks on George's back and neck – either he's a

masochist or something got him down there. You know that?' he said.

She nodded. 'I know.'

29

There was a warm, muggy feel to Camden Tube station. Late night commuters picked their way through the waifs and strays. Jodie looked up at the CCTV cameras. She wondered what they saw in the dead of night when everyone had gone home. Things down here in the old tunnels and on the badly lit platforms took on a life of their own. She thought of all the pins on her father's map and the people who'd seen things. She thought of the wind and the carriage being ripped apart and dreaded going down again, but knew she had to. She had to find out what had happened to her father.

She looked at the advertising hoardings and the whalebone arches of the tunnel and felt two hundred feet of earth pressing down upon her. A wind stirred and the walls began their familiar, querulous shaking. The air moved like it had at Chalk Farm. A Charing Cross train pulled in, blowing refuse before it. The doors opened uniformly and shut behind her with a snap. The carriage was nearly empty. Luca sat beside her with Kamran. Trent and Laura sat opposite. They had no idea what was happening. They had just came to crow, to take another piece out of her.

She looked at the Tube map above their seats. There were 253 stations and over 250 miles of used track on the Underground and her father had been down every one. Tonight, she was going to join him. While the city slept, she was going to walk the lines after him. And they were coming with her.

She felt the electric surge and pull of the engine. People didn't belong down here. It was a twilit world, just like in her nightmares. Fear was pouring from her, just like it must have from her dad. He spent his life fighting people's fears and superstitions, but it had caught up with him. She looked up at the ceiling and thought of what might be out there, waiting for her. Her ears strained against the noise of the train, listening for a jolt, or sounds of scraping.

But nothing came. The train pulled into Euston and let on the late-night drunks. Their voices registered a different kind of fear in her, something more fathomable. She almost welcomed it. She took the spectrum analyser from her bag and switched it on. The familiar jarring of lines broke like waves on the display. The tunnels were deep and the vibrations getting stronger.

She watched people get on and off and wondered whether they knew they were being bombarded with a sound they couldn't hear; that all around them machine guns of infrasound were strafing across the line, and grenades were being thrown between stations, much worse than the wartime blitz. How many millions of people had seen and heard things down here and not reported them? The waves on the display ebbed and flowed. Some stations and tunnels were worse than others. That's what her father's map showed, too.

The train passed through Goodge Street and Tottenham Court Road safely and continued to Charing Cross. They were under the heart of London now, Leicester Square, the bowels of the West End. Nothing bad could happen here, could it? Two hundred feet above, traffic was moving and people were pouring out of theatres and cinemas. That was where she should be.

The train pulled into Embankment. They stood by the doors. Laura stared at her like she wanted to push her through. The carriage creaked to a stop. She thought she heard something, a whisper down the line, and looked out. But there was nothing. The carriage doors opened and shut like a dragon's mouth, and they were spat out on to the platform. She heard footsteps running at the far end and voices shouting down the tunnels. They echoed eerily. George told them to meet him on the concourse. There was no way back.

A warm breeze blew across the river, bringing with it the smell of brine. Gulls squalled overhead and long boats ferried their cargo downstream like tomb ships, their black silhouettes blotting out the lights on the far bank. Jodie looked into the water and felt the threatening swells of the waves against the embankment. There was something uncontrollable about them, something she felt in herself.

Luca was beside her. He hadn't said much since they'd left Camden. Now and again, he held her arm, but it was without much conviction. She was glad Kamran had tagged along. Considering how scared he'd been on the heath, his mood seemed positively buoyant. He glanced over at her and smiled. The goodness in him shone. She looked up at the London Eye. At night, it was even more impressive, like a lambent moon bearing its unearthly carriages up into the sky.

Laura was by the river with Trent. All she did was stare: at her coat, at her hair, at Luca. If she needed any further proof that something was wrong, it was that. Jodie thought she looked like a moon goddess, her figure full and her skin pale. It hurt her to admit her feelings, that she felt inferior to her, that she hated her, that she was jealous.

'Well?'

'Well, what?'

Laura sharpened her nails. 'Where's this friend of yours?'

'It's not eleven, yet.'

They crossed Victoria Embankment and went into the main concourse of the Underground station. She hoped he'd be there.

'If he doesn't turn up, you lose the bet.'

'That's not what we agreed.'

'Yes, it is.'

She was about to reply when Luca touched her shoulder. George had come out of a small office. He was talking to an official-looking man in a fluorescent orange coat. She watched him hand over something and then disappear back into the office.

'Wait here,' she said, and ran over. 'George?'

He didn't seem to see her till she was almost on him.

'I didn't recognise you there, luv. You been out somewhere?'

'I was meant to. Are you okay?'

He was sweating like he'd caught a fever. 'Yes, it's just I

ain't been back in a while. Where's your friend?'

She pointed to the others.

'Blimey, I'm not a tourist guide. They come from the London Dungeon? I thought it was just the two of you?'

'It was. Please. I need them to take readings for me.' She took the spectrum analyser out of her bag.

'Don't show me, luv. I don't want reminding. Just remember it took me a lot to get this key.'

She called them over.

George led them through one of the gates by the ticket machines. He nodded at the attendant and made for the Bakerloo Line escalators. There was a different atmosphere amongst them now. George's presence acted like an armistice; all Laura's and Trent's scepticism eroded as quickly as it came.

George wheezed down the long corridors. They went down another escalator and she felt the familiar wind of passing trains. She didn't know if it was psychosomatic, or just the memories of Chalk Farm and the ripped carriage roof, but a sickness started to spread through her gut. She turned on the spectrum analyser and waited for the bars to flatline. Horribly, they started to crawl upwards. Fifteen decibels.

She showed Luca.

'Bloody hell,' he said. 'We're only in the corridor. Where's he taking us?'

George took them the final, few steps. They were standing next to the entrance of the northbound Bakerloo Line platform.

'This it?' she said.

George shook his head and pointed to a plain white door in the wall. It was set in a semi-circle of blue tiles where a tunnel had been blocked off.

'There.'

She looked round. Trent and Laura didn't look so sure of themselves now. They were all out of their comfort zone.

'Pages Walk,' she whispered.

'I haven't been here for twelve years, luv. You sure about this?'

They were all looking at her.

She nodded.

George put the key in the lock and turned it. She closed her eyes.

The moment they were inside, the temperature dropped like a kite and a black gulf sucked them in. The door banged to. George lit a torch and long shadows scurried for cover. There was a sense of great space reaching out beyond them as if they were in a vault, or under a night sky with no stars. They crossed over a bridge about halfway along the platforms and stopped before a black tunnel. Their footsteps echoed and their breathing became more laboured. The green bars on the spectrum analyser flickered silently.

'This is the start,' George said. 'It's where I left your dad.' He handed a torch to Trent. 'You mind going at the back? Keep it to the ground. There are loose cables on the floor. You trip on them, you'll break your neck.'

Gradually, Jodie's eyes got used to the semi-darkness. George's torch cut a circle into the darkness. The tunnel started to rise and the distant ceiling receded even further, until it seemed to Jodie that they were in one vast railway warehouse like at Stables. There was a smell of damp and oil and must.

She walked with Luca and Kamran, Trent and Laura behind them. Laura's boots echoed loudly. She could make her steps and slips out clearly. Every now and again, George flashed his torch upwards and she had glimpses of cables and girders and the high, cavernous ceiling. The sickness in her stomach was worse now. Anxiety ate at her insides. The temperature in the tunnel rose and fell. There were moments when it felt heavy and warm, like an oven door had been opened, and others when a cold draft emanated from the floor. She could hear passing trains clearly. The tunnel shuddered underneath and the spectrum analyser rose.

She showed Luca. Thirty decibels.

When they got to the top of the slope, George stopped. He was having trouble breathing. 'We're right inside now.'

Trent's torch criss-crossed George's and made a light show on the ceiling. 'So where's the ghost?'

The darkness swallowed his words.

Jodie walked on for a bit, her eyes darting from side to side. She willed something to come out of the shadows, something to drop down from the cables that looped like nooses. Her father had been here and seen something. She wanted to show them, to prove he was right. But the spectrum analyser got no higher than thirty. She wondered if it was different twelve years ago. Maybe there was more infrasound? Maybe there were other tunnels?

It was Kamran who first noticed the change. He was sitting on an old crate by the tunnel wall, holding his head.

'You okay?' she asked.

He nodded. 'Just dizzy. I think it's the heat.'

'It's not the heat,' George said, looking up at the ceiling.

As he said it, there was a clang of metal ahead of them. It rang dully. A few seconds later, a cold draft blew up the tunnel. It was strong enough to move the cables above them. They rippled like jellyfish in an invisible current. George flashed his torch. The light seemed to flounder in the black depths. It was hard to pick anything out. Jodie kept one eye on the spectrum analyser. The green bars were her eyes in the dark places.

There was another clang and the draft changed direction, sucking the air from the tunnel. Kamran flapped the air around him.

'What's the matter with you?' Laura asked.

'I can see something.'

Luca looked around. 'What?'

'Up there.'

They followed his gaze. Luca put his arms out to restrain him but Kamran kept swatting the air.

Laura turned to Jodie. 'Is this your little joke, Bella? Getting Fatty to go all spaz on us?'

Jodie wasn't listening. George gave her a hard look and began walking away from them. 'I never wanted to come down here.' The umbrella of light that protected them receded, and in rushed the waves.

'Where are you going?' she called out.

'I can hear water,' he said, like he was in a trance.

She strained to hear him but the rumble of a train drowned everything out. It rattled her eardrums. She followed him down the tunnel.

His torch flickered. He hit it with his hand and the light returned to full brightness, then suddenly went out. She heard him curse under his breath. The darkness brought something else. At first, it came like an echo, a faint whistling in the joists of the tunnel walls. But with her eyes now blinded by the darkness, her ears burst open and trapped all sound.

'We need to go,' George whispered. His voice was trembling.

The green bars pushed higher and higher up the spectrum analyser.

'I can't. I have to stay.'

There was a shout from behind them. Trent's torch was dancing wildly on the walls. Silhouettes flickered like puppets in a shadow play. She could make Kamran and Luca out. They seemed to be teetering on the brink of some terrible abyss, caught in a deadly embrace. Behind them, for the briefest second, their shadows locked horns.

George ran up the tunnel towards them. The hairs on the back of her neck stood up. She felt something touch her. She ran as fast as she could, but it was too late. There was a crash of crates and another shout, then Laura screaming.

'Jodie!'

At the same moment, Trent's torch went out. The scream harrowed Jodie's bones and shook her. She'd never heard anyone so utterly frightened, yet Laura was twenty metres from her. She stumbled in the dark. The flicker of a mobile phone light suddenly painted the air blue. It was answered by another. Kamran was shaking on the floor. He looked like he was having a heart attack.

Laura looked at her, terrified. The moon goddess was gone: so was the witch. In their place was a frightened girl. 'I saw you.'

'What are you talking about?'

Luca turned round. 'Jodie, Kamran needs help right now.'

George bent to the ground and examined him. There was a cut on his forehead. 'He's having a panic attack. Someone will have to stay with him. I'll go and get help.'

'Why not just ring?' Trent said.

'You won't get a signal down here. You won't get anything.'

Jodie looked down the tunnel nervously. The whistling was still there. 'Can't we take him with us?'

'I'm not staying,' Laura said.

'I will,' said Luca. 'So can Trent.'

It was a challenge, she knew. Trent looked like he'd been floored. Jodie caught the look he gave Laura and the sidelong glance at Luca.

George picked up Trent's torch. It had smashed on the ground. 'You'll need to use your phones.'

They gave out a meagre light. They looked like they were holding birthday candles in a storm.

'Keep him calm,' George said.

They followed him down the tunnel. She looked back to see Luca standing in silent vigil over Kamran, till they disappeared from view.

'I shouldn't have come,' George said.

Jodie felt the darkness close in around her. There was another clang deep in the tunnel and another draft of wind. This time it was stronger. The phone lights flickered as if they were about to be blown out.

'What the hell's that noise?' Laura said.

'The vents,' George said. 'There are some service shafts down here.'

'It sounds like someone's opening doors.'

Jodie stared into the tunnel. They were going downhill.

Laura stumbled in front of her. Her boots scraped across the concrete. The echo died with it.

Thud.

Jodie looked round quickly. The flickering from the phones was now a strobe light. 'Did you hear that?'

Laura bent to adjust her boot. 'What?'

'There.'

It was like a pad on the ground.

'I can't hear anything. I can't see anything.'

George wiped his face with his sleeve. 'We've got to hurry.'

There was panic in his voice.

'I don't think we can.' The sickness spread up Jodie's chest. It felt like something was tugging at her insides, pulling her organs out. The whole tunnel was shaking. She kept her eyes on the spectrum analyser. The readings had leapt to seventy decibels. Had she read it wrong? The light made it difficult to tell. She pointed it in different directions and the green bars jumped up and down. The whistling was louder now and a wind came down the tunnel, blowing her towards a service shaft. There was a panel with numbers written on it, but they were jumbled up like a Sudoku.

Thud.

It was coming from in there. Someone was tugging at her. Their hand had looped itself round her and was pulling her off her feet.

'You can't go in there, luv. You'll electrocute yourself. It's a transformer.'

The words blurred.

'Dad?'

He's not there.

She was ready to heave. The black space of the shaft opened up. She realised she'd seen it somewhere before, long ago. She lashed out with her fists and the hands let her go. The momentum brought her to her knees. Just round the corner, if she could only crawl to it, was the answer.

'Can't you hear anything?'

There was a scream behind her, then a shout further up the tunnel. She was dimly aware of Luca's voice. He was calling for help. Lights flickered and went out. She put her fingers on the wall and pulled. The corner was near. Her eyes shook. The tunnel shook.

'Dad? Are you in there?'

There was a scratching sound. Something was moving. She felt like she was underwater and the world was on the other side of a glassy sea, the whole weight of the ocean pressing on her lungs. The green bars filled the screen. She didn't need them to tell her what was going on now.

'Hello, Jodie.'

'Dad?'

She staggered towards him.

'Why have you come?'

'I came to see you.'

His face changed. She could see him in the darkness. He looked the way he did in the photograph by the sea.

'You shouldn't have come, darling.'

'Why not?'

Her father looked round. He was frightened. His face changed again.

'It's not safe.'

There was a thud and more scraping.

The readings on the spectrum analyser hit one hundred decibels. She stared at the screen. The green was luminous and brighter than her phone. Her eyes zeroed in on the frequency level: 18.98 hertz.

Everything was happening just the way he'd said. She looked up to tell him but he was gone. A horned green face had taken his place. It stared at her, then grew a body and wings. Its red eyes burned and its red melon jaws slit the air.

Sinuous arms stretched out of the darkness to take her. Piece by piece, the demon was taking shape.

This is what he'd seen, the thing that had pursued him?

She wanted to stop it, but was as powerless as a painter painting a canvas. When it was done, it would have a life of its own.

She felt herself drifting into unconsciousness.

30

The moment Jodie left, Luca felt the suffocating weight of George's words. He knelt beside Kamran and did his best to calm him. He loosened his jacket and collar so he could breathe better and pulled him into a sitting position. Kamran took in great gulps of air and shivered. He looked like he'd had the life sucked out of him. The cut on his head had stopped bleeding but his eyes were bloodshot.

'Don't leave me.'

'I'm not going anywhere, Kam.'

Trent held his mobile phone over their heads. 'Is he okay?'

'What do you think?'

Trent bent to look.

Kamran shuddered. There was a metallic clang from the end of the tunnel. It rang along the girders and echoed above them.

'What's that?' said Trent.

'I dunno,' said Luca.

He looked down the tunnel, thought he heard Jodie's voice borne up by the wind.

Trent followed his gaze. 'That machine of hers. It really works?'

'What do you think?'

'How come we can't see anything?'

'Maybe we aren't looking hard enough?'

Luca thought of the séance room and what John had said. The whole thing seemed frighteningly real.

Kamran looked at him distantly. What made him so different?

Trent's boots shuffled on the floor. 'You think they've gone?'

'I guess so.'

'So it's just us?'

Luca nodded.

Trent reached into his pocket. 'That's kind of convenient, I suppose.'

'Convenient? Why?'

'Oh, I dunno. You asked me to stay. Maybe you don't see the irony?'

His tongue flicked out of his mouth. Something glinted in his hand.

'No.'

'Laura, I mean.'

Luca held up his phone. The blue light lit Trent's face. His hair hung down like a dead plant and his skin glistened. There was a large crucifix round his neck. It dangled and turned on its string.

'Laura?'

'Yeah.' Trent's eyes narrowed. 'Don't you remember?'

Luca swallowed. The glint had become a knife. It emerged from Trent's hand like a claw. He backed away slowly. 'What are you doing?'

'She told me everything, pal. All the things you did together. Always playing the nice guy while doin' it behind your girlfriend's back. Nice girl like that doesn't deserve shit like you.'

'I don't know what you're talking about, Trent. Laura's been winding you up.'

Luca backed further down the tunnel, held his phone out like a shield. It shone on the cold steel of the blade. The sight of it sent a paralysing dread through his body. He tried to think of the words to say to make Trent believe him. But his tongue was weighed down. He couldn't say a thing to defend himself.

Trent shuffled towards him.

'Don't.'

'Don't what?'

As he said it, Kamran shook violently. 'Don't leave me! They're coming back!'

Trent's concentration wavered a moment. It was all the time Luca needed. He charged at him. The knife zipped by but the force of the impact sent them both to the ground. Luca dropped his phone and the blue light went out. Trent dropped his, too. Its light dimmed. Luca felt clammy hands on his wrists and the knife turning towards him. He didn't dare let go. If he gave Trent a second, the knife would cut him. He tried to lever himself on top and prise it away. Their bodies writhed and bumped along the tunnel floor. His knee smacked against the concrete and a searing pain shot up his leg. The half-light of Trent's phone sent shadows over the walls.

Kamran started screaming again. The sound of it froze them both. Their limbs locked in a death embrace. The scream was answered by another down the tunnel.

Jodie?

He shouted her name and tore the knife from Trent's hand. Trent didn't stop him. He was looking round, terrified. Luca felt it, too. The tunnel was spinning. From the corners of his eyes, figures started moving. They were all around him, crawling up the walls and reaching down from the ceiling.

'Can you see them?' Trent said, gripping his arm.

Luca nodded.

Kamran swiped the air desperately. Luca ran to save him. The figures were like grey shadows, thin and indistinct. He cut the air with the knife but they just melted away. Then Trent's light went out completely. The air moved even when he couldn't see anything. There was a wind blowing down the tunnel and an ominous thud, then the sound of scraping. He huddled on the ground and closed his eyes and tried to blank it away.

'Please God,' he prayed.

The scraping got closer and closer. It was coming up the tunnel. He could hear it now, put flesh on its bones. Jodie had drawn a picture of it. The wind blew a nauseating odour into his nostrils. He took his cross out. The scraping stopped. He shivered. It was near. He opened his eyes. The darkness couldn't contain it or swallow it up. The luminous green skin shed its own light; the horns reared up and the wings beat the fetid wind. It stood over Trent and felt the air with its claws.

Luca gripped the knife in his hand. Sensing movement, it

turned its head. Fear nailed him to his cross. This couldn't be happening. Any second now, he'd wake from the dream. They'd never been in the tunnel; George had never turned up; he'd never seen Laura; he'd never done anything.

It reached a claw out and touched his face. It didn't feel like a claw. It felt soft like a hand. He opened his eyes fully. The demon was no longer there. It was Laura. He could feel her nails touch his cheeks and her hands round his body. She was drawing him to her. He could smell her perfume and feel her flesh. She pressed her face towards him and her lips opened like fruit. His head spun and his stomach turned. Their lips were touching.

'Don't you want me any more, Luca? I know you've always wanted me.'

He turned his head away. Her breath stank; her skin felt like scales. He struck out with the knife and waited for the scream. It shook the tunnel. Laura disappeared; the demon disappeared.

He looked down, then collapsed on to the floor.

31

The first thing Jodie saw when she woke was the light. It appeared like a pinprick in the distance, then grew bigger and bigger until it shone like a lamp. She held out her hand to shield her eyes. She didn't know how long she'd been out or where she was. She felt something brush her skin and memories come rushing into the void. She jumped back into her body, her lungs filled with air, and her heart started beating again.

She sat up quickly. 'Get off.'

The light retreated and she saw Laura framed in its halo.

'What are you doing?'

'I thought you were dead.'

'Where is everyone?'

'Gone.'

The tunnel rumbled. The trains seemed nearer. She thought they must be by the bridge. There was a smell of sick, stronger than the oil and must. Her coat was full of bile. She covered her mouth and turned her head. Beside her, the spectrum analyser flickered. The infrasound levels hovered round the ten-decibel mark.

'Has it gone?'

Laura backed away. She looked at Jodie like she was about to bite her.

'Where's George?' Jodie strained her ears against the silence. The wind had gone. 'We've got to warn him.' She looked up into the blackness and felt along the wall. She found her phone and turned it on. It glowed dimly. The battery was almost out. 'George? Luca?'

Her voice echoed along the ceiling and down the tunnel.

There was no answer.

Any second she expected to hear the wind rise and the scratching start. She got up and her head spun. She had to hold on to the wall to steady herself. 'Come on.'

They climbed the tunnel in silence. Another train passed. Laura's boots shuffled behind her. After a few minutes, she could hear crying. She felt the tunnel open up above them and knew they were coming to the part where they'd left the others.

'Luca?'

There was a shuffling sound. She felt a hand on her shoulder and jumped.

'Jodie?'

She lifted her phone up. It was Kamran. He was propped up against a crate. The cut on his head was now a deep gash.

He smiled like he was drugged up. 'Hi, Jodie.'

She held his hand. 'Where are the others, Kamran?'

'I don't know. I don't feel too good.'

'We're going to get you out of here.'

'You're not gonna leave me?'

'No.' She turned to Laura. 'We've got to find Luca and Trent.'

Laura shuffled behind her. 'I don't think there's any need.'

A blue light was coming up the tunnel. They watched it nervously. Jodie glanced at the spectrum analyser. The reading hadn't changed.

The blue light dropped. A knife emerged from out of it, then a body. It was Luca.

'Is it you?' he asked.

'What do you think?'

'I don't know.'

'Where have you been?'

His face was black with dirt and blood. 'Looking for Trent.'

'Where is he? Why have you got his knife?' Laura said.

He looked down as if he'd just seen it. 'We've got to get out of here, Jodie. Something attacked us. All the things your dad said, they're true. It was the biggest hallucination ever, like I was in a computer game.'

'It wasn't a game, Luca. The frequency was the same. 18.98.' She turned to Laura. 'You saw it?'

But Laura's eyes were fixed on Luca and the knife in his hands. 'I just saw you on the ground and tried to help you. What have you done to Trent?'

'He's gone,' said Luca. 'I went to the end of the tunnel. There was no one there.'

'You're lying.'

The knife waved in his hand like he was dousing for an answer.

'No,' he said.

Laura unsheathed her own blade. 'Why don't you just tell

her, Luca? Tell her how much you want me.'

Jodie looked at them. 'What?'

Her emotions were igniting just as Laura wanted them to.

His blade dropped. 'Nothing. She's just making it up to hurt you, Jodie. Don't listen to her.'

Jodie looked at him. The knife, the blood. Had they had a fight over her? Isn't that what men did? They pumped themselves into a frenzy and killed. They left you at the altar like Miss Havisham. There was no point believing anything they said. Even girls like Laura got hurt, girls who could have anyone and anything. How stupid was it that she even cared when something so terrifying was out there.

The tunnel rumbled under their feet again.

Nothing was important now.

She turned to a sound in the darkness. Kamran was mumbling again.

'We've got to get him out of here.'

32

John stared at the picture of the demon in the book. The early evening light cast a sickly pallor in the library, more midwinter than midsummer. He skimmed a few pages and cast nervous glances at the oak doors. He tried to see if he could pull them out; it was one of those encyclopaedic books where the spine could lie comfortably flat, but the pages wouldn't budge. He took a small knife out of his coat pocket and ran it down the middle, cutting the page with the demon out. He did it with a surgeon's skill and held it up as if he'd just removed a diseased organ, then folded it up and put it in his pocket.

He looked round the room and checked if he'd left anything. To his father, this was Solomon's treasure chamber, the tomb of Tutankhamen: the price of desecration had been spelt out on more than one occasion. He closed the book and took it back to the shelf, making sure the spine was level with those next to it. He pulled his coat around him and ghosted to the doors. He was no more than a few feet away when the latch turned. There was no time to hide or place to turn, just enough to prepare himself.

His father stood in the doorway like a night watchman discovering the thief in the house.

'Just leaving, John?'

'I thought I'd left something, Father.'

Habborlain sniffed the air for a sign that something had been disturbed. 'Perhaps I can help you find it?'

He closed the doors behind him.

John touched his cheek where the bruise bloomed like a black orchid.

'What was it?'

'Nothing. It wasn't there.'

'You know I hate lies, John.'

'Yes, Father.'

'Like I'd hate to ask you to turn your pockets out.' He went to the shelves and ran his fingers along the spines. 'Everything knows its place in this library. Perhaps it was something your friends left last night and you've been asked to reclaim it?'

'I haven't spoken to them. I thought you were seeing her tonight.'

Habborlain's eyes flickered.

John knew he'd overstepped the mark, but temptation kept him close to the flame. Ever since he'd seen her, she'd occupied his thoughts and wandered about his dreams. He looked for her by the ponds, on the mound, on the top of Parliament Hill. He looked down the slope to Hampstead and imagined her walking up. 'Is she in trouble?'

'Why? Do you have feelings for her, John?'

His father's impassive face yielded to a moment of doubt. John felt the colour stain his skin. 'No, Father.'

Habborlain nodded. 'That's good. Because she's sick. More sick than you could possibly imagine. She won't accept my help so you need to be careful of her. You need to stay out of her way.'

John stared at his father's hands. They were more like a bear's paws than a man's palms, more used to fighting than finesse. Nobody else saw that. They saw the books and statues and paintings and assumed he was an artist, a scholar, a man of learning. He'd conned everybody.

'Why?'

The hands clenched and unclenched. 'Because she's in danger.'

'What kind?'

'The kind that should stop you asking questions.'

John swallowed. He knew he was pressing things too much, but he couldn't stop himself. He felt she would have wanted it. 'Is it to do with the picture she showed you?'

John watched his father's hands grip the desk and the shadows creep from the corners of the room. He remembered the séance and the scratches on the floor.

Habborlain's eyes danced in the candlelight. 'Yes, John. It is. The devil is after her.'

John shuddered.

'One thing is for certain. If what came for her father comes for her, she'll find out soon enough.'

'Shouldn't you warn her?'

'She has been warned. Why do you think I went to see her this evening? Why do you think I tried to help her when you brought her here the other night?'

Habborlain looked at John's hands buried deep in his

pockets. John waited for the order to come, prepared himself for the blows, but neither came. 'If you care about her, maybe you should show her this.' He took a fountain pen from a small table and wrote something on a piece of paper. He folded it up and held it out to him. 'Tell her to keep away. And keep away yourself.'

John dared not look. The dread of revelation, and his father's shaking hands, terrified him. He took the piece of paper and put it in his pocket.

'I want to save her.'

'Very Christian, John. The only way to save a soul is repent. Believe in Jesus.'

'Jesus, Father?'

Habborlain went to the shelves and took a book down. He laid it on the mahogany table and opened it. 'There's a price to pay for everything, John. Every man must face what he has done and try to wipe the slate clean. I should never have given her father the book.'

'Why?'

'Because the blood that was meant for him is now on my hands. I never thought she'd see it.'

'You put a spell on it?'

'I put a spell on *him*. To stop him meddling. To prove to him there is such a thing as a spirit world. I was angry. I never thought it would work. It lay there in the book, waiting for him. Now, it's after her. Maybe then, it will come for me.'

'Aren't there ways you can stop it, Father?'

'Yes, John. Just one. Every man has that choice. If he's brave enough to take it. The choice between life and death.' He read from the book. 'We beg You: Free us, O Lord. From every sort of spell, malefice, witchcraft, and every form of the occult. Remove and bind to the abyss all demons and their devices that had access to me because I believed their lies.'

His voice faded to a whisper.

John knew the audience was over. When his father looked up, he seemed surprised he was still there, and almost irritated.

'Go on, then. Tell her. Isn't that what you wanted?'

John turned. Every step he took was a step into the unknown. His father had never let things lie. There were always questions to answer. As he got to the oak doors, he heard his name called. He saw his father looking up at the ceiling fans.

'John?'

'Yes, Father?'

'There are a lot of things I've done that I shouldn't have. I want to apologise to you for them. I want to apologise for everything.'

John was still. He opened the library doors and slipped out. The doors clanged to behind him. He ran out of the house and didn't look back. The wind whipped his face and the rain dampened the ground. He headed for the cemetery gates. He vaulted gravestones and swung on angels' wings. After a few minutes, he stopped at the plain and unadorned grave and took out the piece of paper. He laid it carefully on top. The wind crumpled it and the rain spotted it, but he could still make out the words. His father's normally articulate type trailed across the page. *Pages Walk*.

In all the books on folklore he'd ever read, and all his father's notes, he'd never come across that. Yet there was something eerily familiar about it, like a distant memory. He put it in his pocket and traced the letters on the grave: *In*

Loving Memory Clara Duprez. He looked round quickly and shifted the headstone to the right. He reached into a hole in the ground and brought out the small metal box. He spilled the contents into a plastic bag and put the headstone back.

He ran through the cemetery to the heath. When he got in the open, the wind blew hard from the east, and he drew his coat tightly around him. It buffeted and swept him up the hill to Boudicca's Mound. The copse of trees protected him from the worst gusts. The fading sun filtered through the branches and brought the gnarled ones to heel. Darkness had not given them the power to transform into wizened arms and legs but they cast shadows along the path.

He took out the picture of the demon and looked at it. The red sun shone through the paper and gave it a weird, preternatural glow. The model, the scratches on the floor in the séance room, it all made sense. He looked across to Hampstead, brought out the paper his father had written on, then ran as fast as he could.

There were other, more practical, ways to save a soul.

33

The loud knock on the front door made Aunt Gene jump. She half hoped it would be Jodie, but she knew it was too early and she had her key. She thought of the police and steeled herself for bad news. The cruel knock came again, more insistent this time. She got up from the kitchen table, tied her dressing gown round her waist, and went into the hall. There was a dark shadow in the entranceway.

'Who is it?'

'It's me, Ms De Dulin.'

Fear gave way to concern. *John*? She undid the latch and opened the door. He looked like a poor mutt lost on the heath, windswept and bedraggled.

'John, what are you doing here?'

'I came for Jodie, Ms De Dulin.'

'At this time?'

'I'm not sure what time it is.'

He looked dazed.

'It's after eleven. She's not back yet. Didn't your father tell you she was going to a party?'

She opened the door fully. He stepped inside, put his hands in his coat pocket, and took out a weather beaten piece of paper.

'No, he didn't. He just told me to give her this.' He handed it to her. 'Have you ever heard of this place?'

Aunt Gene saw the scrawled letters in the faded ink. At the sight of them, she went rigid.

'I think she's in trouble.'

'What kind of trouble?'

He nodded at the paper. 'I think she's gone to Pages Walk. It's not safe for her, or anyone.'

'I told you. She's gone to a party.'

'Ring her, Ms De Dulin. Please. Make sure. I think I know what's wrong with her.' He brought out the plastic bag from his pocket and showed her the contents.

Gene picked them out, piece by piece; like a jigsaw, it suddenly came together. She felt herself going faint. They were from a green Godzilla model.

'Where did you get this?'

'I've always had it. Clara rescued it for me when I was little. I kept it hidden in a box. It was my favourite toy. I never thought about it till Jodie came back. Then I remembered something. On the day she broke it, Clara sat me on her knee and told me: "An ol' monster's gonna get her just like her dad. An ol' monster's gonna get her for her wickedness. You jus' wait".'

Aunt Gene put her back against the wall and felt the years crumble about her. 'Clara was mad. She believed in voodoo and witchcraft.'

'Maybe Jodie's dad did at the end? You have to keep her from going to Pages Walk.'

Aunt Gene looked at him and tried to block out the madness of what he was saying. But tiredness and fear eroded her confidence, and left doubt the sole inheritor of her will. She went to the kitchen and picked up the phone. She brought Jodie's name up and pressed the green dial key. She wouldn't hear her if it was a party. It rang forlornly and cut off. There was no signal.

She trembled. Malcolm was wrong. It was the things you couldn't hear which undid you, not the things you did.

'Ring the police, John. Quickly. My hands are shaking. Let's hope they can find her in time.'

34

They were down to the last phone. The light in Laura's hand was the only thing that stood between them and darkness. Jodie followed it carefully.

Kamran had stopped mumbling. He was propped between her and Luca like a giant sandbag, his feet barely touching the ground. Every ten yards, she had to stop to breathe.

'It would be quicker if we left him,' Laura said.

'Well, we're not going without him.'

'What about your friend George? Where's he when you need him?'

Jodie felt a cold draft coming down the tunnel. 'Maybe he went to get help.'

Or maybe he was still inside?

'You feel like calling him again?'

Their shouts had been eaten up by the tunnel. The names

echoed round the belly of its roof and disappeared into its gullet. Rather than give them strength, it made them feel more vulnerable. Calling out advertised where they were. When Trent's and George's names faded, the silence returned. It felt like the darkness was listening to them.

'There's no point arguing. Just hold the bloody light,' Luca said.

They took a few more paces. If Kamran could only bear some of it, they'd be out in no time. The light flickered. The ceiling seemed to lower. There was a smell of damp in the air.

'I can hear water,' Laura said.

She was right. Water was running down the bricks. One or two drops fell on her face.

'Are we nearly there?' said Jodie.

'I don't know. This is as far as I got,' said Luca.

There was a notice on the wall. It had been mostly obliterated but three words could be made out: *District Line substation*.

'Trent?'

The echo was much less here.

'George?'

There was no answer, just the steady drip of water falling.

They stumbled on, step by step. Luca redoubled his efforts. Kamran's feet made contact with the ground. The cool air seemed to wake him.

'I can see something. There's a door,' said Laura.

She held the light up.

'Wait,' Jodie said.

It was too late. She ran ahead.

Jodie tripped over some cables as she tried to keep up, and felt Kamran slide off her shoulders. Luca groaned. She reached out just in time.

'I can't go on, Jodie. My back's breaking.'

'It's just a little bit further.'

They struggled towards the light. Laura was standing in front of a plain white door like the one they'd come through. Water cascaded down the wall, forming a pool at her feet.

'We don't have a key,' she said.

Luca set Kamran down and tested the handle. It was locked.

'It's a mortise,' he said. 'We'll never get out this way.'

'Then why bring us here?' Laura asked.

Despair and bitterness made her sound even more hostile.

'You wanted to look for Trent,' Jodie said.

'I wanted to get out.'

Luca rubbed his face. 'Shut up, the pair of you.'

It cut them dead. He was brittle with anger.

'Did you bring your father's notebook?'

Jodie nodded.

'Give it to me.'

She searched her bag and took it out. He flicked through the pages. The light began to fade.

'We haven't much time.'

He turned the book upside down and tried to get his bearings. 'He drew a detailed map of this tunnel. There's a service shaft that leads down to the platforms. I think we've just passed it.'

'You want to go back?' Laura asked, incredulously.

'Got any better ideas? Like bang on the door?' He looked at Jodie. 'We can't take Kamran with us.'

'We have to.'

'He'll hold us back. We have to get out before the light goes.'

'I'll carry him myself.'

'I think he'll be safer without you.'

The words stung her. 'What do you mean?'

The light dimmed even more.

'Just.'

He went over to Kamran and sat him up. Kamran stirred. 'Hey, man. You'll be better in a bit. We'll get you an ambulance.'

Kamran's eyes flickered. There seemed to be a smile on his face. Luca touched his shoulder.

'Give me the phone,' he said to Laura.

She handed it to him. Jodie wanted to protest but realised she was no longer in charge. They were reliant on Luca now.

They made quicker progress back up the tunnel. Jodie thought of John and how he knew every twist and turn of the heath. This was Luca's terrain. All that time playing computer games, chasing things on screen, had prepared him for this. They passed the old District Line substation and then he paused. She could feel the ground vibrating. There was an opening on the left. Luca checked the notebook and looked around. The light was getting weaker and weaker.

'I think it's here.'

It was a black space like the service shaft she'd been down.

'I can hear something in there,' she said.

'It'll be the generators,' he said. 'This is the substation.'

'It's not,' she said. 'There's something moving.'

It wasn't scratching or thumping or the wind.

'I can hear it, too,' said Laura.

Jodie looked at the spectrum analyser. The levels were creeping up again. 'I don't think we should go in.'

'We have to,' said Luca. 'We have to get out.'

He took the knife out. He'd only gone a few steps when there was a flurry of movement in front of them. Something shot out of the darkness. Laura screamed. Jodie felt hands on her, reaching for her face. Luca turned the light on her and she could make out a pale, ghostly apparition looking up. It took a few moments to realise who it was.

'Trent?'

Luca pulled him off. 'Where the hell have you been?'

He held the blade above him.

Trent stared at it, terrified. 'Don't cut me again.'

It was then Jodie noticed the ugly lines on his face, like nails had been dragged across it.

'What have you done to him?' Laura said.

'Nothing,' said Luca.

Laura looked at the knife in his hands. 'You tried to kill him.'

'What are you talking about?'

'That's why you went after him.'

'I told you what happened. Something attacked us.'

Trent shivered on the ground.

'They don't look like knife marks,' Jodie said.

'Well, what are they?'

Jodie looked into the tunnel. 'Claw marks.'

Trent's eyes widened. 'We have to get out.'

As he said it, the light finally gave out and they were left in darkness.

'Hold hands,' Luca said. 'Follow my voice.'

Jodie reached out and touched the cold bricks. They were

vibrating. If the tunnel had been dark, the service shaft was darker still. She felt the ceiling lower to just above her head and the walls narrow at either side. She could hear Luca close in front of her and Trent and Laura behind.

'It's not very long.'

Luca's words died in the stultifying air. The vibrations in the wall began to rattle her ears and take hold of her body. She couldn't stop herself shaking.

'Luca?' She looked down at her palms. 'The readings.'

She heard him stop. The green bars had shot off the register. They filled the screen with schizophrenic peaks that the display could no longer contain, like a child's mad scribbling.

'We have to go on.'

She didn't really hear him. The vibrations filled her ears with waves. She dropped the spectrum analyser and heard the wind come roaring down the tunnel like a fury. This time there was no stopping it. It leapt into her consciousness in an instant, flung open the wardrobe doors that had kept it at bay, punched through the rooftop and reached out its arms. She knew by the screams that this time things were different; that it wasn't just she who could see it. Her whole body was convulsing. She heard the screams ringing in her head, up and down tunnel walls that knew no end.

Thud.

She was walking down some steps.

Thud.

She saw a sliver of light ahead of her.

Thud.

She pushed open the door.

35

J odie woke with a start. She was on her back, staring at nothing. For a moment, she thought she'd gone blind. Heart racing, she sat up. The vibrations had gone. The screams had gone. Everyone had gone.

'Luca?'

The silence closed in. She felt the cold floor and reached her hands out. They grasped empty air. There was no way of knowing which way she was facing. She remembered they'd come down a tunnel, but didn't know from which direction. She stood up and tried to quell the panic, imagined long green arms reaching for her neck. Why hadn't it killed her? Something was out there, waiting for her, playing with her.

'Luca?'

She shuffled down the tunnel. The silence was so oppressive, it nearly burst her ears. She imagined waves of infrasound bombarding her, altering her mind. Her hands trailed the wall. She was like Theseus in the labyrinth with no string to guide her back. After a minute, the wall on the right disappeared and she left the service shaft.

'Luca?'

This time her voice carried more conviction and the echo carried down the tunnel. She heard scurrying on the ground. Something had been disturbed. She heard running water and felt the tunnel going down. Luca said it led to the platforms. The air seemed fresher, too. It didn't have the suffocating warmth of the service shaft. Then she stumbled over something. She put her hand out to break her fall and landed on top of it.

She heard it groan.

'Luca?' she whispered.

He put his hand over her mouth and held her tightly.

A scream came down the tunnel and split her ears. It echoed through the concrete and steel and shook the service shaft. It was the most terrifying sound she'd ever heard, made more so by the fact she recognised who was making it: Laura. Luca held her with an iron grip. She choked behind his hand but he wouldn't let go, even when the scream died.

'That's the third,' he whispered.

'Third?'

The implication was clear. It had got them all. It had chased them down.

'They're all . . . '

He held her even tighter. Tears came rolling down her cheeks like the streams on the heath. She had brought them all here. She was responsible.

You shouldn't have come, darling. She should have listened to him.

'What are we going to do?'

'Fight. Get out.'

There was steel in Luca's voice. He reached in his pocket for something. She heard the flick of a switch.

'You dropped it in the tunnel.'

She recognised the green lines. She watched and waited for them to jump like they had in the service shaft, but now they were like ripples on a pond, stagnant and still.

'Time to go,' he said.

She listened for movement down the tunnel. All was quiet. He struggled up.

'What's wrong?'

'Just give me your hand, will you?'

He put his arms round her shoulders and she felt his weight. She did the walking for him. She was a real Walker now. She had no torch or phone or candle to hold back the darkness. It surrounded them on every side. The tunnel wound steadily down into the abyss. Gradually, light seeped in from somewhere and black gave way to dirty grey. They came to some steps that curved down like a spiral. She felt fresh air blowing up them. She stopped.

Luca urged her on. 'Come on.'

She helped him down. For the first time, she saw what was wrong. His left leg was badly gashed, his jeans saturated with blood. She told him to stop. He'd ripped his t-shirt and used it as a tourniquet but it hadn't stopped the bleeding. She took the belt out of her coat and tied it round his thigh, pulled it as tightly as she could. He groaned and his hand gripped her.

She felt, for the first time, a real connection between them. Whatever else he'd done, he was there at the end of the day. Now that day had burst in on them. It wasn't a blue afternoon on the heath, or a grey morning at school. It wasn't summer, winter, autumn or spring. It was the ochre twilight of a train platform: deserted, somnambulant, quiet. She helped him on to the first bench they came to and lay him down. There was an emergency point next to it.

'Call for help.'

Jodie pressed the red button. There was no reply. She pressed again, more forcefully. Again nothing: just static. The third time, a voice crawled out of the Tannoy.

'Help, please help!' she shouted.

The metallic voice squeaked back. 'Where are you?'

More static.

'I don't know. Pages Walk.' She banged on the box. 'Just come, will you?'

The static cut out. She pressed again, once, twice, but no one was there.

She sat next to Luca and held his hand. It was cold.

36

Kamran shivered by the door. Luca's words had kept him going. He knew he wouldn't let him down. The ambulance would be here soon. He felt the spots of water on his face and put his head back to try and catch them. As he did, he heard screams. They ripped through him like knives. He heard running and footsteps coming down the tunnel, then another scream. It sounded like Trent. Then there was silence.

After a few minutes, he heard a shuffling on the ground and a thud. It was too slow to be a train and too heavy to be a person. His felt sick in his stomach. Shapes danced in the corners of his eyes. He hadn't the strength to beat them away, not this time. The thud sounded very close now. He saw it come out of the darkness. First, there were two long arms, reaching out and touching his face. Then a wind brushed him. Inch by inch, two eyes emerged. He closed his and tried to imagine them away, but when he opened them, they were still there. This is what the jinn looked like.

The scream got halfway out of his mouth, then there was a searing pain along his throat, blistering his skin. He choked back tears and tried to breathe, but no air would come. He thought about his mum and dad and his uncles at the takeaway, and how far he was from any of them. Then there was another searing pain across his chest and down his back and he felt himself lifted high into the air. His body emptied like a leaky bucket, spilling entrails on to the ground.

As his life ebbed away, two red eyes stared unblinkingly at him and he stared back, unblinking also. A claw came out of the darkness and played with the shredded tendons of his neck, snapping them one by one till a single thread was left. Then, that too, was gone. His last thoughts were of Luca and Jodie and how he wanted to say goodbye to them properly, but there was no breath in him to say anything.

It was too late.

*

The moment Jodie started convulsing, Laura ran. She grabbed Trent's hand and they stumbled along the passage together, falling over each other in their desperation to get away. She could hear Luca shouting behind her and knew now it was real. She had seen wings and horns wreathed in shadow. Now the world was going black and grey. She screamed, feeling the wind come whipping after her. They came out of the service shaft and turned left. She wanted to get away from the shouting.

She ran as fast as he could, her hands pushing through the darkness, her boots ringing on the ground like they were beating on drum skins. Trent was behind her, then suddenly he wasn't. She heard his scream but didn't stop. Fear kept her going. Wires and cables threatened to trip her up, walls came out of nowhere. It was hard to run straight when she couldn't see where she was going. All she wanted to do was run.

Then the screaming stopped. It had been clawed back. It was just her own heels she could hear. She tried to run quietly but the echoes of her boots kept rebounding back up the tunnel, thumping against her ears. She grazed herself against a wall, bit her lip against the pain, then got her feet caught in a cable noose. She found herself being hauled into the air and she stifled a scream. She was upside down.

No matter how hard she struggled, she couldn't release herself. There were noises coming down the tunnel, things she hadn't heard before: the clinking of chains; a shuffling sound like something being dragged along the ground; a slow thump. Then she was swinging. Something was blowing her. Her nape hairs stuck out like pins. Her eyes felt like they were moving in their sockets. She whimpered. It was breathing on her. There was no point hiding. It pushed her and she swung like a piece of meat in a butcher's shop. Maybe if she played dead, it wouldn't see her?

Do you see me now, Laura?

The voice came out of the darkness.

Not so special now, are you?

Laura recognised her. She had come for her. She wanted her pound of flesh.

Just a piece of meat.

She sobbed. The swinging stopped. A nail touched her face.

There was just enough time left to scream.

297

37

The platform was deserted. No trains had come. Luca was too sick to move. He was mumbling to himself, fighting back the pain. He fumbled in his jacket pocket and handed Jodie the spectrum analyser.

'Take another reading.'

She switched it on and waited for the bars to appear. The levels hadn't changed.

'Well?'

'Nothing.'

He tried to get himself up but the pain kept him down. He held his hand out. 'Pull me up.'

'What about your leg?'

'If I don't get up now, I never will.'

His face contorted in agony. He leant on her and cried. 'We have to get out. The infrasound is triggering it. The demon is appearing whenever it reaches a certain level.'

'Did you see it?'

'Along with a whole load of other stuff. The thing can change shape.'

Jodie thought of her father in the tunnel and how he changed into the demon.

'You remember what George said? He said it was a devil. *Tentacles thicker than a man's waist.*'

'Yes.'

'Maybe he was right. Maybe you see your own nightmare?'

'What do you mean?'

'Well, he saw a tentacled devil, didn't he, and you saw the demon in the book. You can't both be right. Maybe it plays on your subconscious?'

He tried to hobble a few steps. 'The pain's getting worse.'

She looked up and down the platform. 'Can you get to an exit?'

He nodded. There were tears in his eyes. She got him as far as the end of the platform. Then he collapsed.

'I'm sorry, Jodie. I can't go on.'

She sat him on the floor, put his head in her lap.

He looked up at her. 'I am sorry, Jodie.'

She started to cry. She stroked his hair but couldn't see him for the tears. She helped him up and propped him on her shoulder. She shouted for help up the stairs but no one was there. She lay at the bottom with him. She'd have to go on her own. As she thought it, there was a rumble down the platform. A train must be approaching. She looked at the spectrum analyser and saw the levels were rising again. So was the wind. There was no way out. She tried to drag him up the stairs but hadn't the strength for both of them. She sank to her knees a few steps from the top.

'It's too late, Jodie,' he said.

There was a smell of fetid air wafting up the passageway. She turned and saw the shadow of horns on the tunnel wall and knew there was no escape, just like her father knew before her.

She cradled his head. 'No, it's not.'

But she noticed the dark-brown seepage from his wound, and her heart failed.

'What do I do?' she begged.

'You have to fight it.'

'How?'

'It's feeding off the infrasound. From the substation generator, I think. You have to cut the levels.'

His throat convulsed as he gasped for air.

'How do I do that?'

But his voice trailed away.

She stared at his face, lifeless in the half-light, and was reminded of the photo she'd taken of him in Regent's Park, framed in the azure sky. How different he looked now. How cold and how alone. She'd done that to him. She'd done that to all of them, taken them from their normal lives to this nightmare beneath the earth.

She put her lips on his forehead and kissed him. Her tears fell down his cheeks. She watched them run down the steps. Nothing mattered now. They were all on the same train, going the same way, towards the same station. Some passengers were there for the duration, some you had to watch get off, like Luca. Some you never saw, like her parents.

Through her tears, she saw the green lines on the spectrum analyser flicker. It was close to her now. She could feel it. She lay his head gently down on the steps and the madness and panic and fear of twelve years conflated to one final rush of anger. She had to save him, even if she couldn't save herself.

She ran down the steps on to the platform. The horns had gone from the roof. She looked into the black mouth of the train tunnel. A wind was coming down it. With it came the smell of sulphur. She felt movement in the air. Her senses were brittle with anxiety. She clambered on to the tracks and went inside. The inky blackness swallowed her up. She knew to stay away from the far wall. Luca had once told her about the live third rail, how it would burn your body in an instant, melt your fat and fry you.

Maybe the demon wouldn't know.

Her hair blew in the wind. From out of the cavernous emptiness, its wings beat the air. She looked at the spectrum analyser. The green lines were rising again.

She took two faltering steps forward, then froze.

The movement was quicker now. She heard its hooves ringing on the iron floor, beating the girders with a blacksmith's fury. It was coming for her.

The concrete lining of the tunnel walls shook.

She hauled herself back on to the platform and ran.

As she reached the far end, it burst out into the open behind her, stretched its wings across the vaulted ceiling. Darkness fell. In the flesh, it was even more massive and terrible than nightmare had made it. She turned and saw its feet inch closer to the live rail, the claws bent across the metal. Any second, it would ignite.

Please, she thought.

But it sniffed the air and turned its head, its reptilian red eyes glowing like embers. It had noticed something else.

Or someone.

Her heart stopped. It was Luca.

'No!' she cried, running towards it. 'Leave him!'

Its tail crashed against the tunnel wall as it wheeled towards her.

Her head spun, her legs buckled underneath her. Habborlain's words seared into her mind. *If your nightmare knows you want to wake from it, it may come after you first.*

Now, she willed it to.

'Leave him alone. It's me you want. It's me you've always wanted.'

She waved her hands, made sure she had its attention, and ran as fast as she could back to the spiral stairwell. Dirty grey gave way to black again. Her legs ached, her chest heaved. The spectrum analyser was her only light in the dark. Luca had said about the generator. She had to get there, had to destroy it. Every time the green lines flattened, she changed direction. It flickered into life as she got nearer, bobbed uncertainly like a swimmer in a storm. After a few minutes, she detected the low hum. The tunnel walls seemed to vibrate. She sensed movement in the corner of her eye, knew she was getting close.

She felt the breeze on her face. It was whipping down the tunnels towards her. Did it know what she was going to do? She imagined its wings unfurled behind her. It wouldn't be long now. The familiar dizziness spun her round, sent her to the floor. She tried to hold on to the sides of the wall, drag herself into the service shaft. Metal seemed to buckle and crackles of electrical energy pulsed in the darkness. A blue spark soared twenty feet into the air. It hit the roof and shorted out. The wind got stronger. The green lines on the spectrum analyser were almost vertical. She couldn't let herself fall unconscious. She had to keep herself awake long enough to do something.

It was in the shaft with her now. She felt its stale breath on her face, then the acrid taste of sulphur on her lips. Her nostrils dilated. Its horns touched the ceiling and its wings spread like a huge shadow behind it. It seemed to sense her. She tried to hold back the nausea, block out the wind rushing through her head, right the dizziness. She fell to her knees, didn't understand why it didn't put her out of her misery. What was it waiting for?

Then, there was a loud explosion from the generator and a terrible smell of burning. The tunnel walls shook, then burst asunder with a mighty crack. The demon let out an unearthly cry. It was the first time she'd heard it. Was it pain or fear or anger? Its tail swiped the generator and dented the metal. More electrical charges lit up the shaft. The spectrum analyser became white-hot to the touch, and fell from her hand. Her face was pressed to the floor and still the waves of infrasound poured into her. She was drowning in them, unable to see properly, unable to hear and now burning alive.

Stay awake, Jodie.

Orange flames licked the roof. The demon's red eyes bulged out of their sockets, its red melon jaws opened wide, calling out. It crawled across the floor towards her. There was another shudder through the tunnel and more explosions. The heat was unbearable. A bolt of fire ripped down a side tunnel, igniting the tiles.

The demon called out again, its face a mangled, burning mess. They had entered hell together and were going to die together. She crawled away, tried to protect her skin from the heat. Behind her, she heard more rumbles and explosions. They spread through the whole tunnel. Then, there was a huge tremor above her. It felt like the whole of

London was going to come toppling down on her.

She managed to get to her feet. A spark struck her leg and pain seared through her. She turned back, knew she had to get out. There was another mighty explosion which reverberated through the earth like a sonic boom. It threw her off her feet and sent a shower of debris down the tunnel. Pellets of rock and tile flew towards her in a deadly blast. But the larger pieces were absorbed by the demon's wings and the deadly shrapnel missed her. Being so close, it had unwittingly saved her. She heard it give another cry.

Desperation gave her wings of her own. She ran down the tunnel, dodging sparks and jumping flames till the heat relented and she reached the spiral stairwell. She thought of Luca, lying on the platform steps. As she descended a final time, she noticed the dirty grey light was tinged with an orange hue. Fire had spread from Pages Walk to the platform. Maybe the whole Underground was in flames.

She ran to where she'd left him.

He was at the top of the stairs, had somehow clawed his way there. His exit was blocked by angry, Hydra-headed flames. She put her hands under his shoulders and pulled him away, dragged him till she could drag him no more, and propped him against the platform wall.

His eyes opened a fraction.

'Luca?'

But his expression was dead.

She cried then, not just for him, but for herself. The fire crackled and sparks lit up the Tube line. Electromagnetic currents tripped, earthed and ignited. To think she had done all this.

She hauled him up and staggered down the platform with him. At the end, exhaustion finally took her. She lost her footing and felt herself falling. She hit her head and slipped into a grey twilight. Through the dim haze, she thought she caught a despairing smile on Luca's face, and turned her head to see what he was looking at. The demon was collapsed on the platform edge next to her: burned, charred, its red eyes now black.

It had followed her down from Pages Walk.

It was the last she saw before unconsciousness took her.

38

As morning broke, Laura felt herself swaying in the darkness. There was a dull ache in her head and what felt like ice gripping her feet. The thing had gone. She shouted out, hoping that someone would hear her. Instead, a wind came rushing towards her. It brought hot air with it. She realised she was still upside down. A meagre light lit up the ceiling, eating away at the darkness. She blinked away its brightness. The roaring got louder and the wind stronger and stronger. Soon she would be out of there. She started to cry.

*

The Upminster train thundered down the tracks to Embankment station. The driver had done the journey hundreds of times before. There were no red lights, nothing to warn him. The tunnel lit up under the glare. The thing dangled down from the roof like a giant bat, swaying like a pendulum.

Three, two, one. No time to hit the brakes. There was a dull thud and the windows turned red. For a second, two eyes stuck to the glass, then they were gone.

39

Jodie wasn't in the tunnel any more. She was on the heath. The kites were strung along Parliament Hill and she could see the whole of London spread out before her, framed by a skyline of unbroken blue. There were no dark corners or tunnels and the air was fresh and clean. Life was returning to normal. She let the breeze sweep her away and closed her eyes. It was then she heard the beeping sound. It seemed to be coming from beside her. She checked in her pocket but her phone was on silent. Still, the beeping cut through, getting faster and faster.

She couldn't see anything but the joggers and kites. She tried to stand up and found she couldn't. She was stuck. Something was holding her back. She opened her mouth to scream and the moment she did, the shackles came off. London vanished in an instant and she sat up.

She was on a bed. It wasn't like the one at home. It was

hard and cold. Voices crackled through the ether. She didn't recognise any of them. They were speaking too quickly. She looked round. There were other people just like her, lying on beds like mortuary slabs. For a moment, she thought she was dead. This is what it was like. She was surrounded by things she didn't understand. Then it hit her. She was in hospital. She looked to her side and saw the heart monitor bleeping. The metronomic pulse was beating loudly and insistently. There were wires and drips coming in and out of her right arm and some attached to her head. She tried to get off the bed. Then she heard a voice cutting through the noise.

'Jodie.'

She recognised it immediately. It was Aunt Gene's. How many times had she been there for her, beside her, looking after her? She was sitting on a stiff, plastic hospital chair, her face tired and drawn. She'd been crying.

'Are you okay, darling?'

Jodie nodded and stared at a nurse who was standing by her bedside with a needle in her hand.

'This won't hurt.'

She felt a small prick in her arm. It didn't hurt at all.

*

The second time she woke up, everything was different. The heart monitor pulsed slowly and little zigzag lines cut across the screen. It reminded her of the lines on the spectrum analyser. Then the memories came roaring back: the tunnel, the platform, the demon. She choked them back.

'Where am I?'

'In hospital, darling. You're safe now.'

Safe? It wasn't possible.

'There was a fire.'

'It's over now, darling. It's all over.'

'What about the others?'

'The doctors said you needed to rest.'

'I need to know, Aunt Gene.'

'They're fine. Just you get better.'

Jodie looked around the ward. It was visiting hour. There were children sitting on beds and parents trying to keep a brave face and nurses running to and fro. There was a smell of surgical spirit and the sound of cars outside. It was a warm summer's day. Sunlight filtered through the open window like the promise of tomorrow. She turned to Aunt Gene. There was a little more grey at her temples and a few more lines on her face, but she was still there. She was her family.

The ward door opened and a boy entered on crutches. She didn't recognise him at first. He was dressed in a hospital gown. It was only when he saw her and made his way over that she recognised him. Tears came to her eyes.

'Luca?'

He had surgical dressing on his hands and patches of white on his face. He hobbled over, trying to smile.

Aunt Gene made room for him. 'He's been here most days when you were asleep.'

'How long have I been here?'

'Five days.'

'Five?'

The time had gone by without her knowing. The feeling disorientated her. 'I've been asleep?'

He sat down and put his crutches up. 'Yeah. Snoring.'

Aunt Gene didn't exactly smile at him but she wasn't hostile, either. She looked from one to the other. 'Well, I'm going to get something to eat. I'll leave you alone for a bit.

Don't tire her out, Luca. They're going to run some tests later. She's still very poorly.'

He nodded. 'I won't.'

The moment she was gone, his demeanour changed.

'I had to see you.'

'You're in here, too?'

'Yeah, my leg's infected with something. It hurts like hell.'

'What about your hands and face?'

'First-degree burns only. You saved my life.'

She had a flashback of the flames. 'I didn't. I nearly killed you.'

He looked at her strangely.

'What happened to me, Luca?'

He bent his head close to the bed and gestured that she should do the same. 'Your aunt said you were knocked out, but I think it was more. She didn't want me to worry.' His voice dropped to a whisper. 'Remember what you promised? When the time came, you'd hear me out?'

Her heart started to beat faster. The metronome picked up speed. 'Yes.'

'Well, listen very carefully.' He looked round the room as if the walls were listening. 'I think we're in trouble.'

The word loomed large over her again. The room seemed to get darker.

'Actually, it's more *you're* in trouble.'

'What do you mean?'

'The police have been to see me a few times.'

'What did they want?'

'They asked about the fire. How it started. It's been all over the news. Biggest one since King's Cross. It took out the whole network. They think the substation blew and someone vandalised it.'

'It wasn't me,' she protested. 'It was the demon.'

He put a finger to his lips. 'I know. I believe you. But they won't.'

'They have to. It was there on the platform. *You* saw it.'

He shook his head. 'It's gone, Jodie.'

'Gone where?'

'When you passed out on the platform, it vanished. One minute I was looking at it, the next I wasn't.'

'I don't understand.'

'The infrasound hadn't changed. It was you.'

She stopped, stunned. 'So what are you saying?'

'I'm saying you're the key, the cipher, whatever you want to call it. We were all attacked down there. The screams we heard in the tunnel, it went after all of us, didn't it?'

She nodded.

'But it never came after you.'

She clutched at broken straws. 'You said it was our imagination.'

He shook his head, sadly. 'Not our imagination. Yours. It's in you, Jodie. You're the cause of it.'

Her mind couldn't take it in. 'How could I be?'

'I don't know. But your father was right. The answer was down there like it was on his tape. We all saw things. Maybe with some people, and with the right levels of infrasound, it brings more out.'

She shook her head. It couldn't be.

'Remember what Habborlain said? There are people who have the ability to project things into reality. What if you had that?'

'It can't be true.'

But she knew it was. She'd fashioned a monster from her mind and set it loose. 'What happened to the others?'

Luca looked at her.

'Kamran? George?'

'We were the only two they found.'

It didn't register. Nothing did. They were gone, just like her father.

She stared at the heart monitor. 'If infrasound is the trigger, why did I see things in the séance room or the science lab? Or in my attic?'

'I thought about that. Remember the storm, how it knocked a slate out of the roof? Well, maybe the hole caused the roof cavity to resonate? The loose tiles acted like a tuning fork. Whenever the wind blew, it set off infrasound. The same thing happened with the ceiling fans. They acted like conductors. Any vibrations can set it off, if you're sensitive enough to pick them up.'

She thought of how different the attic felt after the builder had sealed the hole up.

'But what about my father? Something had come after him. He disturbed something down there.'

Luca just stared at her.

The metronome beat insistently, sending jagged green triangles across the monitor. The image of her father, staggering across Tube lines just like George, flashed into her head.

Thud.

'I don't think so,' he said.

The green triangles looked like teeth. She stared into its mouth.

'Me?' The shock of it sent her own heart beating in her ears. 'I did it?'

'You weren't responsible, Jodie. No one can control their dreams. The demon was as separate from you as an animal

313

at the zoo. All you did was open its cage.'

Cage? She thought of the tiger at the zoo. She'd done that, too.

She started to cry.

'It's gone now, hasn't it, Luca?'

Her put his arm round her, held her tightly.

'Yes,' he said. 'It's gone now.'

*

Aunt Gene came back with a nurse and two doctors. They looked kindly at Jodie but she didn't look at them. She was thinking of a little girl waking up in the middle of the night, walking down a corridor to see her mother and father. This time she could see it all. As she was wheeled away down corridors of the living, she entered the charnel house she'd prepared for them. She knew now what lay behind that door and what feeling so unwell meant. There'd been no serial killer, just like there'd be no escaped lunatic on the Underground, or madman who killed the tiger. It was she who was responsible, who'd brought the demon into being. It had massacred them in front of her, soaked her with their blood. Better if it had killed her instead. She didn't want to live any more.

40

They put her head into an MRI machine. The nurse said it wouldn't take long. She heard a hum and closed her eyes. She saw her dad on a beach somewhere and her mum making sandcastles and knew she was seeing things as they really were. The waves were crashing on the sand and the wind was blowing the flags. They reminded her of the kites on Parliament Hill.

The wind got stronger and a wave of nausea hit her. The machine hummed and vibrated oddly. She opened her eyes and stared down at her feet. She could just make out the end of the bed. She wanted to knock the side so they could get her out of there, so they could get *themselves* out of there. The claustrophobia was overwhelming. She recognised the vibrations now. The machine was sending infrasound through her. Her eyes started shaking and she heard the wind coming. She was powerless to stop it. Something was in the room with them, something horrible. She heard the screams and didn't dare look.

Fetid air was blown across the room. She tore at the patches and straps on her arms and tried desperately to get out. She smashed her head on the metallic plates and glimpsed green wings opening and closing in their reflection. She heard equipment crashing to the floor and then more screams. The wind got stronger and the sickness billowed up from her gut like a tide of sewage. She scrambled out just as the lights in the room exploded. Then the screams were gone. She heard sobbing and gargling and felt a light spray on her skin. Her head lurched from side to side and she fell off the bed.

Lights short-circuited, monitors pulsed. She looked up through blurry eyes and saw one of the nurses kneeling on the floor. Where her head should have been, blood was squirting up. It shot high into the air like a geyser and fell like rain on the crisp white sheets, on the monitors and machines, and on her nightgown. The nurse's headless body fell to the floor.

Jodie put her hands over her ears and tried to stop the shaking. But the vibrations kept coming, invisible and unstoppable. On the other side of the room, the demon turned its head slowly and stared at her, and its red melon jaws opened. For a brief moment, she felt it, and the shock of it sent the scream echoing through the room. She closed her eyes and let the blood cover her, the way it had in her father's basement.

It recognised her.

EPILOGUE

John left the house late and ran across the heath. The air was alive with magic. The stars seemed more beautiful and the ponds deeper and more mysterious than he'd ever known. The trees whispered to him. He imagined taking her for walks in the twilight and showing her all the secret places he knew. He ran down cycle tracks and cut through copses and crossed ley lines which now possessed psychic, mystical energy. They led him home. The gravestones in Highgate Cemetery stepped aside and welcomed him. He'd saved her soul and was going to meet her again.

It was well after midnight when he got back. His father's car was on the drive. He wondered if he'd stayed in. There was a strange atmosphere in the house, like it was waiting for something. His exultation was replaced with a deep sense of foreboding. He went to the library doors and opened them. The lights were still on. He looked at the table in the middle of the room. His father wasn't there. He took a few steps in and saw a shadow on the ceiling. He thought maybe the fans were on. He looked up and saw the rope hanging down from them, and the body swinging beneath. He didn't need to get any closer. He knew who it was. All the colour had drained from its face.

It was too late to accept the apology. It was too late to do anything. His father held his final séance without him. John knelt on the floor and watched him swing slowly.

ACKNOWLEDGEMENTS

Special thanks to Rachel Calder and David Savage for their patience and diplomacy and sound advice; and to Barry Cunningham and all those at Chicken House who supported the book.

FLASHES by TIM O'ROURKE

Charley has visions: flashes of things she can't explain. She feels certain they're clues to a crime someone's committed against a girl, but no one will believe her. Until she meets Tom, a young detective on his first case – a death on railway tracks, not far from where Charley lives. Was it an accident, a suicide . . . or murder?

The attraction between Charley and Tom is instant, but can they discover what's happened . . . before it happens again?

'Flashes is a gripping and very readable thriller . . . an enjoyable read.'

WE LOVE THIS BOOK

Paperback, ISBN 978-1-908435-82-8, £7.99 • ebook, ISBN 978-1-909489-58-5, £7.99

WHAT MAKES HIM DIFFERENT MAKES HIM DANGEROUS

THE UNICORNE FILES **A DARK INHERITANCE**
CHRIS D'LACEY

A DARK INHERITANCE by CHRIS D'LACEY

When Michael saves a dog in a clifftop rescue, he comes to the attention of his schoolmates, the police and a strange organisation called UNICORNE.

What UNICORNE reveal is extraordinary. They claim they can tell him what happened to his father, who disappeared three years ago, but what they want in return is dangerous. Something supernatural that's hidden in Michael's very bones . . .

Paperback, ISBN 978-1-909489-65-3, £6.99 • ebook, ISBN 978-1-909489-66-0, £6.99

NUMBERS
by RACHEL WARD

Since the day her mother died, Jem has known about the numbers. When she looks in someone's eyes, she can see the date they will die.

Life is hard, until she meets a boy called Spider. Suddenly her world seems brighter.

But on a trip to London, Jem foresees a chain of events that will shatter their lives for ever . . .

'... intelligent and life-affirming.'
PHILIP ARDAGH

'... utterly compelling ...'
THE SUNDAY TELEGRAPH

Paperback, ISBN 978-1-905294-93-0, £6.99 • ebook, ISBN 978-1-908435-02-6, £6.99

ALSO AVAILABLE:

NUMBERS 2: THE CHAOS
Paperback, ISBN 978-1-906427-30-6, £6.99 • ebook, ISBN 978-1-908435-04-0, £6.99

NUMBERS 3: INFINITY
Paperback, ISBN 978-1-906427-66-5, £6.99 • ebook, ISBN 978-1-908435-06-4, £6.99